THE CASE OF
WILLIAM SMITH

Books by Patricia Wentworth:

THE CASE OF WILLIAM SMITH

PATRICIA WENTWORTH

HarperPerennial
A Division of HarperCollins*Publishers*

This book was originally published in 1948 by the J. B. Lippincott Company.

HarperCollins books may be purchased for educational, business, or sales promotional use. For information, please write: Special Markets Department, HarperCollins Publishers, Inc., 10 East 53rd Street, New York, NY 10022.

First HarperPerennial edition published 1991. Second HarperPerennial edition published 1992.

LIBRARY OF CONGRESS CATALOG CARD NUMBER 92-62676
ISBN 0-06-092340-7

92 93 94 95 96 WB/MB 10 9 8 7 6 5 4 3 2 1

THE CASE OF
WILLIAM SMITH

PROLOGUE

A concentration camp in Germany—Christmas Day, 1944.

William Smith was dreaming his dream. Like his fellow prisoners, he had spent more than five hours of Christmas morning standing at attention on the square in his ragged underclothes exposed to a bitter north-east wind. Some of the men who had stood there with him would never stand again. They had dropped and died. William had stuck it out. He was strong and tough, and he was not racked as other men were racked by what might be happening to their families. Since he did not know who he was, he did not so much as know as whether he had a family. When the Commandant had said, addressing them all, "If you have wives and children, forget them—you will never see them again," he was stirred to a just and impersonal anger, but not to any private feeling, because life as far as he was concerned had begun two years ago when he came out of hospital with an identity disc which said he was William Smith. There was a long number as well as the William Smith but he was never able to feel that it belonged to him. They put him in a camp as William Smith, and after he had escaped and been caught the S.S. took him over and put him in a concentration camp. Since then he had been moved twice, and each camp was worse than the last. In this camp he was the only Englishman. He knew some French, and he had learned some German. An old Czech who had a knife which he had stolen at the risk of his life used to lend it to him sometimes. They carved

1

animals. The Czech was better at the carving, but William had a lot of bright ideas. After a bit he got very good at the carving too.

Day followed day, and night followed night. There was always hunger and filth and cold, and cruelty, and a dense fog of human suffering. It was better for William than it was for the others, because he hadn't anyone to worry about except himself, and he hadn't got that sort of worrying temperament, so he didn't really worry at all. And sometimes at night he had his dream.

He was having it now. His body was crushed in among other bodies on a bare and filthy floor, but William wasn't there. He was having his dream, and in his dream he was walking up three steps to an oak door. It always began that way. The steps were old, and hollowed in the middle from all the feet which had passed over them for many generations. They started in the street and they went up to the door, which was the front door of a house. It was a house in a street. He knew that, but he didn't know how he knew it, because he never saw any more than that—three steps going up, and an oak door studded with nails.

The next thing that happened was that he opened the door and went into the house. When he was awake he could remember the three steps up and the door, but after that it was all shadowy, like things are in dreams. What he remembered was that in the dream he had come home. There was a hall, rather dark, and a staircase going up on the right, and he went up the stairs. But it was all vague and dark and shimmering, like a reflection in water when the wind ruffles it. All that he could be sure about was that it was a happy dream.

When he was asleep it was quite different. The dream was as clear and plain as anything that had ever happened to him in all his life. It was much more real than anything that happened in the camp. The hall was dark because it was panelled. The wood wasn't really dark in itself, but it made the hall dark. The stair that went up on the right was made of the same wood. The newel posts were carved with the symbols of the four evangelists—a lion and an ox at the foot of the stair, and an eagle and a man at the head. The man and the ox were on the inner side of the stair. They were only heads, but the lion had a mane flowing down over the newel at the bottom, and the eagle was a whole eagle with folded wings and great horny talons on the left-hand side at the top. At intervals there were portraits let into the panelling, some on the inner side of the stairway, and some in the hall below. In a half light there was an effect of people waiting in the shadows. When he was a little boy it had frightened him.

In his dream he went on up the stair. So far it was always the same. It was after he got to the top that it began to be different. Since his recollection ceased with the dream, he had no means of knowing what the difference was. He only knew each dream whilst he was dreaming it. When he was awake all that remained was the three steps up out of the street, the door, the shadowy hall with the stair going up, and the sense of coming home.

On this Christmas night, with his body lying crowded in between other bodies filthier than his own, he himself sprang up the three steps and came into the hall. He came out of the dark street into warmth and light. The curtains were drawn over a window on either side of the door and all the lights were on. A powdered wig emerged from the gloom of one portrait, the sweep of a faded rose-coloured dress and a child's white muslin frock from another. The lion and the ox at the foot were crowned with holly, and over the stair head there hung a great pale bunch of mistletoe. An extraordinary

3

rush of happiness came over him. It was so strong that it fairly swept him up the stairs. No time to look at old dead and gone relations in the shadows, no eyes for anything except the one who was waiting for him on the top step— between the eagle and the man—under the mistletoe.

CHAPTER 1

Brett Eversley was reading a letter which he had already read quite a number of times. He liked it so little that one would hardly have supposed he would desire to read, and read it again, yet that is what he was doing. The letter had come by the first post. He had opened it with a smile and been immediately thrown into rather a desperate state of mind. Since then he had gone over every word, every phrase, in an attempt to find a different meaning from the one he could not bring himself to accept. Women said one thing and meant another—it was proverbial. They liked to be courted, flattered, pursued. They liked to make a man show his paces— put him through the hoop.

He was a goodlooking man, and he had always had money to spend. Women had run after him, and he had let them run. At forty he had kept his freedom, his figure, and a decidedly good opinion of Brett Eversley. At the moment his handsome face was flushed, his dark eyes brooding, his brows drawn together in a frown. When he looked like that you could see that in the next ten years the regular features might coarsen, the lower part of the face become too heavy, and the colour fixed. On the other hand, grey hair would probably suit him very well and impart an eighteenth-century air. He really was not at all unlike some portrait of a full-flavoured Georgian squire.

As he sat at the desk in his private office at Eversleys' he had the letter spread out before him. However many times he read it, he found himself unable to accept its evidence. It just wasn't possible that Katharine was turning him down. He read what she had written:

"Dear Brett,

I'm afraid it's no use, and the best thing I can do is just to tell you so and say 'Let's go on being friends.' I said I would think it over, and I have. It isn't any use, really. You're a cousin and a friend, and that's what we are to each other. I can't change into being anything else. It's just one of those things. Don't worry about the money—I'm getting a job.

Yours

Katharine."

Not very easy to get anything out of it except a plain down-right "No." He went on trying. It was a mood. Women had moods. They were changeable. She had withdrawn before, and then been kind again. Kind . . . His own word might have warned him, but he was resolute to find what he wanted. She was kind, she was fond of him—what more did she want? She couldn't just go on refusing one man after another. She had known him all her life. As far as he could tell there wasn't anyone she liked better. It would be a most suitable marriage. It wasn't as if she was a girl of twenty. She must be a good eight years older than that. She had had her fling, and he had had his. You had to settle down some time, and if he could bring his mind to it, so could she. He really did

5

find it impossible to believe that her refusal could be final.

He read the letter again.

Katharine Eversley got off the bus at the corner and walked along Ellery Street until she came to Tattlecombe's Toy Bazaar, which was about half way down on the right. It had on one side of it a small draper's, and on the other a rather depressed-looking cleaner's establishment with an ironically fly-blown legend in the window, "We can make your old things new."

The Bazaar had two windows, one on either side of the entrance. On the left there were paintboxes, chalks, a hoop, and miscellaneous toys, but the right-hand window was entirely given up to William Smith's wooden animals, the fame of which was beginning to spread to places quite far removed from Ellery Street and its North London suburb. There were Wurzel Dogs, Marks I, II, III and IV—the gay, jaunty, the pathetic, the rollicking, all with moveable heads and tails. They were black, brown, grey, white, and spotted. They were retrievers, bulldogs, hounds, terriers, poodles, and dachshunds. They were of a heart-smiting oddity. Amongst them paraded the Boomalong Bird, with striding feet and swivel eye, gawky, indomitable, booming along—white, grey, brown, black, parrot-green, flamingo-red, orange, and blue, with black and yellow claws and long erratic beaks. Katharine stood looking in at them, as nearly every stranger did stand there and look in. The people who frequented Ellery Street had got used to the creatures, but strangers always stopped to look at them, and very often went in to buy.

Katharine stood there and thought about being tough. Some people were born tough, some people achieved toughness, and others had it thrust upon them. It was being thrust on her at this moment, and she didn't know what to do with

6

it. She had a sick kind of feeling that she might just let go and be the world's completest flop. And yet all she had to do was to walk into the shop and say she had been told that they were looking for an assistant, and did they think she would do. Anyone who had been through the war as an A.T. ought to be able to manage that. And of course it would have been the easiest thing in the world if only it didn't really matter whether she got the job or not. It mattered so much that her feet were cold and her heart was knocking against her side.

She looked at one of the rollicking Wurzel Dogs, and he looked back at her with his jovial rolling eye. "Get along with it and don't be a fool!" was undoubtedly what he would have said if William could have endowed him with actual speech.

Katharine bit her lip very hard indeed and walked into the shop, where she encountered Miss Cole. William Smith, coming through from the workshop, saw them standing together. Miss Cole, pale, plump, efficient, spectacled, in her tight black dress, her ginger-coloured cardigan, and the tufts of cotton wool which she wore in her ears to keep out the cold. He saw her as he saw her every day and continually. And then he saw Katharine, and heard her say, "Good-morning. I hear you are needing someone to help in the shop." He heard the words, but just for the moment they didn't make any sense, because her voice went through him like music. Thought stopped and feeling took its place. It didn't really matter what she had said. All that mattered was that she should speak again. He heard Miss Cole say, "Well, I don't know, I'm sure," and with that thought took over again, and the sense of what Katharine had said came to him like a delayed echo—"I hear you are needing someone to help in the shop."

He came marching in and added himself to the conference.

Introduced by Miss Cole with a "This is Mr. Smith," he said, "Good-morning," and stood looking at Katharine. Her voice had done things to him. Everything about her was doing things. She was music, poetry, and the enchantment which lies just over the edge of thought. She was applying for the post of assistant at Tattlecombe's Toy Bazaar. He was far too much disturbed himself to be aware that she was dreadfully pale, but it did not escape Miss Cole, who immediately gave her three bad marks. "Delicate. I'm sure we don't want people here who are going to faint. That colour on her cheeks wasn't ever her own. I was sure of it as soon as ever she came in. And lipstick too! Whatever would Mr. Tattlecombe say?"

As Mr. Tattlecombe was laid up in hospital after being knocked down by a car and was not allowed to see anyone except his sister, there was really no answer to this, and much as Miss Cole might deplore the fact, William Smith was in charge. At this very moment he was offering the young woman a chair and saying,

"Were you asking Miss Cole whether we wanted an assistant?"

Katharine was very glad of the chair. Suppose he was going to say that they didn't want anyone, or that she wouldn't do. If it depended on Miss Cole, that was what would be said. That upholstered bust had tightened against her, and the dark beady eyes behind those formidable lenses were the last word in disapproval. She didn't sort any of this out, but it was there. She said,

"Yes. Do you think I would do?"

Miss Cole was quite sure that she would not, but she restrained herself. She looked Katharine up and down, from the small plain hat to the neat plain shoes, took in the fact that her tweed suit was by no means new, and summed up

8

the result as "Come down in the world." Lots of people about like that nowadays—born with silver spoons in their mouths and had everything their own way, and then some kind of slide or some kind of crash, and out they have to go and get a job—sorry for themselves because they've got to do what other girls have always known they'd have to do. Miss Cole had gone out at fourteen and worked to get her experience, but these *ladies*—she gave the word a bitter emphasis—they expected to walk in and get jobs without any experience at all. She said sharply,

"What experience have you had?"

Katharine was frank.

"None for this sort of thing, I'm afraid, but I could learn. I was in the A.T.S. during the war."

"And since?"

"I wasn't demobilized for quite a long time, and then—I took a holiday. Now I want a job—rather badly."

"Money run out," thought Miss Cole. "That's the way with her sort—lipstick and rouge, and not a penny put away."

William let her talk to Miss Cole, because all he really wanted was to look at her. She was tall and graceful. She moved like clouds, like water, like anything lovely and effortless and free. She had brown hair under a little brown hat. She had brown eyes. Bright water, dark water—that was what they made you think about. They changed, and changed again, but they were always beautiful. He watched the colour flow back under the skin until you couldn't see the pink stain which had been there. It just deepened the natural colour, that was all. He liked the soft colour of her lipstick—not splashed on, but following the lines of her most lovely mouth. He liked the rather shabby tweed suit and the little green scarf at her throat. She gave him the feeling of completeness, of everything being just right. He heard Miss Cole say, "I

9

really don't know, I'm sure," and said in his most direct and simple manner,

"What is your name?"

Her colour went again quite suddenly, and then came back in a flood.

"Katharine Eversley."

He turned to Miss Cole.

"It seems to me that Miss Eversley is just what we are wanting."

"Really, Mr. Smith—"

He had a sudden and attractive smile. Miss Cole was not impervious to its charm.

"You will be dreadfully overworked with Mr. Tattlecombe away. What on earth should we do if you knocked up?"

"I have no intention of knocking up."

William said, "Mr. Tattlecombe would never forgive me. You've really got to have some help. So if Miss Eversley—"

It was no good, he meant to have her, Miss Cole could see that. And he was in charge—she couldn't do anything about it. The soft, silly fools men were the minute a pretty face came along—and no notice taken of those that would make a good home and have everything comfortable. No good crying over spilt milk—that's the way they were, and you just had to put up with them. She suppressed a sniff and said abruptly,

"What about references?"

Looking back on it afterwards, William always found it so much easier to recall Katharine than to remember anything else. He had only to open the least little chink in his mind and she came in and filled it. She gave two references. Miss Cole talked to her, and she to Miss Cole, while he stood by. "As you have no experience, you will not expect a high salary. Would thirty-five shillings a week—" He remembered that

10

because of the way Katharine's colour rose as she said, "Oh, yes." And just at the end Miss Cole enraged him by saying in her firmest voice, "No rouge, and no lipstick, Miss Eversley—no make-up of any kind. Mr. Tattlecombe is very strict indeed about that."

Katharine didn't blush this time. She smiled.

"Oh, of course—I don't mind a bit. It's just a fashion, isn't it?"

Then she went away. They were to take up her references, and if they were satisfactory, she was to start work on Monday morning.

William walked on air.

CHAPTER 2

Abel Tattlecombe sat propped up in bed with a cushion and two pillows at his back and a grey and white knitted shawl about his shoulders. The cushion had been brought up by his sister, Mrs. Salt, from the parlour where it belonged. If it had been anyone but Abel, they might have whistled for it. Not that Mrs. Salt would have demeaned herself to use such an expression, but the cushion would have remained on the parlour sofa. Being Abel, it formed, as you might say, a foundation for her two largest feather pillows, and a very solid foundation at that. Constructed of strong canvas, and worked all over in cross-stitch in a pattern of enormous red roses on a purple ground, it had retained to an almost aggressive degree its robust colouring and its even robuster form. Plump, cheerful, compact, it held the pillows in place

11

and made a comfortable back for Mr. Tattlecombe.

He looked out of his very blue eyes at his assistant, William Smith, and said,

"I've been making my will."

William didn't quite know what to say. If he didn't say anything at all, Mr. Tattlecombe would jump to the conclusion that William thought he was dying. If he said, "Oh, yes," or words to that effect, it would amount to very much the same thing. If he said, "Oh, I'm sure there's no need to do that," he would be going against his principles. Because of course people ought to make their wills, if they have anyone to provide for and anything to leave. William hadn't. He returned Mr. Tattlecombe's gaze, thought he had never seen him looking better, and said,

"Well, I daresay it's a good thing to get it off your mind."

Abel shook his head solemnly, not intending any disagreement, but imparting a shade of philosophic doubt. He was an old man with a fresh complexion, a thatch of curly grey hair, and those very blue eyes. He said with a pleasant country accent,

"That's as may be, but I've done it."

There didn't seem to be any more to be said.

Abel heaved a sigh.

"If the Lord wants me he'll call me. Such things as the making of wills or not making them, 'tisn't in reason they'd make any difference to Him."

The solemnity of the tone was embarrassing. William said,

"No, of course not."

Mr. Tattlecombe went through another slow motion of shaking his head.

"I didn't see it that way, but it's <u>come to me</u>. There's not so much time for thinking in the shop, but lying here with nothing else to do, it came over me powerful that I'd be called

12

upon to give an account of my stewardship. It was a nice little business till the war came along, and I looked forward to leaving it to Ernie, but it wasn't to be. When I got the news he'd died in the prison camp I lost heart. What with the bombing, and everything so scarce and no turnover to speak of, I couldn't seem to take any interest. And when the war stopped I couldn't seem to get going. It isn't so easy to start again when everything's different and you're getting on in years. Well, you know how it was, that day you came along and told me you'd been with Ernie in the camp—it meant a lot to me to hear how he'd talked about me and about the shop. And then you brought out those toys of yours and asked me what I thought of 'em. Do you remember what I said?"

William gave the wide, attractive grin which showed how strong and white his teeth were.

"You said, 'It isn't what I think about them, young man, it's what the public thinks. Put 'em in the window and see.'"

"And they were all sold out in half an hour. That's what the public thought of them, and that's what they've gone on thinking of 'em, haven't they? The Wurzel Dog, and the Boomalong Bird—they was the first. I tell you, if ever I saw the hand of the Lord I saw it then. Ernie was gone—the only grandson I ever had—the only bit of my flesh and blood except Abby. And the business gone downhill to such an extent that you might say it had got to the bottom. And then there was you, and there was the Wurzel Dogs and the Boom-along Birds, and the business getting up and, as you might say, beginning to boom along too. Well, if it wasn't the Lord's hand, what was it?"

William said, "We're doing very nicely, sir."

Abel nodded.

"Out of my stony griefs, Bethel I'll raise. I've told the Lord how grateful I am, and now I'm telling you. I made my will yesterday, and I've left the business and what's in the bank to you. Abby's provided for, and she's agreeable. If Matthew Salt did leave his sister Emily hung round her neck for good and all, as you may say, he made up for it as well as he could by providing very comfortably for Abby. He was a warm man was Matthew, and the chapel missed him very much when he went. Being a builder and contractor, they got their Ebenezer built for not much more than cost price. I didn't always see eye to eye with him—he was too fond of his own way— but he was a good brother and a good husband, and he left Abby well provided for. Not that to my mind any amount of providing would make up for having to live with Emily Salt."

"No, sir."

"I couldn't have done it," said Abel Tattlecombe. A blue spark gleamed in his eye. "There was some talk of Abby coming to keep house for me when my poor wife died, but I couldn't have done it—not if it meant Emily along with her, and I said so without any beating about the bush. 'The Lord gave, and the Lord has taken away,' I said, 'but he didn't give me Emily Salt, and I'm not flying in His face by taking her.' Let alone that she thinks any man is something that oughtn't to be going around off the chain, there's something about the look of her that'd turn me from my food. I don't know how Abby's put up with her all these years, but she's done it, and I'm sure it's a credit to her. She's a good woman, and as I started out to say, I've told her my intentions, and she's agreeable."

William really did feel quite overwhelmed. Gratitude and embarrassment made the next few minutes very uncomfortable. He didn't quite know what he said, but he finished up with,

"I hope you'll live to be a hundred, sir."

"That's for the Lord to say, William. I've passed my three score years and ten."

"So did Moses and Abraham. And what about Methuselah and all that lot? They lived practically for ever, didn't they?"

"It's for the Lord to say," said Abel. "I thought he'd called me this time, but seemingly not."

William had a strong feeling that street accidents could hardly be attributed to the Lord, but he wouldn't have ventured to say so.

"You'll have to watch your step, you know—especially at night. You had a very narrow escape."

Abel moved his head on the pillow.

"I was struck down."

Something in the tone, the solemn gaze, made William say,

"You stepped off the pavement, and you were struck down by a car."

"I was struck down," said Abel Tattlecombe. "I can't get from it, and I never shall. The doctor may say what he likes, and Abby can back him up, but I'm telling you that I was struck down. I come out by the side door and over to the kerb, just for a breath of air before I went to bed. The light shone out on the pavement and I could see it was wet, so I just went over to the kerb, meaning to come back again. A very mild air it was, but thickish, with a little rain in it. I left the door open behind me and went as far as the kerb and stood there. There was a car coming along fast. Just before it come up someone pushed me right between the shoulders. I was struck down, and the next thing I know I was in hospital. That's six weeks ago, and a week since I've been here, and you're the first that's listened to me when I said I was struck down. 'Who'd want to strike you down?' they said. That's neither here nor there, and no business of mine, I tell them. There's all sorts of wickedness in the world, and no

15

accounting for it. The imagination of the thoughts of their heart is evil continually, and what hath the righteous done? Struck down I was."

With a feeling that it might be a good plan to change the subject, William said,

"I sent you word by Mrs. Salt about the new assistant."

The blue eyes became shrewd.

"How's she doing? What's her name? I forget."

"Miss Eversley. She's doing very well. But I've put her on to painting the animals—gets the right expression in the eyes. I've got a new creature—the Dumble Duck. He's selling like hot cakes. We can't turn them out fast enough, even with four doing nothing else. I really needed Miss Eversley for the painting. Miss Cole says she can manage in the shop, but we really want more help there."

Abel gloomed.

"I won't be back for a fortnight, and I'll have to go easy. Maybe I'll not be back then. If you want more help you must get it, but I'll not have anyone except a respectable young woman. Nothing but chapel was what I used to say, but I don't hold out for that now—not if it's a respectable, well conducted young woman, which I hope is what you can say about this Miss Eversley."

Katharine Eversley rose before William's mind. She arose and shone. When she came into a room she made a light in it. She came into William's mind and made a light there. He heard himself saying that she was respectable and well conducted. It sounded like a piece out of another book. You didn't use words like that about Katharine. She had words which belonged to her—lovely, lovable, beloved. You couldn't use words about her like respectable and well conducted. He used them in a kind of wonder, and felt as though he was painting a bird of paradise drab.

16

It was actually a relief when Mr. Tattlecombe came back to the will.

"As I've been saying, I've done a bit of thinking whilst I've been laid up, and it came to me that if you knew what your prospects were you might turn your mind to getting settled in life. How old would you be?"

"Well, William Smith would be twenty-nine. I don't know about me."

Mr. Tattlecombe frowned.

"Now, now," he said, "that'll be enough about that. You're old enough to be married, and a good thing if you gave your mind to it in a serious way."

William looked down at the pattern on the carpet and said, partly to Abel and partly to himself,

"It's a bit difficult when you don't know who you are. A girl would have the right to know who she was taking."

Abel thumped the mattress with his clenched fist.

"She'd be taking William Smith, and she'd be getting a decent-living young man with good prospects that'd make her a good husband, and that's a thing any young woman may be thankful for!"

William lifted his eyes.

"Suppose I was engaged—or even married. Have you thought about that, Mr. Tattlecombe?"

Abel's colour had risen. He banged again.

"William Smith wasn't married, and you're not married! Don't you tell me anybody would forget a thing like that—not unless they wanted to, and I'd think better of you than that! Now you just listen to me! I've studied over it, and it's come to me quite plain. If you're William Smith by name and by nature, then you're not the first that went away from his home young and improved himself and come back a bit up in the world and feeling as if he didn't belong. To my mind

17

that's what's happened to you. You've no near kith and kin, and the neighbours don't recognize you because you've changed above a bit, and only natural, and you don't remember on account of your memory being gone. To my mind that's what's happened, and no mystery about it. But just for the sake of argument, let's take it you're not William Smith. To my way of thinking it's the Lord's doing. He taketh up one and putteth down another. If He's taken you up out of whatever you were and put you down as William Smith, then He's got His own purpose in doing it, and not for you and me to be kicking against the pricks."

William did not feel able to comment on this. He had a lot of respect for Mr. Tattlecombe's theology, but he could not always follow its reasoning. He remained silent.

Abel pursued his theme.

"You settle down and commit your way unto the Lord. Suppose it was to come to you after all this time that you were somebody else—how do you suppose you'd fit in? Forty-two was when William Smith was missing. Suppose you were someone else and you'd been missing even longer than that. There's a lot of things might be difficult if you come to think it out. Say you had a bit of money—someone else would have got it. Say there was a young woman you were sweet on—likely enough she'd be married to someone else. You can't come back and find things just the way they were— it isn't in nature. If you have a cut on your finger, the place heals up—it isn't in nature for it to stay open and aching. Same way with you. Supposing for the sake of argument that you wasn't William Smith—your place wouldn't be there any more, and you wouldn't be wanted. I can see that as clear as ever I saw anything in all my life, and it'd be a good thing if you could bring yourself to see it too. William Smith you are, and if it's the Lord's will, William Smith you'll stay."

At this point, to William's relief, the door opened upon Mrs. Salt and a cup of Benger. Abel in petticoats, with the same fresh complexion, blue eyes, and curly grey hair, she wore substantial black, with a fancy apron bought at a sale of work, and a gold brooch and a diamond initial A in a bunch of lace at her throat.

She said, "My brother has talked enough. You'd better be going, Mr. Smith," and William rose.

Mr. Tattlecombe was not pleased. If he had been up and dressed he would have held his own with Abby, but his leg was still in a splint and he didn't so much as know where his trousers were. Dignity forbade a futile protest. He stared at her, but she took no notice. Setting the Benger down, she adjusted the pillows, smoothed a wrinkle from the bedspread, and left the room, shepherding William.

On the way down someone stood in a doorway on the half-landing. She stood for a moment, and stepped back without word or sign, shutting the door. It made no sound, and nor did she. William had a glimpse of her and no more. He never did have more than a glimpse of her. On the three occasions when he had been in this house, at some time either coming or going Emily Salt had peered at him—from a turn in the passage, from over the banisters, from a dark doorway. He saw now as much as he had ever seen of her or wanted to see—a tall, awkward shape with a forward stoop, long arms hanging, a white bony face with deep eye-sockets, raiment of funeral gloom. He thought Abel amply justified in a preference for Mrs. Bastable who housekept for him in the rooms over Tattlecombe's Toy Bazaar. She wasn't the cook that Abigail was, but she was cheerful and willing, and she had no Emily Salt. Abel was very fond of his sister and very grateful to her for ministrations, but he could not do with Emily, and he was beginning to feel that he would be glad to get home.

19

He sipped his Benger and relaxed. Like everything that Abby cooked it was perfect. Mrs. Bastable got lumps in it three times out of four.

On the stairs Mrs. Salt was saying, "I hope you didn't contradict him, Mr. Smith. It isn't good for him to get excited. You had better let three or four days go before you come again."

When they reached the hall she hesitated for a moment and then opened the parlour door.

"I should like a word with you before you go."

William wondered what the word was going to be. He followed her into a room furnished in the Victorian manner with a bright carpet, plush curtains, a handsome solid couch and chairs, a fixture once devoted to gas but now converted to electricity in the middle of the ceiling, and a great variety of enlarged photographs, photogravures and china ornaments which combined uselessness and ugliness to a remarkable degree. The whole scene was reflected in a large gold-framed mirror over the mantelpiece. All the furniture had been inherited from Matthew Salt's parents and dated back to the time of their marriage, but Abigail Salt added regularly to the ornaments whenever she took a holiday or attended a bazaar.

She shut the door behind them, fixed her eyes on William, and said,

"Has my brother been talking to you about his will?"

William did wish that everyone would stop talking about wills. He couldn't say so of course, but it was the only thing he wanted to say. If he hadn't had the rather thick, pale skin which never changes colour he might have blushed. He felt just as uncomfortable as if he had. He said,

"Well, as a matter of fact he did talk about it."

Mrs. Salt's colour deepened. Her gaze was very direct.

20

"Then I hope you'll make him all the return you can. He's taken a wonderful fancy to you, and I hope you'll feel you've got a duty in return. He's got a right to do what he wants with his own, and he's had no objections from me, but I feel obliged to say that in my opinion you will owe him a duty."

William really had no idea what all this was about.

He said, "I'll do all I can," and she said, "Oh, well—" and turned back to the door. She had discharged her conscience and the interview was over. Without a word and without looking back she went along the narrow passage to the front door and opened it.

There was quite a thick drizzle outside. The wet air drew into the house with a smell of soot in it. The light from the hall shone out, showing two shallow steps down into the street. William turned on the top step with his hat in his hand and the light shining on his thick fair hair. He said, "Goodnight, Mrs. Salt, and thank you for letting me come." And Abby Salt said, "Goodnight, Mr. Smith," and shut the door.

William put on his hat and stepped down into the street.

CHAPTER 3

Detective Sergeant Frank Abbott was reflecting on the general unsatisfactoriness of crime. Not only did it flout morality and break the law, but it haled deserving detective sergeants of the Metropolitan Police Force out to remote suburbs in weather wet enough to drown a fish. His errand had nothing whatever to do with the case of William Smith, so there is no more to be said about it than it had got him just nowhere at all. The weather, on the other hand, had improved. The rain no longer came down in sheets. There was much less of it, and what there was no longer descended, it remained in the air and thickened it. It remained on the skin, the eyelashes, the hair, and with every breath it rushed into the lungs. Visibility was particularly poor.

Making for the Tube station, which could now be no more than a few hundred yards away, Frank was aware of a fellow pedestrian. The first thing he noticed was the light from an open door. A man in a waterproof stood black against it. The light dazzled on hair that was either fair or grey. Then he put on a hat and came down into the street, and the door was shut. The immediate effect was that the man had disappeared as if by the agency of one of those cloaks of darkness which used to figure in all the best fairy tales. Then little by little he emerged again, first as a shadow, and then, as they approached a lamp-post, in his original form as a man in a waterproof.

Frank was in process of registering this, when he became aware that there were two men, not walking together but one behind the other. The other man might have been there all along, or he might have slipped out of a cut between two houses, or, like the first man, he might have come out of a house. Frank Abbott wasn't consciously debating the point, but you are not much use as a detective unless you have a noticing habit of mind. The things noticed may never be thought of again, but if needed they will be there.

From the moment of the second man's appearance there was the briefest possible lapse of time before the thing happened. He appeared, he closed on the man in the waterproof, and hit him over the head. The first man dropped. The second man stooped over him, and then at the sound of Frank Abbott's running footsteps straightened up and dashed away across the street.

After a pursuit which almost immediately demonstrated its own futility Frank came back to the body on the pavement. To his relief it was beginning to stir. Then, as he stooped, it reared up and hit out. All quite natural, of course, but a little damping to a good Samaritan. The blow had very little aim. Frank dodged it, stepped back, and said,

"Hold up! The chap who hit you has gone off into the blue—I've just come back from chasing him. How are you—all right? Here, come along under the lamp and let's see."

Whether it was the voice sometimes unkindly described as Oxford, the intonation which undoubtedly bore the brand of culture, or the manner with its touch of assurance, William Smith put down his hands and advanced immediately into the light of the street-lamp. It shone down upon an uncovered head of very thick fair hair. Frank, retrieving a hat which had rolled into the gutter, presented it. But the young man did not immediately put it on. He stood there, rubbing his head and blinking a little, as if the light had come too quick on the heels of his black-out. The blinking eyelids were furnished with thick sandy lashes, the eyes behind them were of an indeterminate bluish grey, the rest of the features to match—rather broad and without much modelling, wide mouth, rather thick colourless skin. Frank, who touched six foot, gave him a couple of inches less. The shoulders under the raincoat were wide and the chest deep. He thought the man who had hit him wouldn't have stood much chance if he hadn't come up behind.

All this at first glance. And then, hard on that, a flash of recognition.

"Hullo! Haven't we met somewhere?"

23

William blinked again. His hand went up to his head and felt it gingerly. He said,

"I don't know—"

"My name's Abbott—Frank Abbott—Detective Sergeant Frank Abbott. Does that strike a chord?"

"I'm afraid it doesn't."

He took a step sideways, shut his eyes, and caught at the lamp-post. By the time Frank reached him he was straightening up again. He grinned suddenly and said,

"I'm all right. I think I'll sit down on a doorstep."

The grin had something very engaging about it. Frank slid an arm round him.

"We can do better than a doorstep. There's a police station just around the corner. If I give you a hand, can you get as far as that?"

There was another grin.

They set out, and after one or two halts arrived. William sank into a chair and closed his eyes. He was aware of people talking, but he wasn't interested. It would have been agreeable if someone could have unscrewed his head and put it away in a nice dark cupboard. For the moment it was of very little use to him, and he felt as if he could do better without it.

Somebody brought him a cup of hot tea. He felt a good deal better after he had drunk it. They wanted to know his name and address.

"William Smith, Tattlecombe's Toy Bazaar, Ellery Street, N.W."

"Do you live there?"

"Over the shop. Mr. Tattlecombe is away ill and I'm in charge. He's at his sister's—Mrs. Salt, 176 Selby Street, just round the corner. I've been out seeing him."

The Police Inspector loomed. He was a large man. He had a large voice. He said,

"Have you any idea who it was that hit you?"

"None whatever."

"Can you think of anyone who would be likely to hit you?"

"Not a soul."

"You say you were visiting your employer. Had you money on you—cash for wages—anything like that?"

"Not a bean."

William shut his eyes again. They talked. The Inspector's voice reminded him of a troop-carrying plane.

Then Frank Abbott was saying,

"What do you feel like about getting home? Is there anyone there to look after you?"

"Oh, yes, there's Mrs. Bastable—Mr. Tattlecombe's house-keeper."

"Well, if you feel like it, they'll ring up for a taxi and I'll see you home."

William blinked and said, "I'm quite all right." Then he grinned that rather boyish grin. "It's frightfully good of you, but you needn't bother—the head is very thick."

Presently he found himself in the taxi with Frank, and quite suddenly he wanted to talk, because it came to him that this was a Scotland Yard detective, and that he had said something about having seen him before. He passed from thought to speech without knowing quite how or when.

"You did, didn't you?"

"I did what?"

"Say you'd seen me before."

"Yes, I did. And I have."

"I wish you'd tell me how—and when—and where."

"Well, I don't know—it was a good long time ago."

"How long?"

25

"Oh, quite a long time. Pre-war, I should say."

William's hand came out and gripped his arm.

"I say—are you sure about that?"

"No—I just think so."

The grip on his arm continued. William said in an urgent voice,

"Do you remember where it was?"

"Oh, town. The Luxe, I think—yes, definitely the Luxe. Yes, that was it—a fairly big do at the Luxe. You danced with a girl in a gold dress, very easy on the eye."

"What was her name?"

"I don't know—I don't think I ever did know. She appeared to be booked about twenty deep."

"Abbott—do you remember my name?"

"My dear chap—"

William Smith took his hand away and put it to his head.

"Because, you see, I don't."

Frank said, "Steady on! You gave your name just now—William Smith."

"Yes, that's what I came out of the war with. What I want to know is how I went in. I don't remember anything before '42—not anything at all. I don't know who I am or where I came from. In the middle of '42 I found myself in a Prisoners of War camp with an identity disc which said I was William Smith, and that's all I know about it. So if you can remember my name—"

Frank Abbott said, "Bill—" and stuck.

"Bill what?"

"I don't know. I'm sure about the Bill, because it came into my head as soon as I saw you under the street-lamp before you spoke or anything."

William began to nod, and then stopped because it hurt.

"Bill feels right, and William feels all right, but Smith

doesn't. Anyhow I'm not the William Smith whose identity disc I came round with. I finished up in a concentration camp, and after I got released, and got home, and got out of hospital I went to look up William Smith's next of kin—said to be a sister, living in Stepney. She'd been bombed out and no one knew where she'd gone. But there were neighbours, and they all said I wasn't William Smith. For one thing they were real bred-in-the-bone Cockneys, and they despised my accent. They were awfully nice people and too polite to say so, but one of the boys gave it away. He said I talked like a B.B.C. announcer. None of them could tell me where the sister had gone. I didn't get the feeling that she was the kind of person who would be missed, and they were all so sure I wasn't William Smith that I didn't really feel I need go on looking for her. If you could remember anyone who might possibly know who I was—''

There was quite a long pause. The street-lights shone into the taxi and were gone again—one down, t'other come on. First in a bright glare, and then in deep shade, William saw his companion come and go. The face which continually emerged and disappeared again was quite unknown to him, yet on the other side of the gap which cut him off from the time when he hadn't been William Smith they had met and spoken. They must have known the same people. Perhaps it was the blow on the head which made him feel giddy when he thought about this. It was a little like Robinson Crusoe finding the footprint on the desert island. He looked at Frank, and thought he was the sort of chap you would remember if you remembered anything. High-toned and classy—oh, definitely. Fair hair slicked back till you could pretty well see your face in it—he remembered that at the station. Long nose in a long, pale face. Very good tailor—

Curiously enough, it was at this point that memory stirred,

if faintly. Somewhere in William's mind was the consciousness that he hadn't always worn the sort of clothes he was
wearing now. They were good durable reach-me-downs,
but—memory looked vaguely back to Savile Row.

Frank Abbott said, "I'm sorry, but I don't seem to get any
farther than Bill."

CHAPTER 4

William got up the next day with a good-sized lump on his
head, but not otherwise any the worse. He wouldn't have
told Mrs. Bastable anything about it, only unfortunately she
happened to be looking out of her bedroom window and not
only saw him come home in a taxi, but having immediately
thrown up the sash, she heard Detective Sergeant Abbott ask
him if he was sure he would be all right now. After which
she met William on the stairs in a condition of palpitant cu-
riosity. If the injurious conjecture that he had been brought
home drunk really did present itself, it was immediately dis-
pelled. She was all concern, she fluttered, she proffered a
variety of nostrums, and she certainly didn't intend to go to
bed, or to allow him to go to bed, until she had been told all
about it. She punctuated the narrative with little cries of
"Fancy that!" and "Oh, good gracious me!"

When he had finished she was all of a twitter.

"Well, there now—what an escape! First Mr. Tattlecombe,
and then—whatever should we have done if you'd been
taken?"

"Well, I wasn't."

Mrs. Bastable heaved a sigh.

"You might have been. It's given me the goose flesh all over. Only fancy if that had been the police come to break the news and Mr. Tattlecombe still in his splint! Oh, my gracious me—whatever would have happened?"

She was a little bit of a thing with a light untidy fluff of hair and a nose which went pink in moments of emotion. It was pink now and it quivered. She dabbed aimlessly at her hair and three of the remaining pins fell out. William stooped to pick them up, and wished he hadn't. He said he thought he would go to bed, and went.

He fell asleep almost as soon as his head touched the pillow and passed into his dream. He had been having it less and less—only twice last year, and this year once, a long time back in the summer. He had it now. But there was something different about it—something troubled and disturbed, like a reflection in troubled water. There were the three steps leading up to the door, but the door wouldn't open. He pushed, and felt it held against him. But not by bolt, or bar, or lock. There was someone pushing against him on the other side of the door. Then the dream changed. Someone laughed, and he thought it was Emily Salt. He had never heard her laugh, but he thought it was Emily. He saw her peep at him round a door—not the door of his dream, but one of the doors in Abby Salt's house. And Abby Salt said, "Poor Emily—she doesn't like men," and William woke up and turned over and went to sleep again and dreamed about being on a desert island with packs of Wurzel Dogs, and flocks of Boomalong Birds, and a pond full of Dumble Ducks. It was an agreeable dream, and he woke in the morning feeling quite all right.

When he had dealt with the post and given everyone time to get going, he went through to the workshop which they had contrived out of what had been a parlour and a rather ramshackle conservatory beyond it. Of course all the glass had been broken during the war, but they had got it mended now, and it was a fine light place, if chilly in winter. Two oil-stoves contended with the cold, one in the parlour, and the other in the conservatory. When Mrs. Bastable looked after them they had diffused a strong smell of paraffin without perceptibly raising the temperature. William took them over because he noticed that Katharine's hands were blue, and it occurred to him that the oily smell was definitely inappropriate. Roses, or lavender, but quite definitely not kerosene oil. He wrested the stoves from Mrs. Bastable, who took umbrage and had to be pacified, but there was no more smell and the temperature went up considerably.

When William came through from the shop an elderly man and a boy were preparing carcasses of dogs and birds at the conservatory end. Katharine Eversley was sitting at a large kitchen table in the parlour putting the finishing touches to a rainbow-coloured Boomalong Bird with an open scarlet beak.

William came and stood beside her.

"That's a good one."

"Yes—he screams, doesn't he? I've just finished with him and then I'll start undercoating the ducks. They're going to be pretty good when we get on to those metallic paints. There—he's done!" She turned so that she could look up at him. "Are you all right? Miss Cole says someone tried to rob you last night."

"Well, I don't know what he was trying to do. He hit me over the head just as I was coming out after seeing Mr. Tattlecombe."

She said quickly, "Did he hurt you?"

"Oh, just a bump. My hat took the worst of it."

"Did you catch him?"

"No—I was out. A detective from Scotland Yard picked me up and brought me home in a taxi. Very nice chap."

"Then you don't know who hit you?"

"No. Abbott said he went off like greased lightning."

Katharine moved the Boomalong Bird away and picked up a waddling duck. She opened a tin of paint and began to lay on a flesh-pink undercoating. William drew a stool up to the other side of the table and started on a duck of his own. After a moment Katharine said,

"It's rather—extraordinary—you and Mr. Tattlecombe both having accidents—like that."

William grinned.

"Mr. Tattlecombe says he was 'struck down.' I certainly was."

"What does he mean, 'struck down'?" said Katharine.

"He thinks someone pushed him. He says he came out of the side door. When he found it was wettish he left it open behind him and went over to the edge of the kerb. He saw a car coming, and then he said he was struck down."

Katharine looked up, her brush suspended. She wore a faded green overall which covered her dress. Her skin and her lips were as they had been made. She was pale. Her eyes had their dark look. William knew all their looks by now—the dark, like shadows on a pool; the bright, like peat-water in the sun; the mournful clouding look; and, loveliest and rarest, something which he couldn't even describe to himself, a kind of trembling tenderness, as if the pool were troubled by an angel. Young men in love have very romantic thoughts.

Katharine Eversley looked at William Smith and said,

"It was at night?"

"Oh, yes."

"He came out in the dark and the door was open behind him? Would there have been a light in the passage?"

31

"Yes, that's how he knew it was wet—the light shone out on the pavement."

She went back to her painting.

"And you came out in the dark last night?"

"Yes."

"With the door open from a lighted passage?"

William looked surprised.

"Yes. Why?"

"I was wondering. It seems odd—"

"What were you wondering?"

She didn't answer that. She said,

"What is Mr. Tattlecombe like?"

"Like?"

She said, "How tall is he?"

"About the same as me—about five-foot-ten."

"Is he about the same build too?"

"Just about."

He was contemplating her steadily now. She went on drawing her brush across the wood in long, even strokes.

"What sort of hair has he got?"

William said soberly, "Very thick and grey. Why?"

"I was wondering about your both being struck—that was his word, wasn't it?"

"Struck down."

"Well, I was wondering—whether there was anyone—who had a grudge against him—or anything like that. If you are about the same height and all, and you were coming out of his front door—your hair is very fair—it wouldn't look so different from grey hair, coming out like that with the light behind you, would it? The person who pushed Mr. Tattlecombe before might have been having another try."

William said cheerfully, "Or it might be the other way

round. The chap who took a swipe at Mr. Tattlecombe might have thought it was me."

Katharine's brush stopped in the middle of a stroke—stopped, and went on again.

"Do you know of anyone who has a grudge against you?"

"No, I don't. But there might be someone. Only it would have to be someone out of my horrid past. Seven years seems rather a long time to keep up a grudge, doesn't it?"

Katharine said nothing. She had finished undercoating her duck. She took another.

William said, "I tell you what I think. It was wet when Mr. Tattlecombe had his accident. I think he slipped on the kerb. When he came round he was all shaken up, and he thought he'd been pushed. That's what I think."

"And you?"

"Just a chance see-what-he's-got affair. Chap on the prowl and no one about, and he thinks he'll try his luck. I might have had a nice fat wallet."

"Did he take anything?"

"No—because Abbott came up." There was a short pause. Then he said, "There was one odd thing—at least I think it's odd, because I can't account for it. You know I was knocked right out, and then I came round and Abbott was there, and my hat had come off and he picked it up—"

"Yes."

"There was a street-lamp not so far ahead, and Abbott had a torch. What I mean to say is, it was pretty murky, but I saw something on the pavement and I picked it up."

"What was it?"

"I thought it was a piece of paper or a bill. As a matter of fact it was a letter. I thought it must have fallen out of my pocket, so I just slipped it back there—I'd got my raincoat on. But this morning when I had a look at it, it was a note from Mrs. Salt to Mr. Tattlecombe—and that's what I thought was odd."

Katharine's brush was arrested.

"Why should Mrs. Salt write him notes when he's lying in bed in her house? Or am I being stupid?"

William laughed.

"That's just what I thought. And then I saw there was a date, and it was quite an old letter. He must have got it just before he had his accident. I remember his saying Mrs. Salt had written to ask him to go up there on the Sunday. What beats me is, how did that note get into my pocket? Because it must have been in my pocket, or it couldn't have fallen to the pavement, and I couldn't have picked it up. Not that it matters of course. There—I've finished my duck!" He reached for another and dipped his brush.

After a little silence Katharine said,

"You know, this is a most dreadfully uneconomic way of turning out these creatures. If they were factory-made, you'd clear about double the profit."

"Yes, I know. Just before his accident I had got Mr. Tattlecombe to the point of agreeing to something of the sort. He didn't like it, but I'd got him to the point of saying I could make enquiries. We're protected by our patents, so there was no reason why we shouldn't go ahead. As I said to him, if the children round about here like the animals, the children in other places probably will too, and if they like them, why shouldn't they have them?"

She looked up and smiled.

"Yes—why shouldn't they? What did you do about it?"

"I wrote to Eversleys'—" He checked on the name. "That's funny, isn't it? I never thought of it before. I don't know why I didn't because when you said your name it did just seem to me—" he drew his thick fair brows together in a frown

34

and gazed at her in a concentrated sort of way—"it did just seem to me as if—well, as if I'd heard it before."

"Did it?"

She spoke so softly that he could hardly hear the words.

"Yes, it did. I didn't connect it with Eversleys' but of course that's what it was. It sounds awfully stupid, but the fact is, I was—well, I was thinking too much about you. I mean, I was thinking you were just exactly what we wanted, and Miss Cole was being a bit difficult, so I hadn't much attention left over for things like names. But it ought to have struck me afterwards, only somehow it didn't. People's surnames don't seem to belong to them the way their other names do."

Katharine's heart beat as hard as if she were seventeen and her first proposal looming. She thought, "He trying to tell me that he thinks of me as Katharine. Oh, my darling, how sweet, and how ridiculous!" She said,

"I know just what you mean. I don't think of my friends by their names at all."

He considered that.

"Don't you? How do you think of them?"

"I don't think I can describe it. Not names—or faces—it's just something that is them and not anyone else."

"Yes—I know what you mean."

"You were going to tell me about Eversleys'. What happened?"

He was still frowning.

"I suppose there's no connection?"

She gave him her lovely smile.

"Well, that's just what there is—a connection."

"But they're in a pretty big way."

"I'm a poor relation. Go on and tell me what happened. You wrote them. What did they say?"

"They asked me to come and see them."

Katharine bent over her duck.

"Did you go?"

"Yes, I went, but it wasn't any good."

She half looked up, checked herself, and looked down again.

"Tell me what happened."

"There's nothing to tell. I went in. I didn't see either of the partners. I came out again, and bumped into an old boy in the street."

She bent lower.

"What sort of an old boy?"

"Looked like a clerk—highly respectable. First I thought he was tight, and then I thought he was ill. He asked me who I was, and I told him. Seemed a bit odd, the whole thing, but he said he was all right and went off."

"But you saw someone inside, in the office?"

"Yes—Mr. Eversley's secretary."

"What was she like?"

He laughed. "She?"

"Wasn't it a woman? Secretaries are as a rule."

"Yes—rather a goodlooking one. Not young, but quite a looker. I was trying to catch you out. I wanted to see if you knew her."

"I know you were. I do. Her name is Miss Jones. She's Cyril Eversley's secretary—he's the senior partner. She's been there a long time—something like fifteen years. Very efficient, and as you say, quite a looker." She lifted her eyes to his face. "What happened when you saw her?"

"Well, just nothing. She'd given me rather a late appointment, just on six o'clock. Neither of the partners was there, and the office was packing up. She didn't seem inclined to give me very much time. I showed her some of the creatures and asked if the firm would be interested in manufacturing

36

them under our patents, but she hardly looked at them."

"What did she look at?" said Katharine.

"Well—me. My word she's got a gimlet eye! I got the feeling I was a base-born black beetle all right. She said she didn't think the things were in their line, but she'd tell Mr. Eversley about them and let me know. A couple of days later I got a line to say that Mr. Eversley wasn't interested."

Katharine went back to her duck.

"When was all this?"

"Oh, just before Mr. Tattlecombe went into hospital."

"Then—who actually wrote the original letter—you, or Mr. Tattlecombe?"

"Oh, I did."

"Wrote it, or typed it?"

She heard him laugh.

"You've never seen my writing, or you wouldn't ask! I didn't actually want them to turn us down, you know. It was in my very best typing, beautiful and legible and clear."

"And the signature?"

"Oh, a quite recognizable William Smith."

Katharine said slowly and carefully,

"That sounds like a frightful cross-examination. But I thought as I do know him, I could perhaps find out whether Cyril Eversley ever saw your letter. He mightn't have, you know—he does leave quite a lot to Miss Jones. And I thought it would be easier if I knew what sort of letter it was, and whether it was signed by you or by Mr. Tattlecombe." She looked up to find him frowning and her colour rose. "Oh, I'm sorry!"

The frown changed to an expression of dismay.

"No—no—why do you say that? It's most awfully good of you. I was just thinking—"

"What?"

37

William registered candid surprise.

"I don't know. I got sort of a come-over. I don't even know what it was about. You said you'd find out if Eversley had ever had my letter and I went into a sort of spin. The result of being cracked over the head, I expect—nothing to do with what you were saying. But I don't think I'll do anything more until Mr. Tattlecombe is about again. I don't think he'd like it if he thought I was doing things while he was out of the way. You don't feel as if I was being ungrateful, do you? Because I shouldn't like you to think anything like that."

Katharine wasn't thinking anything like that. She was thinking rather breathlessly that she had been on the edge of walking enthusiastically over a precipice, and she felt a good deal of gratitude to William's scruples about Mr. Tattlecombe. Suppose he hadn't had them. Suppose she had been confronted with the choice of going back on what she had offered or appearing in Cyril's office as the champion of William Smith. Or, worse than Cyril, Brett. She didn't wish Mr. Tattlecombe's sufferings to be in any way prolonged, but she had a feeling that it would be a pity if he were to come back to work too soon. She just wasn't ready to take William Smith by the hand and lead him into the family circle—yet.

CHAPTER 5

Cyril Eversley put out a hand and touched the bell on his office table. Like everything else about him the hand was long and thin. If his cousin Brett looked like a Georgian squire, he himself had rather the air of a mediaeval scholar— a flowing robe and a skull-cap would have been much more appropriate than a modern suit. He was seven years older than Brett and the senior partner. No one would have guessed that they were related. Where Brett was dark and florid, Cyril had the thinning fair hair, the pallor, and slight stoop of a delicate man who leads a sedentary life. He might have been an artist, a scholar, a dilettante. He was, as a matter of fact, a little of all three. The rather charming water-colour drawing of his daughter Sylvia which faced him across the room was his own work, he could still read Greek for pleasure, and he was a collector of eighteenth-century miniatures and snuff-boxes.

Almost before he had drawn his hand back from the bell the door opened and Miss Jones came in.

"Yes, Mr. Eversley?"

He looked up with his slight habitual frown and said, "Come in and shut the door."

With the click of the latch her manner changed.

That "Yes, Mr. Eversley?" had been any secretary to any employer—voice, manner, and look all just right—the efficient, trusted employee answering a summons. But as soon as the door was shut she became someone else. It was as if she came in and threw off some drab uniform coat, to display the bright dress which had been hidden under it. She seemed a different woman as she came over to stand by the table and say, "What is it?" William's description of her may serve—"Not young, but a looker." A moment ago she might easily have been forty; the change in look and manner took ten years away. Actually she was thirty-seven. There was bright natural colour in the oval face and well cut lips, good lashes to shade the hazel eyes. The tall, upright figure was pleasantly curved, the plain dark dress very well cut. There was some grace of movement, and a noticeable effect of vitality. When it came to the hands and feet, nature had turned suddenly stingy. Neither were well shaped, but she wore good shoes, and did all she could to the hands which a secretary cannot hope to keep out of sight. She groomed them assiduously and used a very discreet nail-polish.

To her "What is it?" Cyril Eversley replied with a shade of petulance,

"Why must it be anything?"

She smiled a little.

"I don't know, but it is."

He threw himself back in his chair.

"For God's sake sit down! I'm worried to death."

"Poor Cyril! As I said before, what is it?"

She was seating herself. If anyone came in, she had writing-pad and pencil before her—a discussion was in progress, presently a decision would be taken and a letter dictated. It had all been going on for so long that every move had become instinctive.

Cyril picked up a letter from his blotting-pad—thick paper covered with a strong, square writing rather reminiscent of cuneiform.

"It's Katharine's trust," he said. "This is from Admiral Holden, who is the third trustee."

"Well?"

"It isn't well at all. He was supposed to be dying, and he hasn't died. He has recovered, and he seems to have heard from Katharine. I don't know what she said to him, but this is what he writes:

'Dear Eversley,

I had a letter from Katharine a couple of months ago. She mentioned that she was giving up her flat and looking for something smaller. She also mentioned that she was going to take a job. I could not understand why this should be necessary, but I was not at the time fully recovered, so I thought that I would wait until I could go into the matter with you in person. Katharine has not written again, and I have not her present address. I shall be in town next week and should like to call upon you on Wednesday morning or Thursday afternoon, whichever would be the more convenient to yourself. I could then go into Katharine's affairs with you and your cousin Brett. After nearly two years of incapacity I should be glad of the opportunity of bringing my trusteeship up to date.

Yours sincerely,

J. G. Holden.'"

Miss Jones repeated her "Well?"

Eversley opened his hand and let the letter fall.

"What are we going to do?" he said.

"The money isn't there?"

"You know it isn't there. You know we had to borrow it in '45. If things had looked up, we could have paid it back. We had to borrow it—you know that as well as I do. It was either that or a smash, and we've always kept up the income payments—until the other day. I told Brett it was folly to cut them, but he's so extravagant—he won't cut out anything himself. If we'd gone on paying Katharine her income, there wouldn't have been any trouble. It's this cutting her down that is bringing Holden into it. He's never done anything before except sign what was put in front of him. Of course all through the war he was serving, and then he had that motor smash and nobody thought he'd ever get up off his bed again—and now he says he's recovered and wants to go into Katharine's affairs. What are we going to do?"

He had the helpless look of a child who has tumbled down and waits for someone to pick him up. She thought, "He's a drifter—he's drifted into this. When firms drift they smash. They've been drifting for years. You can drift on to the rocks, but you don't drift off them. But even if there was a smash, there would be pickings. In any case I'm too far in—" She said,

"You say he's always signed everything you put in front of him."

"He won't now. He'll want to go into it all. We've got to show him figures—he's got to be convinced. Can't you put up something that will make him think it's all right?"

She raised her eyebrows.

"My dear Cyril, you're not asking me to fudge the books!"

She saw him wince at the word. Cyril all over. You had to wrap things up for him—make them sound pretty. A plain thing, and he panicked.

"Mavis—for heaven's sake!"

"Well, that's what you're asking me to do, isn't it?"

He threw out that long, slim hand.

"Don't you see I'm only asking for time to get the money paid back? Now Sylvia is married, I can sell Evendon and move into something smaller. Brett must stop taking so much out of the firm—I've always told him it wouldn't stand it. We must both cut down and get the money paid back. And Katharine must have her income. It was the merest folly to cut it down. But we must have time—don't you see, we must have time."

She sat there looking at him. He said, "Don't you see?" She saw very well. More than he knew—more than he guessed—more than he would have any courage for. She weighed the chances, the probabilities, putting this down on the credit, this on the debit side.

The silence was more than he could bear. He rushed in on it with nervous speech.

"Brett must marry her. That's the solution of course. I don't know why he hasn't fixed it up before it came to this. A man has got to settle down some time, and I don't know what more he wants. He's always admired her—who doesn't? She's a charming creature. If he doesn't take care, someone will get in before him. And if it came to a marriage settlement, and lawyers imported into it—well, as I said to him not long ago, it would be just flat ruin."

"What did he say?"

"He said he had asked her and she had refused him."

Miss Jones considered that carefully. She couldn't decide whether she wanted Brett Eversley to marry Katharine. She disliked Katharine very much—it might serve her right. On the other hand, once you started anything you couldn't always tell where it was going to stop. Perhaps better to play for time.

Cyril couldn't get the word off his tongue.

"Time—that's what we want—time. If we can satisfy Holden and get time to pay the money back we'll be all right. Can't you think of something we can do?"

43

She said, "I could."

"Mavis!"

"What do I get out of it?"

The words came across the table like a pistol-shot. He said her name again in a shocked tone, and she smiled.

"Look here, Cyril, if I do this I'm risking a lot. It's got to be worth my while. I'll be risking a lot, and you know it. Well, I'm not doing it for nothing, and that's flat." The hazel eyes had the hard, dominant look which had impressed William Smith.

Cyril Eversley said, "What do you want?" But he knew before she spoke.

Her smile widened.

"You've been a widower for five years—Sylvia is married. Everybody expects you to marry again."

He said, "It would make too much talk."

"My dear Cyril, men marry their secretaries every day. Who cares about talk?"

He looked down at his own long, nervous fingers. At some moment, he didn't know when, they had picked up a short length of red pencil. He saw them twitch on it, rolling it to and fro.

"I should be lost without you here."

"You needn't let that stand in your way. I like to have a finger in the pie. I would stay on at any rate until we'd got everything straight."

There was more to put straight than he knew about—more than she ever intended him to know. It could be done if she brought this off. The Admiral was a godsend. She pressed her advantage.

"Look here, Cyril, it's a pretty good bargain for you—honestly. Don't you ever get tired of your own company down at Evendon? I should have thought you'd be bored stiff now that you haven't got Sylvia dashing in and out with her crowd."

He looked up with a faint gleam of humour.

"There used to be rather too much dashing in and out, you know."

"I daresay, but there's no sense in going to the opposite extreme. And you want someone to run the house. I don't mind betting you're being robbed right and left."

Inwardly he shrank. Mavis had a coarse streak in her. She attracted him, as vital, domineering women do attract his type of man. Sometimes the attraction was strong enough to blind him to everything else. When it wasn't she could jar him badly. No man likes to be urged to marry, but he had to reckon with long habit and the pressure of her will on his.

She said with half a laugh, "You really want a wife a great deal more than I want a husband. I think I'm a bit of a fool to take it on. I shouldn't if I wasn't fond of you, but there it is."

He said, "I know." And then, "Why can't we just go on as we are? As you say, I haven't got so much to offer you now."

She laughed outright.

"Perhaps not, but I happen to want it. I said it was a bargain, and I said you'd be getting the best of it, and so you will. But I shouldn't be going into it if I wasn't getting something too. You'll get a goodlooking, presentable wife and an efficient mistress for your house, and I'll keep on at the office until we've straightened everything out and I've trained somebody else. Comfort, efficiency, and security—that's your share of the bargain. I give up my independence, and I get a double job, a lot of hard work, and—security. If that satisfies me, it's just your luck. I'm putting all my cards on the table."

45

She had a moment's thought of how surprised he would be if she really did so—surprised, and shocked. That was one of the amusing things about Cyril—the moment you got down to facts they shocked him.

He was staring at his hand again, and at the red pencil. His fingers had tightened on it. He did not speak. She could feel him resisting—not actively, but in a withdrawn kind of way, as if he had gone into another room and locked the door. If they had been anywhere else, she would have let her temper go. Nothing ever enraged her so much, and he knew it. But he knew that she couldn't make a scene in the office. He was afraid of her scenes, but she couldn't make one here. Perhaps one of the things which nerved him to resist her was the knowledge that once they were married she would be perfectly free to make him a scene whenever she chose.

Mavis Jones put out an ugly manicured hand and picked up Admiral Holden's letter. She might have been picking up a weapon. She picked it up, glanced at it, and put it down again.

"Wednesday or Thursday next week," she said crisply. "It doesn't give us too much time."

The thrust went keenly home. He started, dropped the pencil, and said with panic in his voice,

"What can you do?"

It was surrender, and they both knew it. The colour was warm in her face as she leaned across the table and laid her hands on his.

"Don't worry—I'll pull it off. The less you know, the better. I'll go through all the papers and cook something up." She laughed good-humouredly. "There's almost nothing you can't do with figures—especially when you're good at them and the other person isn't."

She had better not have said that—he wasn't any too good at them himself. He might start thinking.

She got up and came round the table and put an arm about his neck.

"Aren't you going to kiss me?"

He turned a harried face.

"Mavis!"

"My poor old man! You needn't worry like that—it'll be all right on the night."

"Are you sure?"

He had been leaning back against her. He turned now as if for shelter and pressed his face into her neck. She held him like that and said,

"Quite sure." And then, "We'd better give notice at the register office today. There has to be a clear day's notice. We can get married on Saturday and go away for the weekend. No need to give it out—better let all this other business fade a bit first. So you don't have to feel you're being rushed."

"Need we—"

She bent and kissed him.

"Darling, I simply can't do it unless I'm your wife. And he's coming next week—that's where the hurry comes in. It's a big thing, and I'll do it for my husband, but—oh, Cyril, you must see that I couldn't do it for anyone else."

Cyril Eversley saw.

CHAPTER 6

On that Thursday morning, the undercoating having dried on the Dumble Ducks, they were being decked out in green and bronze metallic paint, with exciting touches of red and blue, and yellow bills. At the far end of the conservatory old Mr. Bindle was telling the boy Robert all the things that boys had never been allowed to do when he was young. From long habit Robert, whom everyone but Mr. Bindle called Bob, was able to say "Yes" and "No" at the right places and go solidly on thinking about the model aeroplane he was making at home in his spare time. He was a long, rangy boy with a freckled face and competent hands, and, waking or sleeping, he very seldom thought about anything but aeroplanes. Neither he nor Mr. Bindle took any interest in Mr. Smith and Miss Eversley who were painting ducks at the parlour end of the workshop.

William was pleased with his duck. It had a cream breast, brown and green plumage, enormous yellow feet, and a rolling eye. It waddled, and its beak gaped. He was pleased with it, but a good deal of his mind was taken up with something else. Thursday is early-closing day in the outlying parts of London. He wanted to know what Katharine was going to do when she put on her hat and left the shop at one o'clock. Suppose she went to bed at about eleven, that left approximately ten hours in which things could be done. He wondered what sort of things she was going to do.

This happened every Thursday morning. It also happened

on Saturday evening when the long, deserted hours of Sunday began to loom up. Saturday was worse than Thursday, because at the very lowest reckoning there were about fourteen hours of Sunday during which Katharine would not only not be with him, but would be walking, talking, and doing things with other people. Every time a Thursday or a Saturday came round his feelings on the subject became more acute. Today they were rapidly approaching the point where he would no longer be able to keep them to himself. He may never have heard of the poet who declared that he either fears his fate too much or his deserts are small that dares not put it to the touch to gain or lose it all, but he certainly would have agreed with him. The trouble was that he did fear his fate and was most wholeheartedly convinced of the smallness of his deserts. Yet what he had not so far dared put to the touch was no matter of headlong wooing, but the mere "Madam, will you walk, madam will you talk?" on a Thursday or a Sunday afternoon.

By a quarter to one, and his fourth duck, he got it out.

"What do you do on your half day?"

Katharine was putting a bright blue patch on her duck's head and shading it off with green metallic paint. She said,

"Oh, different things—"

Once started, William could go on. In a sledgehammer kind of way he inquired,

"What are you doing this afternoon?"

"I haven't really thought."

"You wouldn't—I suppose—you couldn't—I mean you wouldn't—"

Katharine looked up, wanted to laugh, wanted to cry, looked down again. Her lips quivered into a very faint smile.

"I might."

"Oh, I say—would you really? I've wanted to ask you for

ages, but I didn't know—I mean I thought—I mean you must have lots of friends—"

She looked up again. He had a smear of paint on his left cheek. She said,

"Are you asking me to go out with you?"

"Well, I was—but of course—"

"You can't back out of it now—it would be frightfully rude. Where shall we go?"

"Where would you like to go?"

"I'd like to go somewhere in your car and then come back to my flat and have tea, because it isn't any fun driving after dark."

"You wouldn't really, would you? It's a most frightful old thing, more or less made up out of scrap-iron. Everyone laughs at it, but it goes. Only it isn't the sort of thing—"

"You've got a very unbelieving nature. I've told you what I'd like to do. Did you really mean to paint that duck black? Because that's what you're doing."

William contemplated his work with horror. The duck, funereally black except for a squawking beak and an unpainted eye, leered back at him. He brightened.

"I don't know about meaning to, but touched up with the metallic green he'll be rather effective—the bold, bad buccaneering drake. And I think he'd better have an orange-coloured beak and feet. He'll have to dry first. It isn't worth starting anything else—it's just on one. You're quite sure—"

Katharine said, "Quite," without looking up.

"Then I'll go along and get the car. Miss Cole can shut up. I'll be waiting for you where Canning Row comes in." He grinned suddenly and said, "She goes the other way."

They drove out over Hampstead Heath. The car deserved all that William had said about it, but it was quite obviously the pride of his heart. With his own hands he had assembled it from the scrap-heap, tinkered here, straightened there, contrived, coerced, and finally applied two coats of enamel. Katharine, who remembered other cars, had a ridiculous softening of the heart for this one.

They stopped and had lunch, and then went on again through a winter afternoon with a pale gold sun in a pale blue sky and mist coming up out of the ground. Katharine found that she did not have to talk at all. She only had to sit there and every now and then say, "How lucky," or "That was very clever of you," whilst William recited the saga of how he had picked up his tin kettle bit by bit. He was perfectly happy and completely absorbed. If everything else about him changed, she thought, that was one thing which would never alter, his capacity for being absorbed in whatever it was he happened to be thinking about at the time. If he was thinking about her he could paint a duck black without knowing it, but if he happened to be thinking about the duck he might not notice whether she was there or not. At least—well, she wondered. She was so taken up with her own thoughts that she missed the soul-stirring narrative of how William had acquired a fog-light, which was a pity, because it threw considerable light upon his energy, perseverance, and resource.

They got to the flat, which had been lent to Katharine by a friend who had gone abroad.

"I had to let my own—it was too expensive—so I don't know what I should have done if Carol hadn't come to my rescue."

The flat was a cluster of rooms built over a garage in a mews. William drove between tall brick pillars on to what looked like a cobbled village street with a row of cottages on either side. In the last of the daylight the scene was picturesque. Children bowled hoops and roller-skated. There were lines of washing, and lines from which washing had been

51

taken in, one of them made of two skipping-ropes tied together. There were wide garage doors in many shades of
paint and corresponding degrees of decay. Flights of concrete
steps guarded by iron railings ran up to the flats above. They
had gabled roofs and occasionally window-boxes, empty
now. The railing of Katharine's steps was painted scarlet, and
so was the front door.

Standing at the top while she found her key, she drew
William's attention to the view. Behind the roofs of the houses
opposite tall, bare plane trees stood out black against a stretch
of pale green sky. Between the gables lights sparked like
fireflies. Away to the left someone was hammering on metal,
bang, clang, bang, and two radio sets were contending. The
learned professor who was giving an instructive talk was
obviously being turned up louder and louder in an attempt
to drown the crooner next door, but the saccharine melan-
choly pursued and overtook him.

They went in and shut the door. The sounds receded without being lost. Katharine switched on the light, showing a
narrow passage which turned at right angles. There was a
living-room, two bedrooms, a dressing-room, a kitchen, and
a bathroom. When she had shown William where to wash
his hands she put on the kettle and then went into her bedroom and drew the curtains.

Carol's taste in chintzes was cheerful. Curtains and bed-
spreads were canary-yellow, with a pattern of blue and purple
zig-zags and triangles. All the furniture was briskly modern.
Katharine went over to the bright yellow chest of drawers,
picked up a large standing photograph, and put it away in
a drawer. Then she took off her tweed coat and skirt, hung
it up in the yellow cupboard, and slipped on a long-sleeved
woollen dress. It was half way between blue and green in
colour, and it did very becoming things to her skin. Even

without lipstick and powder she looked all lighted up. But this was not the shop—lipstick and powder there would be.

She found William in the sitting-room, the gas fire lighted, and the curtains drawn. He explained that he thought she would be cold, and helped her to get tea. They might have been doing it for years. Actually, when she came into the room he was sitting at the piano picking out a tune with one finger. As she was pouring out the tea she came back to that.

"Do you play the piano?"

"I shouldn't think so."

"Don't you know?"

"I don't know very much about myself. My memory only goes back to '42."

She said, "Yes—you told me. I wondered how far it went. You see, it's obvious that you must remember quite a lot—reading, writing, arithmetic. What else?"

He said, "Yes, I never thought about that. That sort of thing is all there. The usual history and geography seem to have stuck—schoolboy Latin—maths. I learnt German in the camps, and I rubbed up my French a whole lot. You know, that's one reason I don't think I'm William Smith, because he left school at fourteen and he wouldn't have learned French or Latin. Mine weren't anything to boast about, but I did learn them."

"And the piano?"

He laughed.

"You heard me!"

"You were picking out a tune. Do you know what it was?"

"Well, it was trying to be 'Auld Lang Syne.'"

"Why?"

He gazed at her.

"I don't know—it just came into my head. When you come to think of it, it's odd to remember tunes and forget people,

53

isn't it? There must be people I used to know walking around, and I might bump into them and never know them. That gives you an odd feeling. I used to think about it a lot and wonder if I should run into any of them, but it never happened until the other day."

Katharine put down her cup.

"You met someone—the other day—who knew you?"

He nodded.

"The night I was hit over the head. It was the chap Abbott from Scotland Yard, the one who picked me up and brought me home."

"He knew you?"

"Well, sort of half and half. He said we'd been at a do together at the Luxe before the war, and I danced a lot with a girl in a gold dress who seems to have struck him all of a heap—which, I expect, is why he remembered me. But when it came down to names he couldn't get any farther than Bill. You know, I always have had a feeling that the William part of my name was all right."

"But he must remember some of the other people who were there."

"He says he doesn't. It's a long time ago—he'll have been at hundreds of shows since then. You know how it is—things get run together in your mind. Look here, I could make toast at this fire if you'd like some."

They made toast.

William ate a hearty tea. Afterwards he told Katharine that painting the duck black by accident had given him a very good idea for a really black bird, and which did she think would be the best name—the Rookie Raven, or the Kee Kaw Krow?

When she said she liked the Krow best he demanded pencil and paper and produced sketches. He sat on the hearthrug with a block propped against his knee, his fair hair sticking up on end, and a fiercely concentrated expression on his face. He was, for the moment, apparently quite inaccessible to anything except Krow. Yet when Katharine said idly, "What made you think of the Wurzel Dogs?" he answered her at once in an abstracted voice,

"Oh, I had a dog called Wurzel once."

She almost stopped breathing. She let a little time go by, then she said in the same voice,

"When was that?"

He said, "I was ten," and came to with a start. "Oh, I say— I remembered that!"

"Yes, you did."

He was staring at her, intent and strained.

"I remembered it then, but I don't now. I'm only remembering that I remembered it."

She said quickly, "Don't try like that. It came when you were thinking about something else. I'm sure it won't come when you're trying."

He nodded.

"No—things don't, do they?" He leaned over and laid the sketches on her knee. "Look—what do you think of those?"

He had drawn every conceivable aspect of the Krow—the solemn, the rampant, the jaunty, the belligerent, the predatory. To each of them he had managed to impart the vitality which made all his creatures seem alive even in the wood.

"They're very good indeed."

He said, "Wait a bit," took them back, and plunged again. His hand just touched hers as it gathered the papers. It shook a little. He stopped it almost at once, but it showed him that he couldn't really trust himself. He must do a little more to the Krows, and then he must get up and go away, because if he stayed he couldn't be sure that he wouldn't

55

make love to Katharine, and of course he couldn't do that. She was all alone here, and she had asked him to tea. He couldn't possibly take advantage of her kindness. And of course he couldn't make love to her at the shop. The sort of employer who takes advantage of his position to embarrass the girls who work for him rose with horrifying distinctness. He plunged back into the Krows.

Katharine watched him. It wasn't difficult to guess what he was thinking. It gave her that feeling between laughter and tears which she had so often when she was with William Smith. He was in love with her, and he wanted to tell her about it, but he didn't like to because she worked at Tattlecombe's and it might make it difficult for her. She wasn't quite sure whether she wanted him to say anything yet. It was the kind of moment in their relationship, exquisite and fleeting, which had its own particular charm just because it could not be indefinitely prolonged. It had the quality of a February day. The picture rose before her mind—a light air stirring, a handsbreadth of blue in the sky, the almost imperceptible drifting of the clouds, a little mist to enhance and enchant the half seen landscape—fruit, flower, and leaf all still a dream of the bud. It had its charm—but February passes on its way. Like Faust she could have said, *Schöner Augenblick verweile doch.*

William put his papers together and got up.

"I think I'd better go now."

She smiled, and said, "You can stay to supper if you like."

He stood there frowning a little. The living-room was more soberly suited than Carol's bedroom, the furniture less modern. Katharine's blue dress made a pleasant harmony with the rough brown leather of her chair. The dull background brightened her hair, her eyes. Her lips smiled at him. He said in a stubborn voice,

56

"I'd better go."

"Why? Sit down again and talk a little."

He shook his head.

"No—I'll be going. Thank you very much for asking me."

It was only after the front door had shut that they remembered he had neither said goodbye, nor touched her hand again.

Quite a number of interested heads looked out of the gable windows as he drove away. There were four radios in full blast. A female with a strident voice was informing her offspring that she would cut his liver out if he didn't come in. Behind the plane trees the new moon, curved and shining, was going down the western sky. In the living-room of the flat Katharine listened to the sound of William's gears and his noisy retreat. Everyone in the Mews would know that she had come home with a young man and he had stayed for hours.

She said, "Oh, William *darling*," and laid her head down upon her arm.

CHAPTER 7

By the first post in the morning Katharine received a letter from Cyril Eversley. It ran:

"My dear Katharine,

I am afraid I have not your present address, but I hope this will be forwarded. Brett tells me you have let your flat and gone away to take up some work—

unspecified. So I do not even know whether you are still in town, or whether you would be able to lunch with me at the club on Wednesday next. Admiral Holden is coming up to go into your affairs with Brett and myself, and I thought it would be very nice if you could meet us afterwards for lunch. I know he would appreciate it. I am sure you will be glad to hear that the usual half-yearly dividend has now been paid into your account. I hope you have not been inconvenienced by the slight delay. We shall all look forward to seeing you on Wednesday—1:15 at the club.

Yours affectionately,
Cyril Eversley."

She put the letter away to answer when she got home in the evening.

So Admiral Holden was on the war-path, and her half year's dividend had been paid in. She wondered whether Cyril expected her not to connect the two events. The letter was in his own hand. She had an idea that it might have undergone some modification if it had been dictated to Miss Jones. There were very definitely no flies on Miss Jones. Cyril on the other hand would never really notice whether there were flies or not. She thought a little bitterly about the two Eversley partners and what they were doing to the firm— Cyril with his policy of drift, and Brett to whom it was a bank on which to draw. Instead of pulling up after the war years, they had gone down, and were still going. She wondered a little what would happen if she were to tell Admiral Holden just what she really thought. She wasn't going to do it, but she couldn't help wondering what would happen if she did. She was still wondering as she went out to catch her bus.

William did not receive a letter, but he wrote a great many. He spent a good part of the night writing them. Some of them began one way, and some another, but they were all to Katharine. Since he couldn't make love to her in the shop or in her flat and he had a strong feeling that streets, busses, tubes, and other places of concourse were not in the least appropriate to all the things he wanted to say to her, the idea of putting them in a letter had on its first appearance seemed quite bright.

The trouble was that, like so many bright ideas, it was proving very difficult to translate into words. For one thing, it appeared to be quite impossible to make a start. The torn-up sheets on which he had tried to get going littered not only his table but the floor. He wrote, "Darling," and blushed for his own temerity. He wrote, "Miss Eversley," and thought how cold it looked, and how unlike everything he felt for Katharine. When he had tried several other openings, and torn them up, he took a new sheet and began without any beginning at all.

"I am writing to you because I want you to know that I love you. I hope this will not make you feel uncomfortable in any way, because I should hate to do that, but it seems fairer to let you know how I feel. I do not like to think of your having to work, but if you are going to work anywhere, I would naturally like you to go on doing it here. I hope you will not feel I have made this difficult by writing to tell you how much I love you.

"As far as I know, I am about thirty years old—it might be a year or two more or a year or two less, but that doesn't make much difference. I had a head wound which was the cause of my loss of memory, but except for that it doesn't give me any trouble now. I am very strong and healthy, and never have anything the matter with me, I am glad to say.

"I cannot say anything about my family because my memory only goes back to '42, as I told you, but I seem to have had quite a reasonable education. I don't know at all what I did before the war, but one of the reasons why I feel sure I am not William Smith is that he worked in a tannery, and I am quite sure that I could not work in a tannery without being sick. I went to the place where he worked to see, and I was sick. If I was William Smith I should think I would have got over it—wouldn't you? That is only one of the reasons why I don't think I am William Smith, but I feel quite sure about it myself.

"It is of course a great drawback my not being able to remember anything before I came out of hospital—I mean the German one in '42. When I went to see Mr. Tattlecombe the other day he asked whether I had ever thought about getting married. I told him that I did not know whether I could think about it, because I might have been engaged to someone, or even married, before I lost my memory. I feel I must put this to you because I put it to him, but on thinking it over I do not think it could be so, because I would not be engaged to anyone, or married, unless I was in love with her, and I do not think I could forget anyone I loved like that. I know that I could never forget you, because all the feelings I have are mixed up with loving you, and as long as I felt anything at all I should have those feelings. It would not be a case of remembering or not remembering, it would just be knowing that I loved you. I have thought about this a lot, and I feel quite sure that I never have loved anyone but you. I hope I have put this quite fairly.

"I am not in a very good position as regards money, but I think the prospects are good. I am sure that the animals will bring in a steady income as soon as we can get them manufactured under licence and on the market in sufficient quantities. In a year's time I ought to be very much better off. Through Mr. Tattlecombe's kindness in allowing me to board with him I live very cheaply, and I have been able to save two hundred and fifty pounds. I would look after you and work for you, and I will always love you. I do not know whether you will always have had any idea that I have been thinking of you in this way. It was love at first sight. As soon as I saw you I knew there wasn't anyone else and never could be. You were everything in the world. I love you very much.

William Smith."

This letter he put into Katharine's hand as she was leaving at the end of the day. She did not read it until she got home, but every now and then she put her hand into her bag and felt it to make sure that it was there. It was a thick letter. There was only one explanation of a letter like that, put into her hand without a word as she turned to go. You don't read that sort of letter in the street or on a bus.

She came into her dark flat, put on the light, set a match to the gas fire, and took off her coat and hat. Then she sat down on the hearthrug and read William's letter. It might have touched any woman's heart. It took Katharine's heart and wrung it. Everything she knew about William was there—his simplicity, his honesty, his directness, and the way he loved her. She read the letter a great many times, and cried over it with the sort of tears which leave the eyes bright and the cheeks glowing. What seemed like quite a long time went by. Then the telephone bell rang. Katharine jumped up with her heart beating and her breath coming quickly. It couldn't possibly be William—it couldn't possibly—

But it was. She said, "Hullo!" and heard him say, "Is that you?"

"Yes."

"Have you read my letter?"

"Yes, William."

"I'm not asking you to answer it, or anything like that. You might want to think about it quite a lot—I don't want to hurry you. I just thought I'd say you mustn't think I'd make it difficult for you if you felt you had to say no—I mean I wouldn't bother you."

"Thank you, William—" Her voice gave out.

She heard him say, "That's all. I'm ringing up from a callbox," and all of a sudden she couldn't let him go. She said, "Wait!"

William waited. He heard her catch her breath.

"William—"

"Katharine—"

"William—would you like to come round and have supper with me?"

He arrived in the tin kettle. When Katharine heard it she went into the passage and stood ready to let him in. She had put on the blue dress. The moment she heard his step she opened the door. He came in with the cold night air and the smell of frost. The door shut behind him and she was in his arms.

CHAPTER 8

On the Wednesday morning about half an hour before Admiral Holden arrived, Miss Jones was bracing her employer for the interview. Properly speaking, she was no longer Miss Jones, having become Mrs. Cyril Eversley at a register office on the previous Saturday. The fact gave her an added touch of assurance.

"Now there's really nothing to be nervous about. It's all fixed. If he gets at all awkward, you'll put the whole thing on Mr. Davies. You've only got to say he'd been failing for some time but you didn't like to supersede him after thirty years' service. Then you put in about his dying suddenly six weeks ago, and say it's taken us quite a while to get everything sorted out. If he asks anything you can't answer, ring for me. You can tell him I've been straightening out the muddle."

Cyril Eversley frowned.

"It doesn't seem fair. I don't like it."

She said, a thought impatiently,

"It won't go outside this room. And who is it going to hurt? Not old Davies. Anyhow there's no need to say anything about him unless the Admiral gets tiresome. If you have to, it will be all the better if you're a bit embarrassed at bringing it out. Old servants of the firm and all that sort of thing—it's quite a good touch."

He said, "Don't!" so sharply that she stared for a moment, then came round to drop a kiss on the top of his head.

"Cheer up, darling! It will go with a bang—you see if it doesn't." She bent over to touch the papers lying in front of him. "You say your piece first, and then you show him this. Don't bring in Davies unless you have to, and if you feel you're getting bogged, just say, 'I think Miss Jones knows about that,' and put your finger on the bell."

She turned to smile at him from the doorway, and went out and along a piece of straight passage to Brett Eversley's room.

He looked up as she came in, and said,

"All set?"

She shrugged her shoulders.

"I hope so. He's as nervous as a cat."

His eyebrows rose.

"Well, I suppose we shall all be glad when it's over. Are you going to be there?"

"Not to start with. That's what I've come to talk to you about. I've told him to ring for me if there are any awkward questions. It mayn't be necessary, but if the Admiral gets too pressing, it's easy for either of you to suggest having me in. The line will be that I'm straightening up after Mr. Davies, who was a bit past his work and had left things rather in a muddle."

Brett laughed.

"That's a bright one!"

"Yes—I thought so. But Mr. Eversley doesn't like it."

"He wouldn't."

"So it's not to be brought in unless it's necessary. Of course there wouldn't be any harm in *your* saying that the old man had been getting pretty doddery and had left things in a bit of a mess. Mr. Eversley would show that he was vexed and stick up for Mr. Davies, and that would make the right sort of impression. We'd get across with the idea that it was Davies who had muddled things up. But Mr. Eversley being put out about it would take off any appearance of our wanting to put it on the old man, if you see what I mean."

Brett looked at her with a curious expression in his dark eyes.

"Oh, yes, I see what you mean! Clever—aren't you?" He laughed. "I think I shall always take care to stay your side of the fence!"

She gave him a perfunctory smile.

"There's really nothing to be nervous about. As far as this interview goes, everything will be quite all right—I've told Mr. Eversley so. The trouble is, it doesn't go all the way. Nobody is safe until you've married her."

He pushed back his chair and stood up, his hands in his pockets, a smile on his face.

"*You* tell me that?"

"Of course I do! It's the truth."

"*You* want me to marry Katharine?"

"My dear Brett, talk sense! You've got to marry her."

"And suppose she won't?"

"You've got to make her change her mind. You've always fancied yourself with women. I seem to remember your telling me that you could make any woman fall for you. Well, now you've got to marry Katharine Eversley or go to prison— that's the plain English of it. Turn on some of that charm you're so proud of and see what you can do with it. Because if she marries anybody else, the fat will be in the fire, and I shan't be able to pull it out for you. I can bluff the Admiral, but I couldn't bluff a firm of solicitors, and I'm not going to try. If Katharine Eversley marries, her husband will want to know what has happened to her trust funds, and you won't

65

be able to satisfy him. I haven't said all this to Mr. Eversley because there isn't anything he can do about it and it's no good frightening him. But I'm saying it to you, and you'd better get busy. That's all, Brett."

CHAPTER 9

The lunch went off well. In his relief at having come more than creditably through a much dreaded interview, Cyril Eversley relaxed to play the courteous, gentle-mannered host. In doing so he was not so much playing a part as throwing one off. It was the role of man of business which he found perennially jading and ungrateful. As the scholarly dilettante he was at his ease. Admiral Holden, who had never thought much of him, was surprised to find him such an agreeable host.

The Admiral was feeling pleased with himself—pleased to be up and about again, pleased to be asserting himself with the Eversleys, who had certainly considered him as good as dead and buried (he'd show them!), pleased to be visiting his old haunts and saying what a damned filthy place London was, and very much pleased to see Katharine. When she came into the hall of the club in her blue dress and fur coat, and put her hands in his and kissed him, his weather-beaten face turned quite scarlet with pleasure and he thought to himself, "She's a lovely woman—and be damned to all the rest of them—they can't hold a candle to her." He squeezed her hands very tight, and she said,

"Darling Bunny, you look as if you'd just come back from a voyage round the world."

"Bed on the verandah," he said gruffly—"fair or foul—wet, wind, or snow—or I shouldn't be here today."

After that everything went with a bang. She had called him Bunny ever since she was three years old. It gave him extraordinary pleasure. She had a loving heart, God bless her, and she looked young and happy, and he had gone into her affairs for her. If he had come out of his verandah bed in the nick of time to dance at her wedding, nobody would be better pleased than he. Only he wasn't sure that he would have chosen that fellow Brett—no, he wasn't sure about that. Cyril Eversley seemed to think they had made it up between them, or that they were going to, but that it was all very hush-hush at the moment. He couldn't see why it should be. He thought he would have a word or two with Katharine and find out. Hang it all, she liked the fellow, or she didn't like him. She was old enough to know her own mind. He could find out tactfully. He hoped he could be tactful when he chose. Thoughts like these came and went as he partook vigorously of lobster and partridge and finished up with a couple of ices and some Stilton cheese.

Brett Eversley, making himself charming to Katharine, was aware of scrutiny. Admiral Holden's small bright blue eyes appeared to be sizing him up. He laid himself out to entertain, and succeeded. But when Katharine rose to go the Admiral rose too.

"We'll have a taxi, my dear," he said easily. "I'm going your way."

"Darling Bunny, how do you know which way I'm going?"

"Well, which way are you going?"

"Back to my job."

Brett laughed and said, "He crashes in where we've been afraid to tread! Go on, sir—ask her what she's doing, and where she's been hiding herself away!"

Katharine was smiling.

"Oh, I'm not telling anyone. It's fun for me, because I can keep you all guessing—and it's even more fun for you, because you can invent all sorts of scandalous explanations. They won't any of them be true, but that only makes them more intriguing."

Brett took her hand and held it just a little longer than he need have done.

"You won't tell me where you're living?"

"It would spoil the stories. It's all too, too respectable."

Cyril said, "Have you really got a job? There surely isn't any need?"

She laughed.

"I have an urge to work. Doesn't that prove my respectability? I must rush! Thank you for a lovely lunch."

At the taxi door she said,

"I'll be dropped at the Marble Arch Tube."

Admiral Holden spoke to the driver, and got in after her. Except that he did not move quite as lightly as he had done, he seemed to be perfectly restored. As they drove away, he beamed at her and said,

"Well, I've got everything settled up, and you won't have any more trouble. If those dividends of yours don't come in on the nail, you've got to let me know. Not much of a hand at business, Cyril Eversley. Struck me that secretary of his knew more about everything than he did. Goodlooking woman. They had her in, and she had it all at her fingers' ends. It seems the old clerk—what's his name, Davies—was a bit past his work at the end and things got muddled up. I shouldn't have heard anything about it from Cyril—it was

Brett let the cat out of the bag. Cyril was all for hushing it up and saying how long Davies had worked for them, but reading between the lines, I should say he'd left everything at sixes and sevens, and for all we know he may have been feathering his nest for years—"

Katharine interrupted him with distress in voice and manner.

"Oh, no—he wouldn't!"

"That's what Cyril Eversley said. But it happens, you know. Old trusted servant of the firm—everything left to him—too much left to him. Then he dies suddenly, and the whole thing comes out."

She caught him by the arm.

"Is Mr. Davies dead?"

"That's what they were telling me."

"When?"

"They didn't say. Not so long ago, I should think."

She said, "The last time I went to the office he was there. That was about two months ago. I've known him ever since I could remember. He was good—I'm sure he never did anything wrong in his life."

He patted her knee.

"Well, my dear, we all have to go some time. And I haven't got very long with you—I want to talk. First of all, I want to know where you are and what you are doing, and why there's any mystery about it." He looked at her reproachfully—square shoulders, grey hair cut close to his head, water-blue eyes in a ruddy face. "What's all this about? I don't like it."

"Darling Bunny—"

"Hiding yourself away, taking some hole-and-corner kind of a job—what's it all about? Girl does that sort of thing, it means she's got something up her sleeve. What have you got up yours?"

"What do we generally have?"

"A young man," said the Admiral bluntly. "You'd better tell me who he is, and I'll size him up for you."

"I have sized him up."

"Pack of rubbish! A girl can't size up a man any more than a man can size up a girl. Set a thief to catch a thief, my dear! I'll size him up for you."

He saw her eyes widen with that little smile in them, but she didn't answer. With quick suspicion he came out with,

"Is it that fellow Brett?"

"Oh, no, darling."

"Well, I'm glad about that. Something I don't cotton to there. Very agreeable fellow—very good company. What the women call charming—always been a favourite. A bit too much stuff in the shop window to my way of thinking. I like them a bit plainer."

"So do I, darling."

He patted her hand.

"Very glad to hear it." His voice suddenly took on a definitely quarter-deck note. "Then what the blazes did that fellow Cyril mean by telling me you were engaged?"

"Cyril said I was engaged to Brett?"

"Or as near as makes no difference. Said it was all very hush-hush. Couldn't make out why. Because if you're engaged you're engaged, and if you're going to be engaged you're going to be engaged. Can't see any reason to go mincing round like a cat on hot bricks, which is what that fellow Cyril was doing. So I thought I'd have a word with you and find out what was going on. Tactfully of course—"

"Darling, I do love you when you're being tactful!"

"Meaning I'm no good at it. Well, I daresay I'm not. And I daresay you think you can manage your own affairs without my putting my oar in. Women always think so until they go

70

on the rocks. Now you listen to me! If you've got a man up that sleeve of yours I'd like to meet him. If he's any good he'll want to meet me. I'm not your guardian any longer, but your father was the best shipmate and the best friend I ever had, and if you don't know by now that I'm a good deal fonder of you than most men are of their daughters, you're not so intelligent as I've always given you credit for being. Now, what about it?"

She looked at him sweetly.

"Bunny, you're an angel, and I love you."

He said gruffly, "Fine words butter no parsnips. I said, 'What about it?'"

She took one of his hands and held it tightly in both of hers.

"This," she said. "There is someone. I love him—very much. And he loves me—very much too. I can't tell you any more than that—I can't really. It's the most wonderful time of my life, and I don't want it to be spoiled. I want to have it. I want a little time before I tell people—just a little, you know. And you shall be the very first—I promise you that. And I promise you something else—you'll be terribly, terribly pleased."

"Oh, I will, will I?"

"Yes, Bunny—and here's my Tube station."

"All right, all right."

He followed her out of the taxi, pulled a handful of money out of his pocket, and added a generous tip to the fare. Then he turned back to Katharine.

"A deuce of a hurry you're in."

"I've got to change and get back to my job."

"Can't see what you want with a job myself. Look here, who's in the Cedar House?"

"No one at the moment. I let Aunt Agnes have it because

71

she thought she was going to be at a loose end until March when her tenants go out, but her daughter hasn't been well, and she's gone over to stay with her in Eire."

"So there isn't anyone there. Then why don't you go down for a bit? Take one of the old cousins or a friend. Get the place aired and lived in."

"Mrs. Perkins airs it regularly, darling. She lives next door, you know, over the corn-chandler's. She is his wife's aunt, and she used to be Granny Eversley's cook, which makes her fairly antique, but she still cooks like a dream."

"Then go down and let her cook for you."

"Later on perhaps. Darling, I must rush. Write to me care of the bank and they'll send it on. Blessings! It's been marvellous seeing you!"

CHAPTER 10

Katharine let herself into her flat. She had leave off till three. Miss Cole would look down her nose, but she couldn't go back to Tattlecombe's in these clothes. She got into her old tweed suit, removed the forbidden lipstick, bit her lips to induce a natural substitute, looked at the clock, and turned into the living-room.

The telephone was on her writing-table. Standing there ready to go out, she dialled and took up the receiver. A girl's voice said, "Eversleys'."

"Can I speak to Miss Jones?"

A moment later Mavis Jones on the line:

"Mr. Eversley's secretary speaking."

"Oh, Miss Jones—it's Katharine Eversley. Admiral Holden has just told me of Mr. Davies' death, and I'm so very sorry. It was after I said goodbye to my cousins, so I had no opportunity of asking them about it. When did he die?"

"Well, let me see—it would be about six weeks ago."

"Yes, I saw him the last time I was at the office. He seemed quite well then. What was it?"

"He was knocked down in the street—not looking where he was going, I'm afraid. They took him to hospital, but he never recovered consciousness."

Katharine said, "I am so very sorry—I didn't know." The receiver felt cold and heavy in her hand. She said, "What day was it—when did it happen?"

Miss Jones' voice sharpened a little.

"I don't know that I could say offhand."

"It would be very kind of you if you would find out. The date on his ledger would show when he stopped coming—wouldn't it? I should like to know."

"Oh, certainly."

As she stood waiting, the receiver in her hand became colder and heavier still. She heard Miss Jones go away. She heard her come back. She heard her voice, hard and efficient, with that something which wasn't quite an accent—a little more noticeable on the telephone than it was when you were with her.

"The date would be the sixth of December. That was the last time Mr. Davies was at the office."

Katharine said, "Thank you, Miss Jones," and rang off.

An hour later she looked up from her painting to say to William Smith,

"Do you remember the date you went to Eversleys' and saw Miss Jones?"

William frowned.

"It was just before Mr. Tattlecombe had his accident."

"Well, when did Mr. Tattlecombe have his accident?"

"The seventh of December."

She put down her brush because her hand wasn't quite steady.

"When you say just before, what do you mean, William? Do you mean that it was the day before?"

"Yes, it was."

"Are you sure about that?"

"Yes. Why—does it matter?"

"I don't know." She picked up her brush again. "I just wanted to know."

William had become absorbed. Only a small portion of his mind had been on what he was saying. Now the whole of it was concentrated upon putting the finishing touches to the first of the Krow models. Should there, or should there not, be a touch of metallic green on the head? Nothing that you could swear to, but just the suggestion of a sheen.

He referred the question to Katharine and they debated it earnestly.

Tattlecombe's shut at half past five, and William drove her home. Miss Cole, who had put on her hat and coat and walked briskly away in the opposite direction, took the first turning to the right, and the first to the right again, which brought her into the narrow cut immediately behind the shop. William did not see her because he had to back his car out of the shed in which it lived, but by walking very fast indeed and occasionally breaking into a short run she was able to reach the corner in time to see him stop, lean sideways to open the near door, and let that Miss Eversley in, after which they drove away together.

"And not for the first time, Mr. Tattlecombe!" said Miss Cole, in tones which trembled with moral indignation.

Mrs. Salt hadn't wanted to let her in, but she had got in. A really determined woman can always get in if she wants to. It is just a question of how many of the finer feelings she is prepared to disregard, and how much driving-power she can develop. Miss Cole walked past Abigail Salt at her own door and said she had come to see Mr. Tattlecombe. On being told that in his sister's opinion he should be kept quiet and not encouraged to upset himself about the business, she sniffed and said that he would be a great deal more upset if the business got a bad name, and see him she must. Abigail was displeased, but, handicapped by her ignorance of what had happened and a suspicion that Abel would indeed upset himself if he thought she was interfering between him and his business, she gave way, ushered Miss Cole into her spare room, and left her there. Tempted to close the door sharply, she restrained herself and went down to the parlour, where she applied herself to playing hymn tunes on the harmonium. Her momentary indecision about the door may have resulted in its failing to latch. The tongue of steel engaged and slipped out again, the door remained ajar.

Miss Cole sat in an upright chair beside Mr. Tattlecombe's bed and poured out her soul. She wore a ginger-coloured hat and a thick black coat. Her sallow skin glistened in the gaslight. She washed it night and morning with yellow soap, and considered facepowder immoral. Her hands in black woollen gloves were tightly clasped upon her knee. Her voice trembled with earnest disapproval.

"Every day and all day long—painting at the same table, and their heads as good as touching!"

Abel Tattlecombe leaned against his pillows and said,

"The painting has got to be done, Miss Cole."

"Very true, Mr. Tattlecombe, and I'm not denying it. But when I say that I understood Miss Eversley was engaged to help me in the shop I'm only saying what was clearly understood at the time. And what happens? The very second day she is there Mr. Smith takes her out of the shop and puts her in the workshop and gives her the painting to do, which is what he wouldn't let anyone lay a finger on. Because I offered, and he said oh no, he could manage very nicely." She gave a really dreadful sniff and repeated this telling phrase in a loud tone of scorn. "He could manage very nicely! And how does he manage, Mr. Tattlecombe?" She sniffed again. "Him and her with no more than the width of a table between them, and for all I know dipping their brushes in the same paint-pot! And that boy away at the other end of the shop taking it all in!"

Miss Cole was a fellow chapel member. Abel Tattlecombe gazed at her mildly.

"William Smith is a single young man," he said, "and Miss Eversley is a single young woman. I have spoken to William on the subject of marriage. If he is thinking of Miss Eversley in the light of that conversation, there would be nothing wrong about it."

Miss Cole tossed her head.

"You didn't see her when she came about the place! Painted she was, and no other word for it, and I told her straight out it wasn't what you'd approve of! I wouldn't have engaged her if it had been left to me, but Mr. Smith pushed in and said she was just what we were looking for—right over my head!"

Abel said sharply, "She doesn't wear paint in the shop."

Miss Cole sniffed.

"There's no saying what she might have done if I hadn't spoken up. I told her you wouldn't allow it, and I've kept a pretty sharp look-out to see she didn't get round what I said."

Abel was becoming weary of the bickering voice. He said,

76

"Well, that's all right," and immediately became aware that the remark was optimistic.

Miss Cole looked at him in a pitying manner.

"If you call it all right for him to drive her away in his car and stay out till all hours!"

Abel's temper slipped a little.

"What do you call all hours? And how do you know how long he stays out?"

Miss Cole bridled.

"I suppose Mrs. Bastable has a tongue in her head! Eleven one night, and half past eleven another, and before we know where we are there's no saying whether he'll come home at all. It's not what I call respectable."

Mr. Tattlecombe was a good deal more disquieted than he wished it to appear. He put Miss Cole down for a meddlesome old maid. But the respectability of his shop was very dear to him. It should be beyond question or comment, and here was Miss Cole gossiping with Mrs. Bastable, and both of them questioning and commenting just about as hard as they could go. He wished, as many a man has wished, that something could be done to stop women talking, and he remembered that when he was twenty-four he had taken a girl on the river in June and not brought her back until midnight, and what a blazing row there had been. She was a pretty girl, and she had married a stout middle-aged shopwalker at Prentice & Biddle's and had seven or eight children, all the image of their father. And he had married Mary Sturt and been very happy with her until the Lord took her. He fixed his blue eyes on Miss Cole's face and said,

"Does the young woman live with her parents?"—Because if she did, and William was courting her, he would naturally go there of an evening.

"Parents!" said Miss Cole. "There isn't much of that, Mr.

77

Tattlecombe! A flat in a mews—21, Rasselas Mews—that's where she lives. Lent her by a friend is what she says. And all alone there—because she let that out. So if that's where Mr. Smith stays half the night, *you* may call it respectable, Mr. Tattlecombe, but I don't!"

This outburst was delivered in a series of short gasps. If Mr. Tattlecombe had been at all mobile, it is tolerably certain that he would have left the room. Unable even to leave his bed, he had perforce to sustain the onslaught.

Miss Cole took a good long breath and began again.

"A front door painted scarlet isn't what I'd call respectable either—steps going up to it and the railings as red as any pillar-box! And no hearsay gossip about that, for I saw them with my own eyes, and if you want to know what came into my mind, well, it was the Scarlet Woman! And can you be surprised?"

Abel Tattlecombe primmed up his mouth. If he wasn't surprised, he was certainly shocked. He said so, just like that.

"Miss Cole, I am shocked!"

Miss Cole appeared quite pleased about it.

"I thought you would be."

"I am shocked at the way you are jumping to conclusions. Red paint on the front door of a flat that someone else has lent you—"

Miss Cole interrupted with vigour.

"Don't say lent *me*, Mr. Tattlecombe! We've all heard about flats in mews before this, and we know what to think about them, let alone scarlet paint on the doors!"

Abel restrained himself with difficulty. Miss Cole was a valued assistant. Persons of unblemished moral probity and years of business experience did not grow on gooseberry bushes. If you possessed one you did not lightly let her go. He said with praiseworthy calm,

"I think that's enough about the paint, Miss Cole."

Miss Cole tossed her head.

"Certainly, if that is your wish, Mr. Tattlecombe! Whether it's on Miss Eversley's face or on her front door, I'm sure it's all one to me! And if I thought I had a duty and it's been misunderstood, well, I've done what my conscience told me, and I shan't mention it again."

Abel hoped very much that this was true, but he was not very sanguine. Even his wife, estimable and deeply mourned, had been known to close an argument in this manner, only to reopen it as soon as she had thought of something more to say. He said, "I will speak to William Smith," and took refuge in his character of an invalid, alarming Miss Cole by groaning slightly, closing his eyes, and leaning back against the pillow which happened to be uppermost.

Heart-smitten and alarmed, she retired in disorder to find Mrs. Salt. As she came out upon the landing, a black shirt disappeared into the room opposite. A big bony hand remained in view for a moment. It had been closing the door. It now withdrew. The latch clicked home.

Miss Cole, who knew all about Emily Salt, did not bother her head—Emily always tried to get out of the way if anyone came to the house. She found Abigail, hoped she hadn't tired Mr. Tattlecombe, and hastened to be gone.

Abigail Salt went up with a cup of Benger. She met Emily coming down with a queer sly look on her face, and didn't like it. Sometimes Emily worried her. She went on in to Abel, and found him angry.

"That woman talks too much, Abby."

"Most people do," said Abigail Salt.

CHAPTER 11

William and Katharine sat by the fire and talked. Mr. Tattlecombe would have approved of their demeanour. William had a writing-block and pencil, and appeared to be entirely concentrated on doing sums. Although she was sharing the sofa, Katharine was not even touching him except a fold of her dress and the look which dwelt sweetly with a tinge of humour upon a serious and rugged profile. The single young man and the single young woman were, in fact, engaged upon computing a double income and deciding whether it justified them in getting married without waiting for the Wurzel toys to boom. For purposes of this computation they had taken their joint salaries, and Katharine had confessed rather tentatively to a private income of two hundred pounds a year. To her relief, this was received with approval, William obviously considering with perfect simplicity that it would make it easier for them to get married, and was therefore a very good thing.

Since this had gone down so well, she followed it up with a casual, "I've put it rather low—it's always been more than that really. But there was a hitch this year—some of the things didn't pay. That was one of the reasons why I had to let my flat."

He looked up frowning.

"What do you pay for this one?"

"Well, Carol didn't really want to take anything. She didn't want to let. She said there was always a chance the roof might fall in. They had a land mine about a quarter of a mile away, and there's an idea that it rather shook the whole of this place up."

The frown deepened.

"I don't like your living in a place where the roof might fall in."

"Darling, I think Carol was trying to push the flat on to me without taking any rent for it."

"But she ought to be getting rent for it. I mean, it's all right for you, but when we get married, it will be my business to pay the rent. How long is she going to be away?"

"You never know Carol. That's partly why she didn't want to let. She's gone off to get material for the sort of book she writes—A Roamer in Rome, or, Tramps in Tanganyika, you know. She does it awfully well, with little pen and ink sketches. And sometimes she gets what she wants in six weeks, and sometimes she just stays on and on letting it all soak in."

William put down two pounds a week for "rent of flat." He remarked that it might be very inconvenient if they had to turn out at a moment's notice.

Katharine said, "We might be able to get back into my own flat."

The words were no sooner out of her mouth than she realized that she ought to have kept them in. William immediately wanted to know where it was, how many rooms it had, and what the rent would be. When she told him he said with decision that it would be a good deal too expensive, but they could be looking about for something else.

He finished their budget, looked at her seriously, and said,

"We can do it easily. How soon will you marry me?"

"As soon as you like, William."

"If you really mean that, we could make it next Saturday.

That would give us the week-end." He dropped his pencil and paper and took her hands. "Am I hurrying you? Is it too soon?"

The colour came up into her face and her eyes shone.

"No, it isn't too soon."

He put his arms round her.

"Oh, Katharine!" And quite a long time after that, "I'll tell Mr. Tattlecombe tomorrow."

CHAPTER 12

The interview with Mr. Tattlecombe went off well. Abel had a gratified feeling that his advice had been followed. A little more rapidly than he contemplated, but it was good advice and William was following it. A single young man was exposed to temptations. The Lord had provided the institution of marriage. William Smith would make a good husband. If the young woman was respectable and discreet, the marriage would be blessed. Not even to himself would Mr. Tattlecombe admit the secret fear which sometimes presented itself, that William might get tired of the Toy Bazaar and seek opportunities in a larger sphere. The nearest he got to it was the thought that marriage settled a man.

He was, therefore, gracious and urbane, invited William to bring Miss Eversley to see him, and withheld the comments he might otherwise have made when he discovered how very little William knew about her family or her upbringing.

"She was in the A.T.S. during the war. I don't think she has many relations. The partners in Eversleys' are some connection, but I think it's fairly distant. You remember I went to see them about the Wurzel toys, but the secretary said they wouldn't be interested."

Abel nodded. Families were like that. Some of them went up in the world, and some went down. Those that went down dropped out. It wouldn't be likely that the Eversleys would be taking any interest. Having the same name didn't get you very far. Nor having grand relations. What mattered was whether the young woman had good principles and the kind of disposition which made a man happy in his home. He said so.

When William came away he had a few words with Abigail Salt, and arranged with her to bring Katharine straight on from the shop next day. Abigail's calm, decided manner relaxed sufficiently to display quite a human interest.

Emily Salt did not appear at all. For the first time since he had been coming to the house William left it without being made aware of her presence. There had been no furtive step just round the corner, no door that closed as he came up to it, no tall shape disappearing into an empty room, no bony features peering down from an upper landing, grotesquely illuminated by light striking from below. It was rather like going to a haunted house and finding the ghost away from home. He did not really think about it consciously, but he had that sort of feeling.

He walked down the street past the place where he had been, to quote Mr. Tattlecombe, "struck down," and round the corner into Morden Road, which was better lighted and altogether busier, since it ran into High Street. At the far end it developed shops and became quite crowded. It was in his mind to cross the High Street and take a bus. Quite a number of people seemed to have had the same idea.

The lights changed as he came to the island in the middle

of the road. There was a little crowd behind him, tightly packed. Just as a large motor-bus came rolling up he felt a sharp jab under his left shoulder-blade. It was a very sharp jab, and it had considerable force behind it. He was on the edge of the kerb. Thrust suddenly forward, he lost his balance and would have lurched into the road if the big man next to him had not caught his arm in a powerful grip and held him back. The bus roared past over the spot upon which he had been due to fall. The man who had caught him by the arm maintained his grip on it and said angrily, "For God's sake— what do you think you're doing?"

William turned a sober face.

"Someone pushed me," he said.

And with that the lights changed again and the little crowd broke up, streaming over the crossing—two small boys; a woman with a shopping-basket; a workman with a bag of tools going home from some overtime job; a couple of fly-away girls painted high; one of those dowdy, pathetic old women with draggled skirts and a distintegrating hat; a man who looked like a prosperous tradesman; another who might have been a not so prosperous professional man; a stout woman with a little boy; a young woman with a baby which ought to have been at home in its bed. William could not discern anyone whom he could suspect of having jabbed him in the back. Yet someone *had* jabbed him in the back, and if it hadn't been for the stranger who still gripped his arm he would almost certainly at this moment be lying dead, whilst a crowd collected and a police constable took down the details of his sticky end.

He repeated his previous remark, and added to it.

"Someone pushed me—jabbed me under the shoulder with something hard—I think it was a stick."

The large man who held him by the arm let go. William

was manifestly neither mad nor drunk. He looked him up and down, and the anger went out of him. Odd things happened. He had been in all the big cities of the world, and it was his opinion that London could beat most of them when it came to odd happenings. If he hadn't been in a hurry he would have pursued this theme with William. As it was, he decided regretfully that he hadn't the time. Mortimer was the devil and all if you kept him waiting. If he wasn't in a good temper, the interview would be a flop. He therefore clapped William on the shoulder, said, "You're lucky not to be dead. Better be more careful about what enemies you make," and went off at a swinging stride. That he afterwards interviewed the elusive Mortimer with tact and penetration, wrote a brilliant article on him and his latest discovery, and about a month later published an intriguing sketch entitled "A Jab in the Back with a Blunt Stick" has of course nothing to do with this story.

William caught his bus.

He told Katharine all about his interview with Mr. Tattlecombe, but he didn't tell her about the jab in the back. For one thing it would have seemed a stupid waste of time, and for another it might have frightened her. Also, coming along in the bus, the idea of a spotted animal with horns and a rolling eye had come into his mind, and he wanted to get it down on paper in case it faded. He thought of calling it the Crummocky Cow. Ideas were annoyingly apt to fade if you neglected them. The odd thing was that after doing his sketches, and having supper with Katharine, and talking over their plans in a state of happiness which was quite beyond anything he could have thought possible, he had no sooner said goodnight to her and turned out of the Mews than the jab came back to him. It was partly, of course, that the place was uncommonly sore, but it was also partly that the voice

85

of the erratic stranger who had most probably saved his life persisted in his mind—"Better be more careful about what enemies you make." Well, of course that was absurd, because he hadn't an enemy in the world. Or had he? Someone had knocked him down and knocked him out. Someone had jabbed him in the back, and but for the arm of the erratic stranger he would have pitched forward under a regular juggernaut of a motor-bus.

He walked as far as the Marble Arch and stood there waiting for a bus. Suddenly a voice said, "Hullo, Bill! How are you? None the worse?" He turned to see Frank Abbott, very much off duty, in the most correct and up-to-date of evening clothes, his slim elegance accentuated, his whole appearance that of a leisurely young man about town—the last person on earth, it would be thought, to prompt a confidence. Yet William Smith was so prompted. Perhaps because the matter pressed upon his mind to the point of compelling him to make some effort to throw it off, or perhaps because of the name which belonged to his forgotten past. Be that as it may, he said simply and directly,

"I'm all right, but—something else has happened."

"When?"

"About half past seven this evening. Someone tried to push me under a bus."

"Someone tried to push you?"

"Jabbed me in the back with a stick—I've got no end of a bruise. There was a crowd on an island. He jabbed me, and I'd have been under the bus if the man next to me hadn't been extra strong in the arm."

"Where was this?"

William told him.

"I'd been to see Mr. Tattlecombe again. I walked as far as the High Street, and I was crossing over to get a bus."

"Were you followed?"

"Not that I know of."

"You didn't see who pushed you?"

"The lights changed and everyone streamed off. There didn't seem to be anyone the least bit likely. But of course he could have slipped away—gone back instead of crossing over—there was time before I got my footing and turned round. It—rather took me aback."

Frank was frowning slightly.

"Want to report the matter to the police?"

William shook his head.

"I don't see what they could do."

Frank took out a thin notebook, wrote in it, and tore out the page. He said,

"It looks to me as if someone was finding you inconvenient. If you don't want to go to the police, I wonder if you would care to consult a friend of mine. She used to be a governess. Now she undertakes private enquiries—which she spells with an 'e.' She's been mixed up, one way or another, with more big cases than I should have time to tell you about. The Yard owes her a great deal more than it is likely to acknowledge. She's about the most intelligent person I've ever met, and what she herself would call a gentlewoman. If you feel you are getting out of your depth, I should advise you to go and see her. Here's her name and address—and here's your bus. See you some time."

CHAPTER 13

Frank Abbott had had a very busy week. A corn-chandler's wife in Wapping went missing after a violent quarrel with her husband and had to be traced. Husbands in the most peaceable of professions have been known to murder quarrelsome wives, and Wapping is convenient to the river. After a number of voluble neighbours had been interviewed, some dark suspicions hinted at, and a false trail which finished up at a mortuary at Gravesend investigated, it transpired that Mrs. Wilkins was visiting a friend in Hammersmith with the possibly illusory hope that her husband's heart was being rendered fonder by her absence.

A good deal of energy having been wasted and a good deal of time taken up, Sergeant Abbott would have been in a fair way to forgetting his brief encounter with William Smith if it had not been suddenly recalled to his mind. Then the telephone informed him that his cousin Mildred Darcy had arrived in England after a seven years' absence. She appeared overjoyed to be back, and wanted, in rapid succession, to know whether policemen ever had any time off duty; if they did, when he would be having any; and what about dining with her and George at the Luxe tonight.

Frank was reputed to have more cousins than anyone else in England and to be on good terms with them all. Seven years is a long time, and people are apt to change in the East, but he had always been very good friends with Mildred, and he thought he would like to see her again. She had been flighty, fluffy, and charmingly incompetent. He wondered if her rather notable complexion had survived. George he remembered as a heavy, worthy young man eminently suited to his probable role of providing ballast.

He accepted the invitation to dinner, and at the appointed hour arrived to find George less noticeably earnest, but Mildred a good deal more inconsequent than he remembered her. The complexion was gone, and so was the charm. She looked out of date in more than the matter of clothes and hair, but she was obviously in high spirits and affectionately pleased to see him again. Under an appearance of rather mannered indifference Frank was clannish. He found himself shaking George by the hand and responding to Mildred's pleasure. And then, right across all that, there jigged the recollection of William Smith.

Mildred was saying, "I can't think when we met last," and all of a sudden he remembered that it was at the party where he had seen William Smith, whom he recalled not as William or Smith, but simply Bill. Bill—and a girl in a gold dress. Up to this moment they were the only two whom he could have sworn to out of all the guests who must have been present, and now, like two bits of a jigsaw puzzle slipping into place, Mildred and George came into the picture. He even remembered that Mildred had worn pink. With the barest possible interval, he heard himself say,

"It was here at the Luxe, just before the war—somebody's party. But I can't remember anyone but you and George, and a man called Bill, and a girl in a gold dress."

George was leading the way into the dining-room. As they passed under the mirrored archway, Mildred Darcy looked sideways and saw herself reflected there with Frank. The reflection pleased her. Frank's slim elegance, the excellent cut of his evening clothes, the smoothness of the fair slicked-back hair, his poise and assurance, all pleased her very much. It did not occur to her that her dress was *démodée* and not very fresh, that her hair looked brittle and dry and was done in a fashion which had died a year ago. The girl in a pink dress who had danced here before the war was gone and would never come back. She had been Mildred Abbott. This was Mildred Darcy after seven years out East, but every bit as pleased with herself as Mildred Abbott had been. She glanced into the mirror and glanced back again to tilt her head and say,

"We make a nice pair, don't we?"

Frank decided that he needn't feel sorry for her. He pursued the man Bill. He said,

"We do—we always did. I remember thinking so last time. You had just got engaged to George. You wore a pink dress."

"Fancy your remembering that!"

"It's about the only thing I can remember."

They reached their table and sat down.

"Look here, who gave that party? For the life of me I can't remember."

"Oh, Curtis and Molly Latimer."

"He was killed, wasn't he?"

"So was Molly—in one of the first air raids. Lots of the other people—one way and another. Just as well we didn't all know what was going to happen to us, wasn't it? It would have been frightfully grim if we had. That boy Bill—what happened to him?"

Frank Abbott said, "I fancy he went missing. By the way, what was his name?"

She stared. He remembered the trick, and that it had been attractive. Her eyes were a rather light bright blue, and when she was surprised or flummoxed the whole of the iris showed. She said,

"I haven't an idea, darling. I never saw him before, and I never saw him again. But they called him Bill, and he drew dogs and cats and penguins all over the back of the menu—really frightfully clever. I kept it for ever so long, but you can't travel about with everything, can you?"

"You're sure you don't remember his surname?"

"I don't suppose I ever heard it. You don't, you know—not when you only meet a person once. But I thought he was rather a lamb, and I've often wondered if he came through the war. You say he didn't?"

"I didn't say that."

"You said he was missing. I thought he was rather a pet. George isn't listening, so I can tell you as a completely deadly secret that I rather envied the Lester girl."

"And who was the Lester girl?"

Women shouldn't pout when they are over thirty. It should have been George's business to tell Mildred that her pouting days were over. She made the face which had been freakish and charming when she was twenty, and said,

"But you remembered her. You said so—she had a gold dress. Was her name Lester?"

"I don't remember her name. Who was she, and why did you envy her?"

"Well, she was a daughter of Aunt Sophy's friend—at least I think it was Aunt Sophy. Anyhow she was the daughter of somebody's friend, because they were raving about her. Only now I come to think of it, I don't believe her name *was* Lester, because I think they were the people she was staying with, but I can't be sure. I think it began with an L, because if it didn't, why should I think it was Lester? But it might have been Lyall—or Linkwater—or Satterbee—"

Frank cocked an eyebrow.

"Satterbee doesn't begin with an L."

"No, it doesn't, does it?" She brightened. "You know how it is with names—you think it's an L, and it turns out to be something quite different. Do you think perhaps I said Satterbee because I was running Linkwater into Latimer? It was the Latimers' party, you know."

"Yes, you said so. But I don't know why it should make you think of Satterbee."

"It might—you can't tell with names. Or it mightn't have been an L after all. Something made me think of Marriott just then. No, that was Cousin Barbara's companion who went off her head in the middle of a tea-party and broke four of her best Rockingham cups—that lovely apple-green. Grim, wasn't it? So it wasn't Marriott. But it might have been Carlton—oh, no, it wasn't. I'll tell you what it was—it just came in a flash. Do you find things come to you like that? They do me. It was Elliot! That's where I got the L from!" She paused for breath, and added doubtfully, "But I've got a feeling it might be Lester after all."

"Have you?" Frank had a sardonic gleam in his eye.

Mildred pouted.

"Anyhow George admired her so much that I nearly broke off the engagement—didn't I, George?"

George Darcy, having finished a detailed and painstaking conference with the waiter, turned back to his wife and guest.

"Didn't you what?"

"Nearly break off our engagement because you fell so hard for that Lester girl at the Latimers' party just before we were married."

George looked a little sulky.

"I haven't an idea."

"Well then, I did nearly break it off. And I must say she was awfully pretty." She went back to Frank. "He can say what he likes now, but he fell for her like anything. But of course she was engaged to Bill and no one else got a look in. They danced together practically the whole evening. I can't remember whether they were just engaged, or whether it happened that evening, but I know they were married quite soon after that, because Aunt Sophy—if it was Aunt Sophy—told me so. But of course it may have been Cousin Barbara, or Miss Mackintosh, because they were both about a good deal just then."

With his well known talent for taking up the least important point in any preceding speech, George enquired,

"Who was Miss Mackintosh?"

Mildred poured out information about Miss Mackintosh, who was quite old and kept poodles which had to be combed every day and it took hours, and who couldn't, after all, have imparted any information about Bill and the Lester girl—if she was the Lester girl and not Lyall, Linkwater, Satterbee, Marriott, Carlton, or Rockingham. No—Rockingham was the china smashed by the mad Miss Marriott who was Cousin Barbara's companion.

Frank Abbott extracted an exasperated humour from the proceedings, but he obtained no further enlightenment on the subject of William Smith.

Later on, when he was saying goodnight, he asked quite seriously,

"Look here, Mildred, how sure are you about that chap Bill having got married? Never mind the girl's name or anything of that sort—just concentrate on whether he married her."

She looked up at him doubtfully.

"Well, I think he did—"

"What makes you think so?"

"Well, I remember Aunt Sophy writing out and saying she was giving them some china. She had stacks of it you know."

"You really remember that?"

"Yes, I do, because I wondered which of the sets she was giving them. There was one I wanted myself, and I always hoped she was going to leave it to me."

"If she wrote and told you she was giving them a wedding present she must have mentioned their names."

"Oh, yes, she did."

"Well, then?"

She wrinkled up her forehead, a trick that was going to leave ugly lines, and before very long too. She said,

"You know, I was thinking about the china. The tea-set I wanted was a pet—those little bunches of flowers and a blue edge, and a nubble on the top of the teapot shaped like a strawberry. I didn't really bother about the names, but of course she must have said them."

"Try and think what she did say."

"She said, 'I'm giving them one of the china tea-sets.'"

If Frank ground his teeth, he did it silently.

"Never mind about the tea-set—she didn't begin like that."

"Oh, no—she said I'd be interested to hear they were getting married, because I'd fallen for Bill—I told her I had, you know."

"She did say Bill?"

"Oh, yes—I keep telling you she did."

"Then she would have said the girl's name too. What was it?"

"Darling, I've forgotten."

"You're sure it was that Bill and that girl?"

"Oh, yes!" This time she was quite wholehearted.

"Are you sure they got married?"

"Oh, yes, I am, because Aunt Sophy went to the wedding—she couldn't have done that if they hadn't got married. And I remember she did go, because she wore her sable cape,

94

and I got her letter telling me about it on a simply sweltering day, and I remember thinking how frightful it sounded—and anyhow sable and Aunt Sophy—too, too grim!"

"And still you don't remember their names?"

"There was Bill—"

"Thank you—I got that myself. It's Bill's surname and the girl's names that I want. If you don't know them yourself, what about your Aunt Sophy?"

"Darling, she died five years ago. And she did leave me a tea-set, only I don't know if it's the one I wanted."

"Can you think of anyone else who would know?"

The wrinkles deepened. She shook her head.

"Honestly, darling, I can't. You see, such a lot of people are dead—Cousin Barbara—and the Latimers—and Jim and Bob Barrett—I remember they were there, because Jim said I looked like a rosebud, and George was furious. Does it matter?"

Frank Abbott said, "It might."

CHAPTER 14

William took Katharine round to see Mr. Tattlecombe after the shop closed next day, and found that the visit was in the nature of an Occasion. Mr. Tattlecombe had come out of his splint that morning and had moved across the landing to the upstairs parlour, which dated from the time before Abigail's marriage when old Mrs. Salt had lived with her son and for the best part of fifteen years had never gone downstairs. The carpet was the one she had chosen, and so were the plush armchairs. The crochet antimacassars were her own handi-work. A photographic enlargement of her in a Victorian widow's cap looked down from over the mantelpiece.

Mr. Tattlecombe sat in the largest of the armchairs with his leg up on a foot-rest and a brown and white striped woollen shawl spread over it. Abigail Salt had put on her Sunday dress. There was tea, and cake, and sandwiches, and a cold fish mould, and a jelly, and a trifle, and a plate of Abigail's famous cheese straws, and a pot of her cousin Sarah Hill's famous apple honey.

Mr. Tattlecombe was as pleased as Punch. If favour was deceitful and beauty was vain, it was nevertheless pleasant to the eye. He found Miss Eversley pleasant to the eye. And not one of the flaunting kind—a very modest, quiet-spoken, ladylike young woman. And fond of William—you couldn't be in the room with them without getting hold of that. Abigail Salt agreed. A nice girl, if she was any judge of girls, and she thought she was. Something about her that made you wonder why she hadn't looked higher than William Smith. But easy to see that they were in love. Funny how a thing like that came out, when they weren't so much as looking at each other, and the talk was all about the shop, and those painted toys, and Abel's leg, and Sarah's apple honey, and how did she get her cheese straws so light. She found herself giving Katharine the receipt, which was a thing she wouldn't have believed if anyone had told her.

Then, when everything was going as well as it possibly could, who should open the door and look in on them but poor Emily? Not that she wasn't welcome—Abigail Salt would never have allowed herself to harbour the thought that Emily's room was preferable to her company. If such a thought presented itself, it would be turned out and the door banged in its face. But she didn't know when Emily had done such a thing as join them when there was company. Go away down to the kitchen was what she would do, and make her own tea and go picking over the larder for something to eat. And many a time Abigail had been obliged to make it a subject for prayer, for to have your larder picked over was what would try the patience of a saint. If Abby wasn't a saint she was a kind-hearted woman, and she had put up with Emily and her ways for the best part of thirty years. She lifted her eyes placidly to the tall black figure in the doorway and said,

"Come in, my dear. This is Miss Eversley. And I think you know Mr. Smith—my sister-in-law, Miss Salt."

Emily stood there in a black woollen dress with an uneven hem. It dipped at the back and lifted where her angular hips took it up, the neck sagged, and the sleeves left the bony wrists uncovered. She poked her head forward, with its thatch of dark hair piled up like a grizzled haycock, turned lacklustre eyes on Abel, on Katharine, on William, and came into the room and up to the table. When William offered her a chair she looked at him again. The chair might have been a cup of cold poison or an instrument of torture. William was to consider himself detected and spurned. She went round to the other side of the table, chose a ridiculous small chair a long way after Sheraton, set it down as near to Abigail and as far from William as possible, and began to eat cheese and tomato sandwiches with great rapidity, one down, t'other come on. Without saying anything at all she had contrived to cast a blight. She ate her sandwiches and she drank her tea.

Mr. Tattlecombe, with rising colour, reflected that there were trials that were sent by the Lord and you had to put up with them. But he couldn't feel like that about Emily, and in his opinion she ought to be in a home.

It was whilst Katharine was telling him that they thought

of getting married on Saturday that Emily Salt stopped in the middle of a sandwich to make her first remark. Her voice was harsh and deep, almost as deep as a man's. She said,

"Marry in haste and repent at leisure—there's a proverb about that."

Abel's eyes went as blue as marbles.

"And there's one about least said soonest mended, Emily Salt."

She might not have heard him. She went on eating sandwiches until she had finished the plate. Then she pushed back her chair so roughly that it fell over, and went out of the room as she had come, looking sideways at Abel, at William, at Katharine, turning on the threshold to look again, and then shutting the door so quickly that it seemed as if it must bang. Only it didn't—it didn't make any sound at all. It shut, and there was no sound at all. And no sound from the other side of it. Emily Salt might be standing there, pressed close against the panels, listening. Or she might have gone upstairs, or she might have gone down, or she might have flown away on a broomstick.

Inside the room they went on talking, but everyone's voice had dropped. Emily might be standing there, pressed up against the door.

CHAPTER 15

Late that evening the telephone bell rang in Katharine's flat. William had gone. The noises in the Mews had for the most part died down. One persistent radio still discoursed dance music at a penetrating pitch, and now and again a car came home to one of the old stables turned garage, but most of the daytime noises had ceased. Even if they had not, Katharine would not have noticed them. During these days she was withdrawn from a harsh external world into her own place of happiness and peace. The telephone bell surprised her, because no one knew that she was here. The bank or the post office sent on her letters, but she had not given her address to anyone at all. Of course it might be someone ringing up Carol—

She went over to the writing-table, lifted the receiver, and it was Brett Eversley.

"Katharine—"

She was both surprised and angry. She had refused him in as definite terms as a woman can use, and she had refused to give him her address. By what means he had discovered it she had no idea. It wasn't until her name had been repeated that she spoke.

"What is it, Brett?"

"Have I dragged you out of bed? That's what you sound like."

"No."

"Katharine, you're angry."

"Yes."

"With me?"

"Yes, Brett, with you."

"But why, my dear?"

"I didn't give you my address because I wanted to be left alone. I didn't give you my telephone number."

He laughed.

"And I didn't take no for an answer. Come—it's a compliment, you know. You don't expect a man who's in love with you to resign himself to not knowing where you are, or what you're doing, or even whether you're well or ill."

She bit her lip.

"You saw me on Wednesday. I wasn't ill then."

He said, "Wednesday!" And then, "A tantalizing drop of water to a man who is dying of thirst! How much satisfaction do you think I got out of seeing you hemmed in by Cyril and old Holden?"

She said, "How did you get my telephone number?"

"I don't know. Someone told me Carol had lent you her flat. Look here, I won't bother you, but what's the sense of shutting yourself up like this? Dine with me tomorrow. I'll call for you at seven."

"I'm afraid I can't."

"Can't—or won't?"

"Both, Brett."

His voice changed.

"You're being rather hard on me, Katharine—don't you think so? What do you think I'm made of? You go away suddenly without a word to anyone—it's not very easy to put up with. If we're nothing more, we're cousins and friends, and—I love you."

Her tone softened a little.

"I'm sorry, Brett, it's no use."

100

"You don't give me a chance to make you care."

"Brett, there isn't any chance."

"I don't accept that. There's always a chance. I'm only asking you to give me mine."

She had begun to feel as if she were holding a door against which he was pushing hard. It tired her. She wished very much that he would go away. She had said no, and she had meant no, and he wouldn't take it. Where did you go from there? She said, "It's no use, Brett—there's no chance for me to give you. I'm going to marry someone else."

She heard him say "Who?" but she didn't answer that.

She said in a tired voice, "It isn't any use," and put the receiver back.

CHAPTER 16

William Smith was married to Katharine Eversley at St. James' Church, just round the corner from Rasselas Mews, at half past two on Saturday afternoon. All the morning they painted together in the workshop behind Tattlecombe's Toy Bazaar. At one o'clock William drove Katharine home. They had lunch together, after which he put on his best suit, a neat and quite undistinguished blue serge, in what had been Carol's spare room. It was going to be his dressing-room now. He unpacked and put his things away with the feeling that this unbelievable happiness seemed real and felt real, but all the same he didn't see how it could possibly be true. There was something reassuring about getting out his shaving things and putting shirts away in a drawer. He put everything away very neatly. Every time he folded anything or opened a cupboard door it seemed to make it more probable that he was going to marry Katharine, because if he wasn't he wouldn't be unpacking his things in her flat.

Katharine dressed for her wedding with as much care as if the congregation in whose face she was going to be married to William would fill the church and set up the highest possible standard of distinction and elegance, instead of consisting of Abigail Salt and Mrs. Bastable, together with any stray passerby who might scent a wedding and drop in to see the bride. The dress, of rather a deep shade of blue, threw up her skin and brought out the gold lights in her hair. The long matching coat with the touch of fur at the neck was soft and warm. The small hat, hardly more than a cap, was made of the same stuff, with an odd little knot of the fur.

They walked round to the church together and were married with Abigail Salt and Mrs. Bastable as witnesses. To Katharine the church was not empty, or cold, or dark. It was full of her love and William's.

The immemorial words of the marriage service sounded in the echoing space and trembled away into silence—"I require and charge you both, as ye will answer at the dreadful day of judgment when the secrets of all hearts shall be disclosed, that if either of you know of any impediment, why ye may not be lawfully joined together in Matrimony, ye do now confess it . . ." The silence seemed to echo too.

Katharine lifted her head and looked up into the reds and blues of a stained glass window where Christ turned the water into wine.

Now the old betrothal service followed, and the vows "to have and to hold from this day forward, for better for worse, for richer for poorer, in sickness and in health, to love and to cherish, till death us do part..." William's voice quite steady, quite sure of what he was promising. Then her own, rather soft—"to love, cherish, and to obey, till death us do part according to God's holy ordinance..."

William putting the ring on her finger—"with my body I thee worship..."

And the prayer, the joining of hands, and—"those whom God hath joined together let no man put asunder..."

The young man who took the service had a pleasant voice. It came out strong and full when he pronounced them man and wife and blessed them.

Mrs. Bastable sniffed and dried her eyes. Weddings always made her cry. Abigail Salt sat up very straight in a black coat with a fur collar. Because it was a wedding she had put an unseasonable bunch of cornflowers in her hat. They made her eyes look very blue.

In the vestry Katharine signed her name and looked at it and smiled a little, and stood aside for William to sign too. He wrote his William Smith.

The young parson stopped him as he was turning away.

"Your father's name too, Mr. Smith."

"I'm afraid I don't know it."

William was quite simple and unembarrassed. It was the parson who coloured.

"I'm afraid—" he began, and stopped.

"You see, I've lost my memory. I can put blank Smith if you like."

Well, of course, it wasn't what he liked or didn't like. He really didn't know. He would have to tell the Vicar. After all, if a man didn't know his father's name he didn't.

William wrote Smith with a dash in front of it on the register. And then the young parson called Katharine back.

"You have to give your father's name too, Mrs. Smith."

Still with that small faint smile, Katherine leaned over and wrote. Then she turned round to be congratulated by Mrs. Bastable.

"I'm sure I hope you'll be happy, Mrs. Smith. And I'm sure Mr. Smith is one that anyone could be happy with. Believe it or not, I don't know that I've ever seen him out of temper, and when you think how most men are—well, it's bound to make a difference, isn't it? Mr. Bastable had a very hasty temper. And particular about his food—well you'd hardly believe it. Always talking about his mother's cooking too, and if there's anything more likely to make unpleasantness in the home, well, I don't know what it is. I've always been considered sweet-tempered myself, but when he used to look at my scones and say how much lighter his mother made them, it used to come up on the tip of my tongue to say, 'Then why didn't you stay home with her?' But I never said it. I don't know what he might have done if I had—being so hasty, you know." She dabbed her eyes and sniffed again. "Oh, well, we must let bygones be bygones, mustn't we? And Mr. Bastable's been gone getting on for twenty years."

Abigail Salt had much fewer words. She said,

"I hope you will be very happy, and Mr. Tattlecombe hopes so too."

CHAPTER 17

That same evening Frank Abbott dropped in on Miss Maud Silver at her flat at Montague Mansions. Whatever happened in the outer world, here time stood still. But not in any sluggish, lotus-eating manner—"Oh dear, no," as Miss Silver herself might have said. He found in her a constant stimulus to thought, and whilst her idiosyncrasies were a continual entertainment, he did actually and in sober truth revere the little woman who, beginning her working life in what she herself termed the private side of the scholastic profession, was now a much sought-after enquiry agent.

Where time had been halted was on the threshold of this room. The furniture inherited from more than one great-aunt was of the type strangely popular in the sixties of the previous century. The chairs, with their walnut frames, bow legs, and spreading upholstered laps, suggested long departed crinolines and peg-top trousers. Engravings of famous Victorian pictures in yellow maple frames looked down upon a carpet not of contemporary age but of a truly contemporary pattern. The pictures, interchanged from time to time with those in her bedroom, included the late Sir John Millais' "Bubbles," Mr. G. F. Watts' "Hope," together with "The Stag at Bay" and "The Soul's Awakening." The carpet, new a year ago, was of a lively shade of peacock-blue, with a pattern of pink and white roses in wreaths caught together with bows of green ribbon. The curtains, of the same blue but duller in tone, had survived the war, and though not actually shabby were due to be replaced as soon as Miss Silver felt justified in spending so much money upon herself. Two of her niece Ethel Burkett's boys were now at school, and a baby girl had been added to the family during the past year. School outfits were expensive, and much as the Burketts rejoiced over having a daughter after three boys in succession, the year had placed a considerable strain on their finances, and it was not in Miss Silver's nature to allow them to bear it unaided. The curtains could very well do another year, or even two.

As she sat in her comfortable chair beside her comfortable fire, her heart was full of gratitude. She had lived for twenty years in other people's houses, and had expected to live twenty more before retiring on a pittance. The hand of Providence had, however, translated her into a new profession, and to circumstances of modest comfort. The mantel-shelf, the book-case, two occasional tables, and a whatnot were crowded with photographs of grateful clients incredibly framed in fretwork, in hammered or patterned silver, in silver filagree upon plush. A good many of them were photographs of young men and girls, and of the babies who would never have been born if this little old maid had not brought her intelligence and skill to bear upon their parents' problems.

Frank Abbott was received very much as if he had been a nephew. He accepted the cup of coffee brought him by Emma Meadows, Miss Silver's valued housekeeper, and sat back sipping it and feeling pleasantly at home. On the other side of the hearth Miss Silver was knitting a pair of infant's leggings in pale blue wool. After completing three pairs of stockings each for Johnny, Derek and Roger, she was now equipping little Josephine for the coming spring—so treach-

106

erous and changeable. With four children to make and mend for, to say nothing of her husband and all the household work, Ethel really had no time for knitting.

There was a pleasant silence in the room. A coal fell in the fire. Miss Silver's needles clicked above the pale blue wool. Frank finished his coffee and leaned sideways to put down the cup. Then he said,

"How did you find out that the way to make people talk is to sit there knitting and make them feel everything is as safe as houses and it doesn't matter what they say?"

A faint smile just touched her lips. She went on knitting. He laughed.

"You know, I've been here hundreds of times and it's only just come to me that the thing you conjure with is security. That's what you're putting across. Your pictures, your furniture—they've come down from a settled past. They belong to the time when there practically wasn't an income tax and European wars were just something you read about in the *Times*. There's all that—and then the one practical modern touch, your office table. That makes them feel that the security doesn't just exist in the past—it can be brought up to date and put to work for them."

Miss Silver coughed.

"I find that a little fanciful."

He smiled.

"How many frightened people have you had in this room?"

Her eyes dwelt on him for a moment.

"A good many."

He nodded.

"Well, I wouldn't mind betting that very few of them went away as frightened as they came."

Her needles clicked, the pale blue wool revolved. She said,

"I think you have something on your mind. What is it?"

He did not speak at once, but leaned back, looking at her. No one could have suited her room better—the small neat features, the rather pale smooth skin, washed twice a day with soap and water, belonged to a period when a lady did not use make-up and even powder was considered "fast." Her hair conformed more to the Edwardian than the Victorian age, being banked up in a fringe like the late Queen Alexandra's and coiled neatly at the back, the whole controlled by an invisible net. During the years he had known her Frank had not observed that she had any more grey hairs than the few which he remembered to have been there at their first meeting, nor did she seem to be older in any other way. She might have stepped out of any family group at the end of the last century or at the beginning of this. It was her practice to wear a summer silk in the winter evenings. The current garment, of the type sold by pushing saleswomen to elderly ladies who are not very much interested in dress, was of a boiled spinach colour with an orange pattern of dots and dashes which suggested Morse. It came modestly to the ankles and revealed black woollen stockings and glacé shoes with beaded toes. The V neck had been rendered high by the insertion of a net front with a boned collar. The pince-nez, used only for fine print, was looped to the bosom of the dress by a gold bar brooch set with pearls, and the base of the V was decorated by Miss Silver's favorite ornament, a rose carved in black bog oak with an Irish pearl at its heart. Since the January evening was cold, a black velvet coatee reinforced the thin silk of the dress. It was a cherished garment—so comfortable, so warm—but it must be confessed that its better days were definitely past and gone, and that it was now a mere relic. No self-consciousness on that score, however, disturbed Miss Silver's appreciation of its comfort.

With no need to keep her eyes upon the knitting, she

smiled at Frank, maintained her affectionate regard, and waited for him to speak. When he did so, it was in an odd doubtful tone.

"I've run up against something—I don't quite know what."

Miss Silver pulled on her ball of pale blue wool.

"It is disturbing you?"

"I suppose it is. The fact is, I don't know whether there's anything in it or not. There might be nothing—or something. I don't know quite what to do, or whether I ought to do anything at all."

"Perhaps you would feel clearer about it if you were to put your conjectures on the subject into words. If you would care to tell me about it—"

He laughed a little.

"I've come here on purpose, and you know it."

Miss Silver coughed with the faintest hint of reproof.

"Then, my dear Frank, suppose you begin."

He said, "There's probably nothing in it, but I'd like to get it off my chest. About a week ago I was coming along Selby Street, which is a respectable suburban road on the way out to Hampstead, when a man came out of a house on my left and walked along in front of me. I saw him with the open door of the house behind him. He had fair hair, and the light caught it. Anyone else could have seen him too. That's one of the points—anyone could have seen what I did. After the door was shut and he was out in the street visibility wasn't too good. It was a thickish night with rain in the air, but we were coming up to a lamp-post and I could see him ahead of me—perhaps twenty feet away, perhaps a little more. Then all of a sudden there was someone else, and I don't know where he came from—out of one of the other houses—out of a cut between the houses—out of somebody's porch—I don't know. The first I saw of him, he was there between me

109

and the light, closing up on the first man. All I can swear to is that he was wearing a raincoat and some kind of a hat. Then in a flash he swung up his arm and brought it down again. The first man dropped, I ran up, and the fellow who had hit him ran away. I lost him almost at once. As soon as you got away from the lamp-post you couldn't see a thing. I went back to the man on the pavement, and he'd had a pretty lucky escape—hit over the head with something hard enough to break it if it had been the sort that breaks easily. He told me himself that it was tough. His hat had taken the worst of it."

Miss Silver listened attentively, but made no comment.

Frank leaned forward.

"Well, he was a bit dazed and shaken. I took him round to the police station and they gave him a cup of tea, and then I took him home to Tattlecombe's Toy Bazaar, where he is an assistant temporarily in charge. He had been visiting his employer in Selby Street, where he has been laid up after a road accident. I expect you wonder what all this is about—and here it is. The chap said his name was William Smith, but it isn't. I'd seen him before and I recognized him. I told him so, and he told me that he came out of a German hospital in '42 as William Smith, and that was as much as he knew. He hadn't got any past, and he naturally wanted to know who I thought he was."

Miss Silver's needles clicked.

"And who do you think he is?"

"That's the bother of it—I can't get any farther than Bill. You know how it is, everybody using Christian names—I don't suppose I ever heard his surname." He told her about the party at the Luxe. "And you can take it from me that's the sort of crowd where he belonged, and that quite definitely you wouldn't expect to find him assisting in a suburban Toy

Bazaar. He told me himself that he wasn't the William Smith whose identity he had somehow acquired. This man came from Stepney, and Bill went down there to make enquiries. Only relative, a sister, had moved away during the blitz and been lost sight of, but the neighbours all laughed at the idea of his being their William Smith. They were thorough-paced Cockneys and were proud of it, and they despised what they called his B.B.C. accent."

Miss Silver looked at him across her knitting.

"A curious story, Frank."

"Yes, but you've only heard half of it. I met the chap again on Thursday night. I'd been dining out, and I was coming home, when I saw William Smith in a bus queue at the Marble Arch. I went up and asked him how he was and he said he was all right, but something had happened—earlier that evening. He'd been to see his employer again. Coming back, he was standing in a crowd on an island waiting for the lights to change, when, he says, someone jabbed him in the back with a stick. He lost his footing and would have fallen under a bus if the man next to him hadn't grabbed him. By the time he'd got steadied up enough to look the lights had changed, everyone was streaming away, and there wasn't anyone who looked as if they could have done it. I asked him if he was going to report the incident to the police, and he said no— he couldn't see what they could do." He paused, and added, "I gave him your address."

Miss Silver coughed.

"My dear Frank!"

"Well, I thought you might be interested. That's not all, you know. I've given you the last incident for what it's worth, but two rather uncomfortable points emerge from what I've come across myself. Here's the first. After William Smith dropped and I was running up, the man who had hit him

111

was going to hit him again. That's all wrong, you know. The chap was down and out—very completely out. If the motive was robbery, the thief ought to have been going through his pockets. Well, I don't think the motive was robbery—I think it was murder. He'd got what looked like a stick, but it must have been something a good deal more lethal—probably a length of lead piping—and he was going to polish him off, and another blow like the first on a head with a paving stone under it would have polished him off. The fellow was so intent on what he was doing that he couldn't have known I was there until I started to run, and even then he as near as a toucher took the time for that second blow. When he heard me he lost his nerve and made off across the road."

Miss Silver knitted in silence for a moment or two.

"Do you think that this man was lying in wait for William Smith—that he saw him come out of the house and attempted to murder him?"

"I can't go as far as that—there's no evidence. He could have seen him, he could have recognized him, and I think he certainly tried to murder him. That's as far as I can go."

After a slight pause she said,

"That is your first uncomfortable point. What is the second?"

He said, "Bill—the chap I met at the pre-war party at the Luxe—was married."

Miss Silver said, "Dear me!"

"There was a girl there in a gold dress—very attractive. They danced together most of the evening. No one else got a look in with her—I know I didn't. Now last night I dined with my cousin Mildred Darcy and her husband, just home after seven years out East. They were at that party. They were engaged at the time. Mildred remembers Bill—she rather fell for him—but she doesn't remember his surname

112

any more than I do. It's the other way round with the girl in the gold dress. She has no views of any kind about her Christian name, but she produced at least half a dozen surnames, of which the most probable seemed to be Lester—if it wasn't Elliot. There was some connection with Mildred's Aunt Sophy, and she's sure the girl and Bill were married, because Aunt Sophy wrote out and told her she had given them a tea-set. My cousin Mildred has the world's most inconsequent mind. She really doesn't remember Bill's name or the girl's but she sticks to it that she remembers them, as apart from their names, and that she is sure they got married— largely, I think, because of the tea-set." Miss Silver knitted thoughtfully. Then she said,

"He has lost his memory—he does not know who he was before the war. But you believe that you met him at a party at the Luxe in '39, and your cousin Mrs. Darcy, who was also present, informs you that he married the girl to whom he was then engaged. You knew him only as Bill, and you do not remember the girl's name at all. Mrs. Darcy remembers too many names, and is not sure about any of them. You are of the opinion that his life has recently been attempted."

Frank said, "An admirable summing-up."

Miss Silver coughed.

"As to your two uncomfortable points—have you told him that you consider the attack you witnessed was an attempt at murder?"

He said, "No."

"And you are wondering if you should put him on his guard."

"Perhaps."

"And you are also wondering whether you should pass on Mrs. Darcy's information as to his marriage."

Frank lifted a hand and let it fall again.

"Correct on both counts. But what is there to say? I can tell him that the chap who hit him once was going to hit him again. It doesn't prove anything—does it? I rather blench at telling him that my cousin Mildred says he is a married man, because—well, you used the word information, but anything Mildred produces is entirely without form and void. I told you she had an inconsequent mind. That's putting it much too mildly. When it comes to anything like evidence, she hasn't really got a mind at all—she just dives into a sort of lumber-room and brings out odds and ends. If you put them together they make something, but nobody—least of all Mildred herself—can do more than guess at whether the result bears any relation to fact. I think she really does remember that Bill did marry the girl in the gold dress, but I can't be sure, and I don't see that I'm justified in passing it on unless I am sure. On the other hand, if I did pass it on it might be a clue to his identity, or it might give his memory a jog, so I don't see that I am justified in keeping it to myself. I am in fact exhibiting extreme infirmity of purpose, and as I usually don't find any difficulty in making up my mind I don't like it."

Miss Silver knitted briskly.

"There are interesting possibilities. On the other hand your cousin may be mistaken, and the attack you witnessed have been a mere sporadic act of violence, the initial purpose robbery, with the brutal instinct to strike a second time overpowering reason. This has been, and is, a factor in many crimes."

"I agree. But I am left with my impression. Would you like to discourse on the interesting possibilities?"

Miss Silver turned the pale blue leggings, which had now assumed a definite shape. She said,

"You recognized him. Someone else may have done so."

"Yes."

"After seven or eight years a return from the grave would not always be welcome. On the purely material side, it might be inconvenient, or even disastrous. You have, I suppose, no idea of this young man's circumstances?"

"You mean when he was Bill? Well, no. The Latimers—Mildred said it was their party—well, they were in a fairly moneyed set. His father made a pile in soap. Most of their friends would be well-to-do. But—" he laughed—"well, I was there! Bill may have been on the same footing. His girl looked expensive. But there again—you can't tell with girls. My cousin Rachel who hasn't a bean turns out looking like a million dollars, and I know women who spend hundreds and miss the bus every time. Bill's girl may have made her own dress, or Aunt Sophy may have given it to her—or any of the other ladies whom Mildred reeled off. There was a cousin Barbara, I remember, queer and rather rich. Mildred's mother had a whole tribe of relations, and they are all dead, so it's no good saying go and ask them what about it. The whole thing could hardly be vaguer—could it? What I can't account for is the fact that it has left me with these impressions, which are not vague at all, but quite definite and sharp. Do you know what it reminds me of? Looking up at a lighted window out of a dark street and seeing someone or something, or watching a train go past and getting a glimpse of a face you can't forget."

Miss Silver had a Victorian habit of quotation. She employed it now. The late Lord Tennyson was her favorite poet, but on this occasion it was Longfellow who came aptly to her lips:

"'Ships that pass in the night, and speak each
    other in passing . . .
So on the ocean of life we pass and speak one
    another . . . '"

CHAPTER 18

Katharine woke with the night turning towards day. It was
the hour when even a great city is quiet—a still hour, but
not dark, because the sky was clear. Somewhere behind all
those houses the moon was going down. From where she
lay she could see the tracery of leafless trees above the roof-
line over the way. The trees were in the garden of Rasselas
House. They were old, and tall, and beautiful. She looked at
them now and was at peace. The window was open and a
soft air came in. She turned a little. On the other side of
Carol's wide, low bed William was very deeply asleep. One
of his hands was tucked under the pillow, the other lay across
his chest. She had to listen to catch the quiet, even breathing.
If she put out her own hand it would touch him. But her
thought could not reach him at all. Or could it? She wondered. When you loved someone as much as this it didn't
seem possible that he could go where you couldn't reach
him. All through time—all through space—The thought
broke off. Time and space were frightening things—cold, far,
endless. No, not that, because time must come to an end.
There was a verse about it in the Bible—the angel standing
upon the sea and upon the earth and lifting up his hand to

swear that there should be time no longer. A little shiver went over her. Time and space were cold and far away. She and William were here. This was their hour. Her thoughts swung back again. His body was here. William was somewhere else—perhaps in the very deep places of sleep where they say there are no dreams. How do they know? All they can really tell is that you don't remember what you dream in those deep places. Perhaps William was there.

William came up into the shallows where dreams begin. The dream that met him there was the one he knew, only this time it was different. Always before it had begun in the street. He would be walking up the steps and going into the house because someone was holding the door against him. That hadn't ever happened before, and it worried him. This time was quite different, because he was not only in the house, but he was right up at the top of the stairs. As a rule, that was when he woke. Always in the dream someone was waiting for him, and when he got to the top, or nearly to the top, he woke up.

This time it was different. He stood at the top of the stairs and looked down. He could see all the way down the stairs into the hall. There was plenty of light—but not daylight—there wasn't ever daylight in his dream. Everything was all right. And then quite suddenly it wasn't. The dream took a slant, the way dreams sometimes do. The newel-posts which were carved with the four Evangelists went queer. He was standing at the head of the stairs between the eagle and the man, looking down to the lion and the ox at the foot, and all at once they were different. The eagle had changed into a Boomalong Bird, and the man was Mr. Tattlecombe, looking indignant, as well he might, with his grey hair standing up and his eyes very blue. And down there on either side of the bottom step there was a Wurzel Dog and a Crummocky Cow.

He came down the stairs into the hall, and someone knocked three times on the door. They wanted to get in, but the door was barred. Then they came through the door—just like that—the door didn't open, they came through it with their arms linked—three of them, with the woman in the middle. He knew her at once. She was Miss Jones, the secretary who had told him that Eversleys' wouldn't be interested in the Wurzel toys. He knew her, but he didn't know the men, because there wasn't anything to know. They were just trousers and coats, and faces painted smooth and featureless with the paint they used in the workshop for undercoating the toys. It was a horrid pinkish colour and it glistened. The faces had no eyes and no features. They were just paint. They came towards him. He called out, "No—no—*no!*" and the dream broke up. He opened his eyes on the room, the glimmering square of the window, the light air coming in.

Katharine slipped her arm under his head and drew it to her shoulder.

"What is it? You called out."

"What did I say?"

"You said, 'No—no—*no!*'"

He said, "I was dreaming."

"Tell me."

"Well, it's rather odd. It's a dream I have sometimes about going up three steps into a house. There's an old door—oak, with nails in it—and I go through into a hall with a staircase going up on the right. The hall has panelling—it goes all the way up the stairs too. There are pictures let into it. There's a girl in a pink dress. The stair goes up on the right, and the newel-posts are carved with the four Evangelists—a lion and an ox at the bottom, and an eagle and a man at the top—" He broke off suddenly. "Katharine, I've never remembered that before. It's been in the dream, but I haven't remembered

118

it when I was awake—not till now. That's funny, isn't it?"

"I don't know—"

"I've never remembered it before, but it was there. I used to remember going up the steps and into the house, and that I was coming home. Do you think it's something real and I remember it when I'm asleep?"

She felt his rough fair hair under her cheek. She said, "Does it feel like that?"

"I don't know—I don't know what it would feel like. It's always felt good—until tonight."

"What happened tonight?"

"Well, as a rule I come in and I go upstairs, and then I wake up. It doesn't sound much, but it feels good. Tonight it all went queer. Three of the Evangelists turned into Wurzel toys, and the man was Mr. Tattlecombe. And then it all got horrid. Three people came through the door—I mean really right through it, when it was shut. Two of them were men, with their faces all smoothed out with undercoating paint—no features or anything—but the one in the middle was that Miss Jones I saw when I went to Eversleys'."

Katharine drew a sharp breath.

He said, "What's that for?"

"It was rather horrid."

"Yes. But I woke up—don't let's bother about it any more. I love you."

"Do you?"

"Yes. I feel as if I'd loved you always."

CHAPTER 19

They went back to the shop on Monday morning, and received the acid congratulations of Miss Cole.

"So very sudden. Quite unexpected, if I may say so. But Mrs. Bastable tells me she saw you married. And Mrs. Salt there too! Really I had no idea at all, though I naturally thought it very strange when you and Miss Eversley both took the afternoon off. If there had been a rush of business, I don't know how I should have managed."

This from Miss Cole who had steadily refused to have help in the shop. She hoped they would be happy in tones which suggested that she feared the worst. They escaped thankfully to the workshop.

At eleven o'clock Mrs. Salt rang up to say that Mr. Tattlecombe would be coming home that afternoon. She made no explanation, merely remarking that she had ordered a taxi for half past three, and that she would of course accompany her brother. This diverted Miss Cole's attention, and sent Mrs. Bastable into a perfect fever of preparation.

Mr. Tattlecombe arrived triumphantly at four o'clock. He kissed his sister and thanked her for all she had done for him, but he did not press her to stay. William helped him upstairs, gave him a footstool and a rug, and attended to his frank opinion of Emily Salt.

"Listens at doors," said Abel, looking exactly like he had looked in William's dream—hair sticking up on end and blue indignant eyes. "I always thought she did, and now I've

120

caught her. Last night it was, after Abigail got back from chapel. I got talking to her about you getting married, and natural enough we got on to my leaving you the business."

William began, "I hope Mrs. Salt—" but Mr. Tattlecombe put up a hand to stop him.

"Abby's agreeable. I told you she was when we talked about it before. The one that isn't is Emily Salt." Two bright patches came up into his cheeks. "Emily Salt, if you please, that's no more relation to me than she is to you! 'Don't talk about it in front of Emily,' my sister says. Well, that's what I've never done, and so I told her. 'Well,' she said, 'Emily knows, and it's upset her.' 'What's it got to do with her for her to be upset about it?' I said. 'I'll thank her to mind her own business—she's no call to upset herself about mine. What does she know about it anyway?' Abby didn't say anything, so I told her straight out. 'She listens at doors,' I said."

Abel had quite obviously enjoyed himself. He had wanted to say what he thought about Emily Salt for a long time. Well, now he had said it. And Abby had just sat there looking down into her lap. She hadn't said anything because she couldn't say anything. He explained this to William with a good deal of satisfaction.

"Doctor came Saturday, and said I'd got to use my leg, so I got up out of the chair and tried it. Wasn't too good, and wasn't too bad. What I was aiming at was getting near the door, for there's a stair that creaks, and I'd heard it. Abby's a bit hard of hearing, but I'm not, thank the Lord. I'd heard that stair, but I hadn't heard the one that goes on up, so I'd a pretty good idea where Emily was. I began talking about you again, and I raised my voice a bit, thinking it would be a pity for her to miss anything. I said I wondered if it would ever come out who you were. And that's when I got to the door and pulled it open. I tell you I nearly had her in on top of me."

"Emily Salt?"

Abel nodded emphatically.

"Right up against the door, with her hand on the knob, listening. Good thing for my leg she didn't fall right on the top of me."

William kept a straight face.

"What did you do, sir?"

"I said, 'You'll hear more comfortably if you come inside, Emily Salt.' She stared the way she does and said she was just coming in. So I told her what I thought about that. 'Listening at the door,' I told her—'that's what you were doing, and not the first time either. And I'll thank you to keep your hands off my affairs, Miss Salt.' Abby came along then to get me back to my chair. 'Now, Emily,' she says, and Emily flew right off the handle. I never heard anything like it—screamed like a wild cat and said I was doing Abby out of her rights. 'And what's it got to do with you if I am?' I said—and I could have said a whole lot more if my leg had been different. As soon as I got back to my chair Abby took Emily away. I could hear her screaming and going on all the way down the stairs."

"Mr. Tattlecombe—"

Abel put up an imperious hand.

"If it's anything about my will, you can keep it to yourself. I'm agreeable, and Abby's agreeable. And as for Emily Salt, she ought to be in a home, and so I told Abby when she came back. We didn't have words about it, but we might have done if I'd stayed on, so I said I'd come home. . . . That picture over the mantelpiece isn't straight, and those two photograph albums have got changed over. The one with the gilt corners goes at the back of the table."

He looked about him with a critical pleasure as William

made these adjustments. None of the furniture was as handsome as Abigail Salt's. The Brussels carpet was a good deal worn, the upholstery of the chairs was dingy. But it was his own place. The picture over the mantelpiece was an enlargement of the photograph taken of himself and Mary on their wedding day—an earnest young man in an ill-cut suit, and a plain, sweet-faced young woman in balloon sleeves and a dreadful hat. The furniture was what they had bought together. He nodded approvingly, and said,

"There's no place like your own, William."

CHAPTER 20

That evening when they had had their supper and had cleared it away and washed up, William told Katharine all about Emily Salt and her listening at doors. He was making sketches of Crummocky Cows, sitting in a low chair and leaning forward with a writing-pad on his knee.

"Of course she's balmy," he said. "I don't know how Mrs. Salt stands her. Whenever I've been there she's either been peering round a door or disappearing round a corner. But all the same I don't feel so happy about Mr. Tattlecombe's will. He's left me the business—did I tell you?"

Katharine said, "No."

"Well, he has. He told me about it that time I got knocked on the head. It's awfully embarrassing when people tell you they've left you things in their wills."

"He told you that evening?"

"Yes. He said Mrs. Salt was comfortably provided for, and

a lot of things about our having worked the business up together and he wanted me to have it. Of course it's got nothing to do with Emily Salt who he leaves it to—he told her that—but I can't help wishing she didn't feel like she does about it."

"It isn't her business," said Katharine firmly.

She was plumping up the cushions and doing the sort of things that women do to a room which has been empty all day. Now she came to look over William's shoulder at the sketches he was making. She put a hand on his back to steady herself and felt him wince. She said in a startled voice,

"Did I hurt you? Why?"

He put up his left hand and caught hers.

"It's nothing. I've got a bruise, and you just hit it off."

She stood beside him, looking puzzled, her hand in his.

"What an extraordinary place to get a bruise. How did you get it?"

"Someone jabbed me in the back with a stick."

"Why?"

"Well, I think he was trying to push me under a bus."

"William!"

"It didn't come off, so you needn't look like that."

She was quite white. Her hand trembled. She said,

"When was it? Why didn't you tell me?"

"Thursday, I think—yes, Thursday, because I met that Scotland Yard chap Abbott when I was going back from here and told him all about it. Darling, you're shaking." He pulled her down beside him and put his arm around her.

"What did he say?"

"Abbott? There wasn't anything he could say. I was jabbed, but I couldn't see who jabbed me."

"Tell me what happened."

He told her. When he had finished she said,

124

"How far had you gone before it happened?"

"It's about a ten minutes' walk from Selby Street to where I was getting the bus."

She said, "You could have been followed."

He nodded.

"Well, I shan't be going that way again."

She thought to herself that it might happen anywhere—anywhere at all. Then, to William,

"When you told Mr. Abbott, he must have said something—didn't he?"

She was sitting on the ground beside him now, leaning against his knee, and he was trying different shaped patches on a cow. His voice was a little absent as he said,

"Oh, he gave me the address of a Miss Silver. Governess turned detective, only he called it enquiry agent. He said she was a friend of his. He seemed to think she might be interested, but as I said, I don't see what she or anybody else can do. There isn't any motive, and I didn't see anyone either time. I just got hit over the head and jabbed in the back. There's nothing to go on."

"No, darling. Where does this woman live?"

"I've forgotten. I expect it's in one of my pockets—I had this suit on." He put down the pencil and dived. "Yes, here it is—Miss Maud Silver, 15 Montague Mansions, and a telephone number."

Katharine put out her hand for it.

"I'll put it away. We might want it—you never know."

He said, "Not likely," and began on a different arrangement of patches.

On Thursday afternoon, which was early closing at the Toy Bazaar but not in the neighbourhood of the Mews, Katharine got rid of William by sending him to buy a cake for tea, and then went off in the opposite direction, leaving a note inside the door to say she had remembered something urgent and would be back as soon as she could.

She rang Miss Silver up from the first call-box she came to, and went on her way feeling very much as if she had jumped into a deep pool without knowing how to swim. If it had been a matter of herself, she would have turned back long before she got to Montague Mansions. If it had been anyone else but William, she would never have got there at all.

She did get there, was admitted by Emma Meadows, who looked the comfortable countrywoman she was, and was ushered in upon Miss Silver and her Victorian room. Miss Silver, laying down her knitting on the arm of her chair and rising to shake hands, saw a tall, graceful girl with a heightened colour. She said, "Mrs. Smith?" and Katharine said,

"I rang up. It is very good of you to see me at such short notice."

Miss Silver coughed.

"I shall be glad if I can help you in any way. Will you not sit down?"

She picked up her knitting again and looked at her visitor in a kind and encouraging manner. The bright colour came and went. Mrs. Smith was nervous. She had breeding as well as very engaging looks. Her hair—really very pretty indeed—brown, but not at all a usual shade—so bright with those golden lights in it. Her clothes too—very becoming and well chosen, though not new—a good Scotch tweed, made by a first-class tailor—and the hat, very plain, but not the sort of hat which can be bought in a cheap shop. Miss Silver's eyes passed to the shoes, the stockings, the handbag. She knew quality when she saw it, and she saw it now. The shoes and the handbag were not new. All this was received and registered as her visitor took the chair on the other side of the hearth.

It was no more than a moment before Katharine said,

"I don't know whether anyone can—but I thought I would come and see you. Mr. Abbott—I think he is Detective Sergeant Abbott—gave my husband your address—" She paused and added, "My husband doesn't know that I have come."

Miss Silver was knitting briskly. She had finished the pair of blue leggings for little Josephine and had begun a coatee to match them. It was still in a very embryo stage, and appeared as a pale blue frill no more than a couple of inches deep. She said,

"You are Mrs. William Smith?"

Katharine looked startled. Her colour brightened, faded, brightened again.

"Yes."

"Sergeant Abbott has spoken of your husband. Perhaps that will make it easier for you to talk to me."

"What did he say?"

"He told me that he had witnessed an assault upon Mr. Smith, and that he had subsequently recognized him, but without being able to remember his name. He was a good deal interested, and so was I. Your husband will have told you of the incident."

"Yes, he told me. He—he doesn't know who he is, you see. He had a head wound, and he doesn't remember anything until he came out of a German hospital in '42. That's where his memory begins—it's all quite clear after that. He had an identity disc which described him as William Smith. That's all wrong. He kept the name because he hadn't any other, but the real William Smith was quite an uneducated man. He was a Cockney, and he worked in a tannery. William went down to the place. They all said he wasn't their William Smith." She hesitated a little, and then went on. "My hus-

127

band hasn't the kind of looks that change at all. Anyone who knew him as a boy would know him now. I expect you know the type—rather blunt features, very thick fair hair that won't lie down, very strong build, very friendly expression. It's the type that doesn't change at all—it just gets older. I'm telling you this to explain Mr. Abbott's recognizing him like that. I think anyone who had met him would remember him. Frank Abbott did, but he didn't remember his name. It's quite possible he never heard it, because everyone was just calling him Bill—it was at a party at the Luxe, you know."

Now that she had made a start, it wasn't so difficult at all. The room was exactly like rooms which she remembered when she was a little girl and went visiting with her grandmother. Gran herself had possessed photograph-frames in silver filagree on plush, and had cherished a photogravure of "The Stag at Bay." Old Miss Emsley who had been one of Gran's bridesmaids had possessed chairs of the same family as these, with curly walnut legs and spreading laps. Great-aunt Cecilia had worn beaded slippers and net fronts with little bones to keep the collar stiff. These familiar associations promoted confidence. Miss Silver diffused it to a quite extraordinary degree. By some means best known to herself she possessed the art of turning back the clock until the state of tension and fear in which so many of her visitors found themselves gave way insensibly to the atmosphere of the schoolroom. Here the problem became the teacher's affair, to propound, to explain, and to resolve. The responsibility was hers, the solution already known.

Katharine did not put any of this into words, but she felt its influence. When she had told Miss Silver about Tattlecombe's Toy Bazaar, the Wurzel toys, Mr. Tattlecombe's accident, and what William had told her about being hit over the head, Miss Silver gave her gentle cough.

"I think that is not all."

Katharine said, "No."

She locked her hands tightly together in her lap and told Miss Silver about the jab in the back. Then she told her about Emily Salt.

"She is really a very queer sort of person. I don't think she's right in her head. William says she has dreadfully creepy ways, and Mr. Tattlecombe says she ought to be in a home. He says she listens at doors too. I believe she is very angry because Mr. Tattlecombe has made a will leaving the business to William. I—I wondered—"

"Yes, Mrs. Smith?"

"She really isn't right in her head—I'm sure about that. Mr. Tattlecombe had been telling William about his will that first time he was attacked. I did just wonder if she had been listening at the door and—and—oh, it does seem dreadful, but I can't help thinking of it!"

Miss Silver knitted thoughtfully.

"And the second attack—that also occurred after he had been visiting Mr. Tattlecombe?"

"Yes. She could have followed him."

"Would she be physically capable of such an assault?"

"She is a tall, bony woman."

After a moment Miss Silver said, "Sergeant Abbott, who witnessed the attack, appeared to have no doubt that the person he saw was a man."

The quick colour came to Katharine's cheeks.

"It was dark and wet. Mr. Tattlecombe's waterproof was hanging in the hall—I saw it myself when we went there to tea."

Miss Silver knitted in silence for a little while. Then she said,

"When did Mr. Tattlecombe sign the will benefitting your husband?"

"The day before he told William about it."

"In fact the day before the first attack."

"Yes."

"It *was* the first attack, Mrs. Smith? There had been no previous indications of enmity or ill will from any quarter?"

Katharine was taken by surprise. When she looked startled, as she did now, her eyebrows took an upward tilt, her eyes widened and brightened. William called it her fly-away look. It really did give her the air of a creature poised for flight. It was not lost on Miss Silver. She said with some firmness,

"Was the blow on the head the first attempt?"

The colour drained out of Katharine's face. She said in a distressed voice,

"I don't know."

"I think it might clarify your ideas if you put them into words. You have some incident in mind—it would be better if you would tell me what it was."

Katharine felt as she had often felt when bathing. You walked into shallow water which was deceptively warm and tranquil, then, as it rose about your body, it became colder and the cold rose too. If you went too far, any step might take you out of your depth. She thought this step was safe. But was it? She didn't. She looked at Miss Silver in some distress of mind, and then without any premeditation found herself saying,

"I was thinking about Mr. Tattlecombe's accident."

"Yes?"

"It happened just outside the shop. He lives over it, and he always goes out for a breath of air the last thing at night. It was about half past ten, and it was a very dark, damp night. He came out by the private door with the light on in the passage behind him, and he went to the edge of the kerb and fell under a car. He says he was 'struck down.' He had concussion, and he was badly bruised, and there was an injury to his leg. He might easily have been killed. Of course he may have slipped—"

"You connect this incident with the other one?"

Katharine looked away from her into the fire.

"He is the same height and build as William is, and he has the same kind of hair, only it's grey—but with the light shining on it from behind—"

Miss Silver inclined her head.

"Quite so. The face would be in shadow, and fair hair would be indistinguishable from grey."

"Yes."

A little shiver ran over Katharine. She put out her hands as if to warm them. The logs in the grate sent out a comfortable glow. But the cold was inside her. She was afraid—afraid of what she was thinking, afraid of what she was saying, afraid of where it might be taking her. It mustn't take her too far—it mustn't, it mustn't. And then she knew that it had already done so. Miss Silver was saying,

"You mean that someone who had planned the attack mistook Mr. Tattlecombe for Mr. Smith. That would mean that the person who attacked him was not at all familiar either with Mr. Tattlecombe or his habits. He or she must have been expecting to see Mr. Smith. But Emily Salt would know Mr. Tattlecombe, since she had lived for so many years with his sister. Did she at that time know Mr. Smith?"

Katharine had that distressed look again.

"I don't know—I don't think so. William said he hadn't ever seen her until Mr. Tattlecombe went to his sister's house after he left the hospital."

"But Mr. Tattlecombe visited at his sister's house? Emily Salt would have known him?"

"Yes."

"Someone who knew Mr. Tattlecombe and did not know Mr. Smith might, in the circumstances, have taken Mr. Smith for Mr. Tattlecombe, but I fail to see how he could have taken Mr. Tattlecombe for Mr. Smith."

Katharine's hands were clasped again in her lap. Her words came in a soft hurry.

"Then—then it couldn't have been anything, could it? It was stupid of me to think that it could. That's the worst of this sort of thing—it sets one's imagination to work." She caught at the word and clung to it. "I've been imagining things—it was just my imagination. I quite see what you mean—it couldn't have been anything else."

She put a hand on the arm of her chair as if she was going to rise. A hortatory cough arrested the moment. She felt called to order. Her hand stayed where it was. She had that startled look. Yet there was nothing alarming about the question which followed the cough.

"At the time of Mr. Tattlecombe's accident were you already working at the Toy Bazaar?"

"Oh, no."

"How long have you been there?"

"About six weeks. I came just afterwards. They were short-handed."

"You answered an advertisement?"

The waters were getting deep again. Katharine said,

"No."

"You were recommended—perhaps by Mr. William Smith?"

Her colour came too quickly. So did her words.

132

"Oh, no—he didn't know I existed. I just asked—if they wanted anybody."

"Had you any previous experience?" said Miss Silver.

"No, I hadn't. I—I needed a job."

Miss Silver smiled.

"Pray do not think me very intrusive. I am wondering what took you to Tattlecombe's Toy Bazaar."

Katharine felt as if a wave had broken right over her head. It was a moment before she could get enough breath to say,

"I—I needed a job. I—I just went in and asked."

Miss Silver said, "I see."

For a moment Katharine felt that the small nondescript-coloured eyes really did see right through her. She felt the kind of panic which comes in dreams when you find yourself naked amongst the clothed. Her hand clenched on the arm of the chair. She got up.

"Miss Silver, I mustn't stop. My husband doesn't know I've come to see you. If—if you think there is anything you can do, will you do it?"

Miss Silver got up too. She said in a very quiet and composed manner,

"What do you think I can do?"

Katharine looked at her.

"I don't know. I thought if you could find out—about Emily Salt—"

Miss Silver met the look.

"You would like me to find out that it is Miss Salt who has been attempting your husband's life. She is an unhinged person who ought to be placed under restraint. It would be a simple and satisfactory solution, would it not? But I cannot undertake to provide this solution. I can only promise that I will do my best to arrive at the truth. And I cannot undertake any case where I am deliberately kept in the dark."

133

"Miss Silver—"

Her rather stern look softened.

"You are thinking that you have no reason to trust me. You must decide whether you will or not. Let me quote the late Lord Tennyson—'Trust me not at all, or all in all.'"

"Miss Silver—"

She was met with a sudden disarming smile.

"There is no reason for you to trust me. Pray do not think that I would urge your confidence, but you must not think that I can accept the half confidence which aims at concealment. You have kept a good deal from me, have you not? I think you know much more about your husband than you have told me. He has lost his memory, but you have not lost yours. You say that he has not changed—that it would be easy for anyone who knew him before he disappeared to recognize him now. What gives you this assurance? You feel no need to press Frank Abbott for the name he has forgotten—to insist that he should go through every friend and acquaintance he has in order to find the evidence which would restore the lost identity of William Smith. Why? Because, I think, you do not need this evidence. I think you know very well who your husband is. If you want my help, come to me again. I shall be glad to do what I can. Go home and think about what I have said."

CHAPTER 21

Katharine went home feeling rather dazed. She walked all the way because she wanted to think, but the turmoil in her mind was too great. Her thoughts were dashed this way and that by tides of feeling over which she had no control. In the end it all came out to the same thing, she didn't know what to do.

She went on walking. The air was soft and damp—one of those mild January days which easily turn to fog. She would have been glad of the sharp feel of frost on her face, or a keen wind to buffet her. There was only that mild, gentle air. If she went back to Miss Silver she did not know what might come of it. At the worst there might be publicity, disgrace, things that William would find it hard to forgive. If she held back she might be taking risks with his life.

She came to the flat to find him gone—a note where hers had been.

"I thought I'd just go over the car. Mr. Tattlecombe said something about giving us Saturday afternoon."

He came in late for tea, kissed her cheerfully, and went to wash. It wasn't until he was helping himself to jam that he asked her where she had been. She had wondered whether he would ask, and what she was going to say. But when it happened she knew. She couldn't lie to William and she couldn't shuffle. The answer was as simple as the question. She said,

"I went to see Miss Silver."

"Miss Silver?"

"Mr. Abbott's friend—the one whose address he gave you."

William put jam on his bread—a good deal of jam. Then he said,

"Oh, her—why did you do that?"

"Because of what you told me."

"Do you mean about my being pushed?"

"Yes."

"It was rum, wasn't it? This is good jam. Where did you get it?"

"It's some I made last summer when I was down in the country."

"I thought it didn't taste like grocer's jam. Talking about things being rum, that is."

"What is?" Her laugh shook a little. "You're being incoherent—we were talking about jam."

"That's what I meant—your making it last summer, and I didn't even know that there was any you to make jam, and if I had known I wouldn't have known you were making it for me, and you wouldn't either. What were you doing in the country?"

"I was staying with an aunt."

"Where?"

"At Ledstow."

He crinkled up his eyes.

"Ought I to know where Ledstow is?"

"It's about seven miles from Ledlington."

He nodded.

"I've been down to Ledlington on business, just for the day. Rather a nice old market square, but a frightful statue in the middle of it—Sir Albert Something-or-other in marble trousers. What's this Miss Silver person like?"

136

She changed colour.

"Like an elderly governess."

William passed up his cup.

"That's what she used to be. It doesn't sound as if she'd be much good."

She ought to have let that go. If she had, perhaps he wouldn't have thought about any of it again. Something in her wouldn't let it go. She said,

"She's—impressive."

"How?"

"Well, she is. She knows things. She knows what you're telling her, and what you're keeping back. I didn't tell her everything, and she knew what I was keeping back."

William helped himself to more jam.

"Perhaps that chap Abbott told her. Darling, you're not eating anything."

"I'm not hungry. No, he couldn't—he didn't know."

"Why aren't you hungry?"

She smiled at him.

"Just not."

"If he didn't tell her, how did she know?"

"She puts things together—things you don't notice when you're saying them—you don't think they're going to mean anything to anyone else. She puts them together, and she's got something you didn't mean to tell her."

William cut himself another slice of bread.

"What did you tell her, and what did she get out of it? Darling, you're pale. What is it?"

"Nothing. She knew about your being hit over the head. Frank Abbott had told her."

William looked interested.

"Is that his name? Does she call him Frank?"

"I don't—know."

137

"Must have, or you wouldn't have known it was his name. I wonder why he told her about me."

"He thought she would be interested."

"Did you tell her about my being jabbed in the back?"

"Yes. William, I told her about Emily Salt—about her being queer in the head. I thought perhaps she could find out whether she was more than just queer, and—well, where she was when you were pushed."

He shook his head.

"It wouldn't be any good. Suppose she was out posting a letter—it wouldn't prove anything. What did Miss Silver say?"

Katharine coloured. The things Miss Silver had said came back vividly—"*I think you know much more than you have told me*"—"*Your husband has lost his memory, but you have not lost yours*"—"*Go home and think about what I have said*" . . . Go home and think—she couldn't stop thinking. Her colour faded. She was pale again as she answered William's question.

"She said I hadn't told her everything. She said she couldn't take the case unless I did. She told me to go home and think whether I wanted her to take it or not."

He looked at her and said,

"What didn't you tell her?"

She met his look with distress.

"It isn't easy. I thought it was fair to tell her about Emily Salt. I don't know about other people—"

"What do you mean by other people?"

Her colour came again.

"There might be somebody else—I don't know—I want to be fair—"

"Someone who wanted me out of the way?"

"There might be. I don't even like to think about it."

"Why? I mean, why would anyone want to get rid of me?

138

Unless it was a chap who was fond of you and thought it would be a bright idea to bump me off." There was half a laugh in his voice, but it went before the end. His fair brows came together in a frown. "Darling, that's barmy."

She said, "Someone pushed you."

They sat looking at each other. Then he said slowly,

"Something else happened this afternoon—at least I found it out this afternoon. I didn't mean to tell you, but I think I'd better. You know I was going to go over the car. Well, I did, and the near front wheel was loose."

She echoed the last word, "Loose—"

"Someone had loosened the studs. They were all right last time I had her out. Someone must have done it."

"William!"

He nodded.

"It's all right—you needn't look like that. They all chaff me about the way I go over the car. All the parts being old, you've got to be careful. It's as well I am, because that wheel would just about have got us out into the traffic before it went to glory. It didn't, so it's all right. But someone must have been at those studs—" He was frowning and intent. "Of course it would be easy enough. The place is open most of the time because of Harman keeping his ladders there. Anyone could have slipped in and done the trick."

Thoughts came and went in Katharine's mind. They turned into words. "Would Emily Salt know how to loosen a wheel?"

"I shouldn't think so—she doesn't look as if she would."

"She might."

William burst out laughing.

"I should think she would be afraid the car would bite her!" Then all at once he was serious. "I don't see how it could be Emily. She's been in bed with a cold ever since Mr. Tattlecombe came home, and the car was all right then. Don't you remember, Mrs. Salt rang up Tuesday and said she couldn't come and see Mr. Tattlecombe because poor Emily was in bed with a temperature, and what a good thing he came home when he did—in case of his getting whatever it was."

Katharine remembered. She took William's cup and filled it mechanically.

"So it couldn't have been Emily Salt," he said.

CHAPTER 22

Katharine knocked on the door of Mr. Tattlecombe's sitting-room. When he had said "Come in!" she found him in his favourite chair with his leg up and a rug over it. He looked up from a large ledger and a litter of papers.

"Good-morning, Mrs. Smith. What is it?"

She said, "I wondered if I could talk to you about something." She thought he looked surprised, and made haste to say, "About William."

Right on that she was reminded in the most ridiculous way of Red Riding Hood in the nursery tale:

> "What big eyes you've got, Grandmamma."
> "The better to see you with, my dear."

Mr. Tattlecombe's eyes were like bright blue saucers. He asked her to sit down, and he asked her if anything was wrong. And out it came.

"I think someone is trying to kill him."

140

Mr. Tattlecombe looked dreadfully shocked.

"My dear Mrs. Smith!"

But he listened whilst she told him about William being hit over the head, about William being jabbed in the back, about the wheel being loosened on his car. When she had finished, he had stopped looking shocked. He said quite deliberately,

"You're thinking about Emily Salt, and so am I. But I never heard of her doing anything like that. And she couldn't have had anything to do with the car—she's been ill. To say nothing of not knowing the front end from the back."

"She really *is* ill?" Katharine's tone was tentative.

Abel nodded.

"Abby says so. She'd know too—there isn't much she doesn't know about sickness. And I should say there's nothing she don't know about Emily. She's lived with her for thirty years. How she's done it, I don't know, but there it is, she has. And I don't think Emily could take her in—not after thirty years. But she's coming to tea this afternoon—I'll put it to her. Was that what you wanted?"

"I'd be very glad if you would. It's—it's serious, Mr. Tattlecombe. What I really came to ask you was whether I might have part of the afternoon off. We've got to get to the bottom of this, and I've got an introduction to someone who I think might be able to help us."

"In what way, Mrs. Smith?"

Katharine did her best to explain Miss Silver. The extraordinary thing was that as she did so her own expectation of being helped was strongly increased. She didn't know whether she was convincing Mr. Tattlecombe, but she was aware that she was convincing herself.

Abel was looking very doubtful.

"Abby wouldn't like the police brought into it," he said.

Katharine's colour rose brightly.

141

"Miss Silver isn't connected with the police. She is a private enquiry agent. But if anyone is trying to do murder, the police are much more likely to come into it if the murderer isn't stopped—in time."

Abel Tattlecombe nodded solemnly. If Emily had been up to tricks they would have to be put a stop to, and he had always said that she ought to be in a home. He frowned.

"There's a thing you haven't mentioned, but I won't say I haven't thought about it since William was struck down after coming to see me. It seems to me it's a bit too much of a coincidence, me being struck down and William being struck down, and no connection between the two. It's too similar for me—I don't seem able to take it in. Seems to me it was one of us was aimed at both times. Seems to me now that it was William. We'd look pretty much about the same coming out into the street at night with the light behind us. But if it was William that was aimed at when I was struck down, then it couldn't have been Emily Salt that did it."

"Why couldn't it?"

Abel brought his hand down on his knee—the sound one.

"Because it was the night of the chapel social and Emily was there. Behaved very odd too by all accounts. Regularly put out about it, Abby was—said if Emily came, the least she could do was to behave herself and not sit there staring as if she didn't know what was going on round her, and then come to and say something rude. I've never known Abby go so far about Emily before—she was down right provoked. And there's no doubt about it, Emily Salt was at the social. I don't say that Emily has got any love for me, nor any reason for it, but I wouldn't think she'd go so far as to come along here at half past ten of a wet night to strike me down. And if it was William that was aimed at, what cause would she have to aim at him then? I didn't alter my will or so much

142

as mention the matter to Abby till I came out of the hospital. So, let alone the chapel social, there wasn't any reason for her to do it. And what with her being sick in bed, and not knowing one end of a car from the other, I don't see her meddling with William's wheel. Why, she won't so much as touch Abby's sewing-machine. So I don't see it could be Emily Salt." He nodded several times and looked at Katharine out of those very blue eyes.

After a moment she said,

"May I have the afternoon off?"

He nodded again.

"Yes, yes—to be sure. But I don't see how it's going to help. I don't see how it could be Emily."

Her voice was very low as she said, "It might be somebody else—"

Mr. Tattlecombe gave her a sharp glance. He thought, "She's got someone else in her mind." Aloud he said,

"Someone wanting William out of the way? Jealous perhaps." His tone sharpened too. "Jealousy's a bad thing—works on them till they don't rightly know what they're doing. Cruel as the grave, like it says in the Bible. The heart is deceitful above all things, and desperately wicked." He became colloquial again. "You'd be surprised the things I've known jealous people do. You go and see this detective lady—seems a queer job for a woman, but there's nothing they don't do nowadays. But don't get mixed up with the police if you can help it. And don't let them go worrying Abby for she won't like it, and I don't see how it could have been Emily Salt."

CHAPTER 23

Katharine sat in one of Miss Silver's curly walnut chairs and told her about the loosened wheel, and about Emily Salt being ill in bed and not knowing anything about cars. After which she repeated Mr. Tattlecombe's observations about his own accident and the chapel social.

When she had finished she sat looking at Miss Silver, who was wearing the same dark green dress and tucked net front but a different brooch. This one had a heavy gold border with a centre of smoothly plaited hair under glass. Some of the hair was fair, and some was dark, the two shades belonging in fact to Miss Silver's grandparents, and by them bequeathed in this portable and enduring form. There was a good deal more of the blue knitting—little Josephine's coatee had made good progress. The busy needles clicked. Miss Silver looked across them and said,

"You are very much troubled, are you not?"

"Yes. If he had gone out into the traffic in that car there would have been an accident. He might very easily have been killed."

Miss Silver let that stand without comment. She continued to knit. She did not fail to observe that Mrs. Smith remained consistently pale, and that she was undoubtedly suffering from strain. She allowed the silence to do its work. Katharine broke it.

"You said not to come back unless I made up my mind to trust you. But you see, it isn't as simple as that. I think someone is trying to kill William. I thought it would be fair to ask you to find out whether it could be Emily Salt. She is—peculiar. She is angry about Mr. Tattlecombe's will and the two attacks on William took place when he was coming away from Selby Street. But the attack on Mr. Tattlecombe and this wheel business—well, it doesn't seem as if she could have had anything to do with them. If I bring in other people, you may come across things which you wouldn't feel justified in keeping to yourself. That's my position now—I don't know if I'm justified in speaking. If I tell you things—I can't take them back again. You may think they're all nonsense, or you may think they're so serious that you can't keep them to yourself. I've thought about it all until I can't be sure I'm thinking straight. And I'm frightened about William. You were quite right when you said I wanted to think it was Emily Salt. I did—I do. She's a stranger, and she isn't right in her head. But now it doesn't seem as if it could be Emily."

Miss Silver inclined her head.

"You have put it very clearly."

Katharine took a quick breath.

"I don't feel clear. I've come back because I'm so frightened about William. When you're frightened you can't think straight."

Miss Silver coughed.

"You said just now that if you told me certain things, I might feel it my duty to go to the police. If that would be my duty, would it not be your duty also?"

A long sighing breath was released. Katharine said, "Yes—"

"Your telling me would not add to your obligation. It would merely serve to clarify it."

"Yes—"

"And you believe your husband's life to be in danger."

A shudder went over Katharine. She said, "Yes—" again. And then, "I don't know where to begin."

Miss Silver's needles clicked, the blue coatee revolved. She said in an encouraging voice,

"If you will make a start, I think you will find it is easier to go on. It is the first step which seems so difficult."

Katharine said, "Yes—" again. She was sitting up very straight with her hands clasped in her lap. "I think I had better begin on the sixth of December, the day before Mr. Tattlecombe had his accident. I think I've told you William designs toys. They are very good indeed. Up to now they've been making them in a place behind the shop—William, and an old man, and a boy, and, after I went there, me. Well, of course, they ought to be much more widely known. I don't suppose you've ever heard of a firm called Eversleys'. They are manufacturers on a big scale. One of the things they do is toys. William persuaded Mr. Tattlecombe to agree to his approaching them with a view to getting them to make his Wurzel toys under licence, and on the sixth of December he had an appointment to go and see them. It was rather a late appointment—six o'clock. He went there, and he saw the senior partner's secretary—her name is Miss Jones. She has been there for fifteen years, and she is highly competent. The partners are Cyril and Brett Eversley. They are first cousins. Miss Jones is Cyril's secretary. I should say she knew a good deal more about the business than he does. She saw William, and she told him that she didn't think they would be interested in the Wurzel toys. A few days later she wrote and confirmed this."

Katharine came to the end of what she had started out to say. She came to an end, and stopped.

Miss Silver said, "Yes?" on an enquiring note.

Katharine drew in her breath again.

"It doesn't get easier—it gets more difficult."

"Nevertheless I beg that you will continue."

Katharine bent her head. However difficult it was, she must go on—she knew that. She went on.

"When William came out into the street he almost ran into someone who was coming in. He didn't know who it was, but I do. It was Mr. Davies, the Eversleys' head clerk. He has been with them for about thirty years. When he saw William he nearly dropped down in a faint. He caught at William's arm to steady himself. I don't know what he said—William couldn't make anything of it. He held him up till the giddiness went off. The first thing he really said was, 'Who are you?' William said, 'I'm William Smith—Tattlecombe's Toy Bazaar, Ellery Street.' Mr. Davies said 'What?' and William repeated it. He wanted Mr. Davies to go in and sit down, but he wouldn't. He didn't want to see anyone, he wanted to get away. He went to a call-box and rang me up."

Miss Silver coughed.

"Mr. Davies rang you up?"

"Yes. I wasn't in the flat I'm in now—I was in my own flat." Her voice went down low. "The telephone bell rang—just like any telephone bell ringing. I lifted the receiver, and there was Mr. Davies telling me he had just seen William—"

Miss Silver said, "Yes?"

Katharine looked at her, but she didn't really see her. She saw a room with a shaded lamp, and her own hand lifting the receiver. She heard Mr. Davies' shaken voice. Her own voice shook as his had done.

"He said, 'I've just seen Mr. William.' I said, 'What do you mean?' He said, 'I took hold of his arm, and it was real. It was in the street outside the office. I nearly dropped. I took hold of his arm to save myself, and it felt real. But he didn't

147

know me—he didn't know me at all—not at all.' He kept on repeating that. I said, 'You're not well,' and he said, 'No—it's been a shock—it's been a great shock. He didn't know me at all—we were there, right under the light, and he didn't know me. I don't know what I felt like—I don't know what I said. I'd some kind of idea I was seeing a spirit—but his arm felt real. I said, "Who are you?" and he said, "William Smith—Tattlecombe's Toy Bazaar, Ellery Street." That's what he said. I couldn't have thought of that if he hadn't said it, could I? He said he was William Smith, Tattlecombe's Toy Bazaar, Ellery Street. And he didn't know me at all. He wanted to take me into the office, but I wouldn't go. I didn't want to see anyone—I wanted to get away. When I'd walked a little, I thought about you.'" She took a long breath. "I told him to go home and rest." She stopped again.

Miss Silver did not speak. Her needles clicked above the pale blue wool.

Katharine said, "I don't know how I lived until the morning. I knew I couldn't do anything till then—the shops would all be shut—I knew I must wait. I went down to Ellery Street at half past nine. The Toy Bazaar had a window full of William's toys. As soon as I saw them I knew that Mr. Davies hadn't made any mistake. William always liked drawing queer animals. There was a draper's shop on one side and a cleaner's on the other. The girl in the cleaner's was quite pleased to talk—it's a boring job waiting for people to come in. I asked about having something dyed and looked at patterns. And then I asked about the toys in the window next door, and she told me all about William, and how he'd worked the business up. She said he'd been in a Prisoners of War camp with Mr. Tattlecombe's grandson who died there, and she said he'd lost his memory, and Mr. Tattlecombe thought the world of him. I asked her whether there would be any chance of getting a job there, and she said there might be. She thought they were short-handed. So I went home and made my plans."

Miss Silver coughed.

"What plans did you make?"

Katharine smiled—a brief, rather tremulous smile.

"I rang up a friend who was looking for a flat and told her she could have mine. I rang up another friend who was just going abroad and asked if I could have hers. I told her I didn't want anyone to know where I was, and she said, 'All right.' I told my relations I had let my flat and was taking a job, and I didn't say where. And I wrote to Mr. Davies at his private address and told him not to say anything to anybody, because it was my affair and I wanted to manage it my own way. In the afternoon I drove to Victoria Station with my luggage, and when the taxi had gone I took another to Carol's flat in Rasselas Mews. And then I went to Ellery Street to ask if they wanted an assistant at Tattlecombe's Toy Bazaar. And it was Thursday—I'd forgotten all about Thursday being early closing in those outlying places. All the shops were shut. I didn't feel as if I could bear it, but there just wasn't anything to be done. I had to go back and get through another perfectly interminable night. That was the night Mr. Tattlecombe had his accident—but of course I didn't know about it until afterwards. That left them very shorthanded indeed. In the morning I went to Ellery Street and went into the shop to ask if they wanted an assistant. There was a Miss Cole there." Katharine gave a little laugh. "She didn't like me a bit—it stuck out all over her. And then"—her voice checked, steadied, and went on again—"William came in."

CHAPTER 24

There was a rather long silence. Then Katharine leaned forward and said,

"He didn't know me, but—he fell in love with me. He didn't remember me, but he remembered loving me."

Miss Silver looked across her knitting and smiled the smile which had won her many confidences, many friends. The dowdy little governess wasn't there any more. Intelligence, understanding, a sustaining and comprehensive sympathy, just blotted her out. It was rather like seeing the light come through a stained glass window.

Katharine experienced a sense of release. It wasn't going to be difficult any more. She could say anything, and what she said would be understood—she could let go and say just what came into her mind. Everything in her was quieted. She said,

"Miss Cole was horrified because William engaged me on the spot. She couldn't help seeing that he had fallen for me, and she thought I was a vamp. I went to work—William and I painted toys together. We were frightfully happy."

"Yes?"

"I gave my real name, Katharine Eversley. Cyril and Brett are—distant cousins. Even the name didn't mean anything to William—things that happened before '42 just don't exist. But he fell in love with me all over again."

Miss Silver looked at her.

"Why did you not tell him?"

150

The bright colour came up.

"How could I? He'd forgotten me. I couldn't say, 'You loved me—you've forgotten.' That was at first. Then when I knew that he was loving me again, I thought if he remembered that, he would remember me. Every time he kissed me I thought he would remember. And then I didn't care. I only wanted us to have this time together. You see, when he knows who he is there will be a lot of business, a lot of worry. It's going to be a shock to the people who thought he was dead, and who won't be particularly glad to find that he is alive—" She broke off with that startled glance. "I oughtn't to have said that—I don't know that it would be like that. Things come into your mind—you can't help it. If you put them into words it makes too much of them. You see, I haven't anything to go on. I don't know that they wouldn't be glad, so I oughtn't to say so."

Miss Silver gave her slight cough.

"You are speaking of Mr. Cyril and Mr. Brett Eversley?"

"Yes."

"Mrs. Smith—who is your husband?"

The startled look was intensified. Katharine coloured vividly, but she answered at once and with complete simplicity.

"He is William Eversley. He is their first cousin."

Miss Silver smiled.

"I thought so. Pray continue."

"His father was the eldest of the three brothers who built up the firm. He was the senior partner and the driving force, and he owned sixty per cent of the shares. He didn't marry till he was fifty, which is why William is so much younger than Cyril and Brett. He died in '38, when William was twenty-three and had been a partner for a couple of years. William joined up in '39, and was missing in '42. The firm turned over to government work during the war, and I don't

151

think they've been very successful in getting back to ordinary conditions. Cyril isn't a business man. He likes a quiet, pleasant life without too much to do. He paints in water-colour rather well, he collects eighteenth-century miniatures and snuff-boxes, he fancies himself at interior decoration. His house at Evendon is really very charming. He has always given me the impression that business bores him to tears." She paused, frowned, and went on again. "Brett's different— younger—plenty of vitality, but—" she laughed a little—"I should say he thought the business was there to provide him with an income. He enjoys himself a lot—has a great many friends, gets asked everywhere. He is very goodlooking, very charming, very good company."

Miss Silver coughed,

"You have quite a gift for description."

Katharine took a quick breath.

"Have I? I've known them all my life. My father was an Eversley too, quite a distant cousin. But he and my mother were killed in a train smash when I was a baby, and William's father and mother brought me up. I'm two years younger."

Miss Silver got up and went over to the writing-table, a massive block with pedestal drawers and leather top. From a drawer on the left she extracted an exercise-book with a bright blue cover, spread it out flat upon the blotting-pad, and wrote. Presently she looked up.

"It is as well to fix facts firmly whilst they are fresh in the mind. Perhaps you will give me some particulars about Miss Jones."

She turned back to the exercise-book to write the name, adding the words: "Secretary—15 years' service—efficient. Interviewed William Smith December 6th."

When she had finished she read them aloud.

"Is there anything you would care to add?"

Katharine had come over to the table. She leaned upon it lightly with one hand and said in a troubled voice,

"Care? Oh, yes. I don't like her—I never have. It's always easy to say things about people you don't like."

Miss Silver sat with the pencil in her hand.

"Pray sit down, Mrs. Eversley." Then, as Katharine took the chair which so many clients had occupied, "Why do you not like Miss Jones?"

She got a sudden flash of humour.

"She doesn't like me—she never has, and nor have I. I'll tell you about her as fairly as I can. I don't know how old she is, but she doesn't look it. She's very—handsome. She's Cyril's secretary and she runs him. I shouldn't think there's anything about the business she doesn't know, and of course that gives her a pull. She's efficient. Cyril never could be, and Brett doesn't bother. The result is you are apt to get the impression that she runs the firm. In a secretary it's irritating. You must allow for that, because if someone irritates you, it just isn't possible to be quite fair."

"Miss Jones irritates you?"

Katharine nodded.

"Intensely. She has always treated me as if I was an illiterate black beetle, if you know what I mean. It doesn't encourage a friendly feeling."

Miss Silver coughed.

"What are her relations with Mr. Cyril and Mr. Brett?"

Katharine lifted her hand from the table and let it fall again.

"I don't know. There was some talk about her and Brett a year or two ago. He took her about a bit. I ran into them at a road-house once. Stupid, because that sort of thing always gets out. I don't suppose there was anything in it. And he's a bachelor—it would be nobody's business. Cyril's wife died five years ago. His daughter married last year. He isn't the flirtatious kind, but he depends on Miss Jones a good deal."

"Will you give me her Christian name?"

"Mavis."

Miss Silver wrote it down.

"And now, Mrs. Eversley, will you continue? What makes you think that Mr. William Eversley's return would inconvenience the firm?"

"He inherited the controlling interest—sixty per cent of the shares."

"Yes. What happened to them when his death was presumed?"

"Half of them were divided between Cyril and Brett—half of them came to me in trust. There was also government stock."

"Who were the trustees?"

"Cyril, Brett, and Admiral Holden, who is a very old friend of the family."

"And have you been getting your dividends?"

"There was a hold-up in the autumn. It left me rather short of money. Admiral Holden had been ill for nearly two years—nobody thought he was going to live. Then he made a marvellous recovery. When I heard I wrote to him about my affairs, and he came bumbling up to town to see the Eversleys. That was about ten days ago. The first thing that happened was that my dividends were paid in—the whole lot of them. Cyril asked me to lunch with Brett and Bunny Holden at his club. Everyone was charming. Afterwards Bunny and I went off in a taxi together, and he told me he thought there had been a bit of mixup, but it would be all right now. He told me he gathered that Mr. Davies had muddled the accounts—that he'd been getting past his work for some time, and that his death had left things in a state of confusion."

Miss Silver coughed.

"That was the elderly clerk who encountered Mr. William Eversley after his visit to the firm on the sixth of December?"

"Yes. I was very much upset. I didn't know that he was dead. After I wrote and told him not to say anything about seeing William I had no communication with him. I didn't want anyone to know where I was or what I was doing. But he never got my letter."

Miss Silver looked at her searchingly.

"How do you know that, Mrs. Eversley?"

"It wouldn't be delivered until the evening of the seventh. He never got it. I ought to have told him when he rang me up not to tell anyone, but I didn't think about it. I didn't think about anything except William."

"When did Mr. Davies die?"

"On the seventh of December. Bunny didn't know, but as soon as I got in I rang up Eversleys'. I got Miss Jones. She said oh, yes, Mr. Davies was dead. She wasn't very forthcoming, but I pressed her. I wanted to know what had happened, and when he died. When she saw I was going on until I got what I wanted she went away, and came back and said that the last day Mr. Davies was at the office would be the seventh of December. He was knocked down in the street on the way home and died without recovering consciousness."

Miss Silver coughed.

"How extremely shocking!"

Katharine made an impulsive movement.

"Miss Silver—all these accidents—I can't believe in them! Can you? On the sixth of December William goes to Eversleys' and Mr. Davies recognizes him. On the seventh Mr. Davies goes to the office as usual. We don't know what he said or whom he said it to—Cyril—Brett—Miss Jones. On his way home he is knocked down and killed. At half past ten that

155

night Mr. Tattlecombe is 'struck down' outside the Toy Bazaar. With the light the way it was, it would be easy to mistake him for William. Then William is attacked twice. And now there's this business of the wheel on his car. I just can't believe in a run of accidents like that."

Miss Silver coughed.

"Very succinct—very clearly put. But the last three can hardly be described as accidents. Do you want my advice?"

"That is why I'm here."

The small nondescript-coloured eyes contemplated her gravely.

"Tell your husband what you have just been telling me."

Katharine caught her breath.

"I know—I must. I wanted just a little longer. I thought— I hoped—he would remember."

Miss Silver said, "How long have you been married?"

Katharine's colour rose, pure and bright.

"Last Saturday—"

Miss Silver stopped her.

"I do not allude to any ceremony you may have gone through then. I think you married Mr. William Eversley in '39, did you not?"

Katharine said, "July. We had a month, and then one or two short leaves. He was missing in '42. How did you know?"

Miss Silver smiled.

"There were a number of indications. That party at the Luxe at which Frank Abbott remembers seeing your husband—he spoke of a girl in a gold dress. That was you, was it not?"

"Yes. We got engaged that evening."

"A cousin of Frank Abbott's was there—a Miss Mildred Abbott and her fiancé. She is now Mrs. Darcy. She has just come home from the East. She remembers the party, and Bill

156

as they all seemed to call him, and you in your gold dress. She couldn't remember his surname or your names, but she said an aunt of hers wrote afterwards and told her she had been at your wedding. She said she had given you a tea-set."

Katharine nodded.

"Old Mrs. Willoughby Abbott. It was a very lovely set. And all that crowd called him Bill. I never did."

"When you spoke of *Frank* Abbott I knew that you must at least have been in contact with friends of his."

"Yes—it was a slip. I never really met him, but I knew a good many of his friends and relations. There was a lot of chaff and talk about his being a policeman. His grandmother, Lady Evelyn Abbott, was supposed to have cut him out of her will, but the young ones all thought it was a joke. Miss Silver, you say I ought to tell William, but don't you see how difficult it's going to be if the Eversleys just dig their toes in and say they don't recognize him? They might, you know."

Miss Silver coughed.

"From that point of view the second marriage ceremony was unwise."

Katharine gave a shaky little laugh.

"William wouldn't have felt married without it. And think how shocked Mr. Tattlecombe would have been."

Miss Silver looked grave.

"I quite see your point of view. But you have taken a good deal of responsibility, Mrs. Eversley. It was, in fact, this readiness to take responsibility on his behalf which convinced me that your marriage was no new thing."

Katharine said slowly, "I thought when we were married he would remember that we had been married before. If he got his memory back it would be all quite easy. There's just one more thing I can do. He has a recurrent dream—he's had it all these years. It's about a house in a village street—

157

three steps up and into a panelled hall, and a staircase going up on the right, with the newel-posts carved with the four Evangelists—a lion and an ox at the bottom, and an eagle and a man at the top. I thought if I could take him down there and take him into the house, he might remember."

"It is a real house, with associations for him?"

"Yes. It belonged to his grandmother. We used to go there a lot when we were children. She left it to William, and he left it to me. It's at Ledstow. It's called the Cedar House. We spent our honeymoon there. Mr. Tattlecombe has given us Saturday afternoon off. I want to take William down there this week-end and see if he remembers." She stopped, her eyes shinning, her look intent. "I think it's a real chance. He wouldn't have that dream about it if it didn't mean something to him—something special. It's as if it was the one sensitive spot. I've got a sort of feeling that his memory might come back to him there."

Miss Silver said, "Yes. These cases of loss of memory are strange. Sometimes a mental or a physical shock will bring the lost faculty back. Your plan is, I think, worth trying. But pray do not be too disappointed if it does not succeed. In that case I must urge you most strongly to lose no more time. Your husband has a right to decide for himself what is best for him to do. His own family and his own firm are involved. You cannot continue to take the sole responsibility."

Katharine said "No—" on a long sigh. It turned into a laugh. "I shan't have much choice about telling him. Everybody in Ledstow will know him at sight. William Smith will be an exploded myth from the moment my Mrs. Perkins sets eyes on him. She lives next door and comes in and does for me when I'm there, and she has known William since he was five years old. But you're quite right—he's got to know. Only it would be so much better if he hadn't got to be told."

Miss Silver gave a short, brisk cough.

"Very true. Meanwhile there is something he should do without delay. He should inform the local police of the fact that the wheel of his car had been loosened. They will make the usual routine enquiries. It is possible that the person who tampered with the wheel was observed. In what kind of street is the garage?"

"It isn't a garage at all, only a shed where a local builder keeps odds and ends—ladders amongst other things. And you can't call it a street. It's just a narrow cut running along the back yards of the houses fronting on Ellery Street."

Miss Silver looked attentive.

"Not the kind of place which a stranger would frequent. The person we are looking for may have attracted attention. By all means get your husband to notify the police. In the second place, I would like your permission to talk the whole matter over with Frank Abbott."

"Oh, no!"

Miss Silver held up her pencil in a hortatory manner.

"Pray think again, Mrs. Eversley. There have been three attempts on your husband's life, an attempt on Mr. Tattlecombe of which your husband may have been the real object, and a fatal accident to Mr. Davies—the day after he had recognized him as William Eversley. I am not saying from what quarter these attacks have come. By changing your address you may have obscured your own connection with William Smith for a time, but it must be clear to you that anyone who is taking a serious interest in his identity with William Eversley cannot remain long in ignorance of the part you have undertaken to play. As soon as that is known, and as soon as it is known that you have gone through a form of marriage with him and are living as his wife, it will be evident to the person or persons who have been attempting his life that the time remaining to them is short. He, or they, must know that you will not remain silent. As soon as you speak and William Smith comes forward as William Eversley they cannot any longer hope to act in the dark. Attention will be focussed upon anyone who has an interest in resisting his claim. Do you not see that the sooner that claim is made, the harder it will be to make any fresh attempt upon his life? Where a common street accident to William Smith could very well pass unsuspected of being anything more than an accident, his sudden death immediately after he has claimed to be William Eversley, whose return from the dead was likely to involve his relatives in a good deal of financial embarrassment, could hardly fail to attract the attention of the police."

Katharine said, "Yes."

Miss Silver laid down her pencil with an air of finality.

"It will, I think, be quite a good plan for you to leave town tomorrow for the week-end. Pray do not tell anyone where you are going. Meanwhile I should like to talk the matter over with Frank Abbott—I do not care to accept the responsibility alone. I think you may rest assured that no action will be taken without reference to your husband and yourself. If Frank thinks as I do he may discuss the matter with Chief Inspector Lamb, a most worthy and dependable officer. He has great experience, and I feel sure that you need not be afraid that he will authorize any precipitate action. Routine procedure may, however, produce some interesting evidence. Have I your permission?"

Katharine looked at her for a full long minute. Then she said,

"Yes."

CHAPTER 25

They drove to Ledstow on the grey Saturday afternoon. Katharine need not have troubled herself to find excuses for starting late. William brought the car up to the Mews and spent considerably more than an hour in going over everything that could be gone over. She didn't want to arrive in daylight, and by the time they started it was quite certain that if they made Ledstow before nightfall they would be fortunate. They talked a little until they were clear of the London belt. William had thought it quite a good plan to let the local police know that the car had been tampered with. He had gone round to the police station before fetching it. He talked about his interview with a monumental sergeant.

"He made me feel about ten years old—" he branched off suddenly—"I wonder what I was doing when I was ten. You'd think you'd get used to not remembering anything, but you don't. It's like running into a blank wall when you know there ought to be a window there. Sometimes it makes me feel as if I was going to bang my head."

"Does it?"

He gave a quick emphatic nod. After a moment he said,

"You wouldn't think I'd mind so much now. I mean you wouldn't think I could mind anything now I've got you. But I do—I mind worse. It's idiotic, isn't it?"

"No, I don't think so. You mean because of me?"

"Yes. You've got a sort of pig in a poke, haven't you? And then if we had children, I'd mind awfully for them."

She said, "You'll remember."

He turned a momentary look on her and she saw the trouble in his eyes.

"Remember—what?" he said. "Perhaps I oughtn't to have married you."

Katharine put her hand on his knee.

"Don't be stupid, darling—you'll remember all right. And it won't be anything to worry about, you'll see."

They came clear of the houses and the traffic and drove on.

Afterwards Katharine looked back and thought what a strange drive it had been—the air mild and full of moisture, mist rising from the fields, and cloud hanging low—the world like a silver-point drawing, no colour anywhere, grey cloud and leafless trees, hedgerows hung with drops like crystal beads, a river streaked with silver and lead, mist on the fields like smoke rising.

William said once, "It won't turn to fog till after dark," but for most of the way neither of them spoke. There was a curious sense of being cut off, not from one another, but from the familiar shape of things. Presently there was no distance. Outlines began to blur. The damp in the air frosted the windscreen and had to be wiped away. The road which Katharine knew so well took on a strangeness, like something remembered but not quite real. She had stopped planning what to do and what to say. It wasn't any use. The road would take them to the house, and when she got there she would know what to say and what to do. She remembered driving down to the Cedar House with William after their July wedding— July 1939, and every one thinking and talking of war—a bright, clear day and the July sun sloping to the west over fields almost ripe for harvesting. "Thrust in thy sickle, and reap . . . for the harvest of the earth is ripe." That was in the

Bible, in the book of Revelations. It had been a bitter and a bloody reaping. She looked back. There had been an agony of love, an agony of parting, a long-drawn agony of slowly fading hope. Now they were here together in a mist, travelling the old road to the old house on a January afternoon.

They came through Ledlington with the last of the daylight and the lamps shining in the streets. William drove right through the town and out on the other side without a check, and when they were clear of the straggle of new houses which had sprung up all round the old town he drove straight on over the seven miles of lonely road into the middle of the village street and stopped there, the headlights of the car making a straight shining beam in which the mist dazzled like motes in the sun.

Katharine said, "We're here."

He didn't answer her. He got down and opened the door. His arm came round her. Then he said,

"I'll just put the car away. I won't be long."

Her heart stood still. A July evening—confetti in her hat— sunlight slanting down the village street—the new, shining car—William opening the door and putting his arm round her as she got out—"I'll just put the car away. I won't be long..."

The garage was across the street, the doors open, waiting not for the new shining Alvis but for William's old tin kettle assembled bit by bit from the scrap-heap. She smiled in the dark, held his arm for a moment, and went up the three steps to the Cedar House. She saw William back the car and turn in, as he had done a hundred times.

She lifted the latch of the door and went into the house. The lights were on in the hall. She turned them out, to leave only one. Then she crossed to a door at the far end and went down a stone-paved passage to the kitchen.

Mrs. Perkins, stout and rosy in a blue dress and a white apron, turned round from the range.

"Oh, Miss Kathy—and I never heard you come!"

Katharine kissed her and stood holding both her hands.

"Perky darling, I told you I'd got a big surprise for you, and I've only got about half a minute to tell you what it is. You won't faint, will you?"

Mrs. Perkins chuckled.

"I'm not the fainting kind. It don't do when you're as stout as me. Who's going to pick you up when you weigh as much as what I do?" Then, with a sudden change of voice, "Oh, Miss Kathy, what is it?"

Katharine said, "William—"

"Oh, my dear—you've heard something?"

Katharine nodded. She had stared dry-eyed at the telegram which told her William was missing. Now the tears sprang unchecked. Her eyes shone with them. They ran down and were salt on her quivering lips.

"He's come back—"

CHAPTER 26

Katharine was in the hall again. She dropped her fur coat on a black and gold lacquer chair under the portrait of great-great-uncle Ambrose Talbot in the uniform he had worn at Waterloo—tight white breeches, scarlet coat, high stock, and a fair, almost girlish face—not quite eighteen when the picture was painted, after Napoleon had gone to St. Helena and his shadow had passed from the world. The Cedar House had belonged to Talbots ever since William Talbot built it for a country lodging nearly four hundred years ago. It took its name from the great cedar he had planted at the end of the lawn, and from the panelling which kept moths away and to this day diffused its own faint sweetness everywhere.

William's grandmother was the last of the long Talbot line. He himself had the name of its founder. He was William Talbot Eversley. The house, and its portraits, and its memories were his. There were a lot of portraits, a lot of memories—a judge in a scarlet robe and a portentous Georgian wig—an admiral with a pigtail and a brown crumpled face, holding a spy-glass in his hand and looking out of the picture with William's eyes. The girl in the pink dress of the middle eighteenth century was Amanda Talbot who made a romantic runaway marriage with a black-browed Highland Jacobite and lived with him in exile after the '45. She had lovely, arch eyes and a sweet smiling mouth. Her portrait hung above the fireplace. A log burned there. Katharine stood by it and waited. The door was latched but not locked. Presently it would swing in. It was all very quiet, very familiar—the stairway going up on the other side of the hall, the door to the dining-room just beyond the stair foot. On the other side, behind the wall with the chimney-breast, the drawing-room, where the panelling had been painted ivory-white and the china which Gran used to show them when they were children was ranged against it in cabinets of Amanda's date.

Katharine's heart beat fast, then quieted. There was nothing to be troubled about. William was coming home.

When the door opened she went to meet him. He took her in his arms and held her without speaking. It was one of those moments for which there are no words. When at last he lifted his head and spoke it was like coming out of a dream. Something slipped away from them to join the other mem-

165

ories of the house. He said her name, and then,

"This was the place to come to. It always did feel like coming home." With his arms still round her, he looked across her shoulder to the glowing bed of the fire, where the logs were heaped, one a shell, red-hot, another black against tongues of flame from below. His voice broke on a half laugh as he said,

"That looks good. But what a climate! Nobody would think it was July!"

July—and they had driven here through the winter dusk. Half past five o'clock, and outside the January night had closed down. Katharine drew away lest he should feel that she was shaking. She waited with caught breath for what he would say next. It came in his most cheerful voice.

"Gosh—I'm hungry! I hope Perky's got something for us. It's not too late, is it?" He turned his wrist, glanced at the watch on it, and exclaimed, "What time is it? This thing's stopped at twenty to six. It must be all of ten o'clock."

"Why?"

"Pitch-dark outside. We must have made very bad time."

The fair brows drew together in a puzzled frown, then relaxed.

"It doesn't matter as long as we are here. Go and see what Perky can do about it. I'll just take our cases upstairs and get a wash."

Katharine went through to the kitchen and found Mrs. Perkins filling a kettle and weeping into the sink.

"Perky, listen—you mustn't cry."

"Oh, Miss Kathy my dear, it's because I'm so glad."

She set the kettle down and put out both her hands. Katharine took them and held them hard.

"Perky—*listen!* I told you he didn't remember anything before '42. *Well, he does now.* It's the last few years that have gone. At least I think they have—I don't know. But he thinks it's July. He thinks we've just been married. He thinks we've come here for our honeymoon, and he thinks it's ten o'clock at night because it's dark outside. Perky, you've got to help."

Mrs. Perkins gazed at her.

"What can I do, my dear?"

Katharine's voice trembled into laughter.

"He says he's hungry. He wants to know what you can give us for supper."

The rosy face cleared.

"Then you'd best let me be getting on with it. There's soup all ready to hot up, and a nice rabbit pie. Would he like it cold, or shall I put it in the oven?"

"We'll ask him."

"And chocolate shape I made—the way you've always liked it, Miss Kathy."

"Lovely!"

And then William came in, kissed Mrs. Perkins as Katharine had done, and sat on the corner of the kitchen table as he had been scolded for doing as long as Katharine could remember. He laughed and said,

"Horrid weather you've conjured up for us. I couldn't see my hand before my face coming over the road, and Katharine couldn't see her wedding ring. Has she shown it to you? She's frightfully proud of being a married woman." He took her left hand and held it up. "Looks good, doesn't it? Sounds good too—Mrs. William Eversley. And, Perky darling, it's not a bit romantic, but we're simply starving. I can't think why we took so long to get here. STARVED TO DEATH ON HIS WEDDING DAY is going to be my epitaph if I don't get something to eat pretty soon."

Mrs. Perkins rallied nobly.

"Then you'll have to get out of my kitchen, Mr. William,

167

and off of that table, or you won't get nothing."

It was the strangest evening. They went into the drawing-room, and William made love to her as the young William of seven years ago had done when life was the gayest, most carefree adventure in the world. And then suddenly in the middle of it all he fell silent, looked puzzled, and walked away from her down to the far end of the room where faded sea-green curtains screened the door into the garden and the casement windows on either side of it. He parted them and stood there looking out. What Katharine got was the impression that the night looked in. It was certain that he could see nothing, unless it were the picture stamped indelibly upon mind and memory through all his growing years. Standing behind him, Katharine could see it too—the small formal terrace with its stone jars which in July would be brimming over with bloom, then the lavender hedge, the two tall myrtle-bushes, the even, velvety lawn, and the great cedar tree. As she touched him, he turned abruptly and said,

"It's all right isn't it—the cedar wasn't blitzed?"

She was almost too startled to answer, but she managed to keep her voice level.

"No, it's all right. You'll see it tomorrow."

The puzzled look was intensified.

"See what?"

"The cedar. You asked if it was all right."

"Did I? Why shouldn't it be?" He went over to one of the china cabinets and stood there. "Remember how Gran taught us to feel the glaze? You know, it's an awfully odd thing—I can remember with the tips of my fingers just the difference between those plates and these cups. She wouldn't ever let us touch them unless she was there. Funny to think how many people have touched them since they were made, and now they're ours."

When Mrs. Perkins summoned them to the dining-room it all seemed stranger still. Gran watched them from her picture on the chimney-breast. Amory's masterpiece—Gran at ninety, with a lace scarf over the white curls she had been so proud of, a lace shawl over her blue dress, her face still vividly alive, her eyes still blue. She sat in her big chair and watched the room. To Katharine her look said, "You needn't think you'll ever get rid of me. I love you all too much." She watched them now.

All through the meal William talked eagerly, cheerfully, about what they would do in the garden.

"I saw a place where they have rows of white lilies growing in front of a dark hedge—it looked pretty good. I thought we might try it down at the bottom against the arbor vitae. What do you think? I'm rather keen on lilies. There's a good apricot-coloured sort too—they grow it a lot in the north— I'd like to have some of them. It's a pity it's too far for me to go up and down every day, but we could do weekends in the summer. I'd like to play about with the garden. I've got an idea for a pool—water-lilies and things. Wait till we've finished, and I'll do a sketch for you." He looked at her suddenly and laughed. "It's going to be fun, isn't it?"

When he talked like that he might have been William Smith, or he might have been William Eversley, or a third William walking the debatable ground between the other two. She encouraged him to go on talking about the garden.

Afterwards, in the drawing-room, she played to him. When they went upstairs together he said the strangest thing of all. They had reached the last step, when he halted and stood there looking round him. The arm about her shoulders dropped to his side, the fair brows drew together. He said,

"I had an awfully funny dream about this place. I can't remember what it was."

169

"I shouldn't try."

He nodded, came up on to the landing, and turned again. His eye went from the eagle on the right-hand newel-post to the man on the left.

"It was something about the Evangelists," he said slowly. "Something—about—" he gave a sudden laugh—"I know— I dreamt the man was Mr. Tattlecombe! Barmy—wasn't it?"

Katharine said, "Quite."

Still laughing, he put his arm round her and they kissed, and went on together into the room which was theirs, a long room over the drawing-room with the windows looking down the garden to the cedar tree. It didn't matter any longer which of the Williams he was, or which way the pendulum of his memory swung. He was the William who loved her and whom she loved. He was the William who had always loved her and would love her always.

CHAPTER 27

William woke up to the sound of the grandfather clock on the landing striking eight. It had a very deep, solemn note, and he must have waked just before the first stroke, because he found himself counting up to eight. He knew he hadn't missed any of the strokes, because it always did a sort of whirring grunt before it started to strike, and that was the first thing he had heard. He was lying on his right side, with the curtains drawn back from the row of windows which looked towards the garden. Two of them were open. The sky was a slaty grey. He could see the upper branches of the cedar stretched out over the garden like black wings. It isn't dark at eight o'clock in January, but it isn't really light.

He turned and saw Katharine lying beside him with her hands together under her chin and her hair loose on the pillow. Perhaps it happened at that moment, or perhaps it had really happened when he was asleep—he didn't know, and it didn't matter—but, turning like that and seeing Katharine, he was aware that what he had called the blank wall no longer existed. William Smith remembered William Eversley, and William Eversley knew all about William Smith. The two halves of his memory had come together and merged into one. The only thing that wasn't clear was that time in the German hospital. He remembered everything right up to the time they were bombed, and he knew he had been in a German hospital, because he remembered coming out of it labelled William Smith, but the bit between was as vague as a last year's dream. It had probably been very unpleasant, and he decided that he could do very well without it. Meanwhile there were a lot of things to be sorted out. He began on them methodically.

There was Katharine—but that had come all right. It mightn't have, because of course she might have married someone else. But she hadn't. They had married each other all over again. Then there was Eversleys'. That wasn't so easy. He wondered what Cyril and Brett had made of the war years and the difficult change over. He had no very exalted opinion of either of them when it came to business. Cyril simply hadn't got it in him, and Brett didn't bother. He might have had to of course, but William didn't feel very sanguine about it. He wondered what they were going to say when they knew that he had come back. The family side of them would be pleased of course, but he thought the business side was going to take a bit of a knock. It didn't make it any easier his

171

being the youngest of the three, and by a good many years. And then he thought about Miss Jones. She came sliding into his mind as he had seen her at six o'clock on the evening of December the sixth. There wasn't the faintest shadow of doubt that she had recognized him—or was there? He thought about that. He could remember what he used to look like, and he could remember what he looked like yesterday when he was shaving. He really hadn't changed enough to give Miss Jones the benefit of the doubt. She had known him for at least seven years before he went missing. Frank Abbott had recognized him after only seeing him once. Davies—that was old Davies he had blundered into in the street—he had known him again, just like that, all in a flash under a street-lamp. Miss Jones must certainly have known him.

He had got to the point where it occurred to him that being dead for seven years and then coming to life again is bound to complicate other people's affairs as well as your own, when Katharine stirred, threw out a hand, and woke.

Just for a moment she didn't know where she was. Then William was hugging her and saying, "Darling, wake up—wake up quickly! I've remembered!"

She couldn't think of anything to say. She felt dazed, and happy, and safe, because it didn't really matter about anything as long as William was there. She said,

"I *am* awake."

"You're not. But you've got to be. Kath, I've remembered!"

She woke right up then.

"Oh, darling!"

"Yes. And it's a pretty kettle of fish, isn't it—what with our being bigamists—"

"We're not!"

"My child, we are. A bigamist is someone who goes through a form of marriage whilst a previous husband or wife is alive. I'm a previous husband, and you're a previous wife, and we're both alive, so we're bigamists."

"We're not. It doesn't matter how often you marry the same person. I found out in a roundabout sort of way."

His voice changed.

"Katharine, why didn't you tell me?"

"I wanted you to remember."

"Suppose I hadn't?"

"I would have told you today anyhow. Miss Silver said I must."

"Miss Silver? What did you tell her?"

"Everything. She seemed to know most of it already."

"How could she?"

"She puts things together. She said I'd got to tell you. And I was going to, only I hoped you'd remember first—and you have."

There was a long pause before he said,

"I didn't really forget you."

"I know you didn't."

"I loved you the minute you came into the shop. I hadn't ever stopped loving you. It was there all the time, and then— you came—" His voice broke. "Katharine, *why* didn't you tell me?"

She said very softly, "Silly! How could I walk into a shop and say to William Smith, 'You don't think you've ever seen me before, but I'm your wife'?" She put her cheek against his. "What would Miss Cole have said!"

William thought of several things that Miss Cole might have said. They laughed together with the sort of laughter which comes like a ripple on the surface of emotion. It came, and it went. Katharine said,

"I wanted you to fall in love with me all over again, and when you did I wanted you to marry me. I thought you would remember then, but you didn't and every day you didn't it was harder to tell you. But I would have told you today. It wouldn't have been fair to let you go on being William Smith."

He said slowly, "No—it wouldn't have been fair." And then, "I say, Kath, there's going to be a bit of a mess to clear up. I've been thinking—"

"Don't think too much."

He gave his head the quick impatient shake which had always reminded her of a dog coming out of the water.

"I've been thinking—that time I went to Eversleys' and saw Miss Jones—she must have known me. Or do you think—"

"No, I don't. You haven't changed a bit. You never have, and I don't suppose you ever will."

Like an echo there came back out of the past her own voice saying on a note of anger, "It's no use, William never changes!" It was something she wanted to do and he wouldn't let her. She couldn't remember what it was, but she could remember being ten years old, and angry, and saying, "William never changes!"

She came back to Mr. Davies' name.

"Old Davies knew me—at least I suppose he did. He bumped into me in the street. He nearly dropped, and he asked me who I was."

"And you said William Smith, Tattlecombe's Toy Bazaar, Ellery Street. And first he thought you were a ghost, and then he went and found a call-box and rang me up."

"He rang you up?"

She said, "That's how I knew," and hid her face against him.

It was a little while before they got back to Miss Jones.

"You know," Katharine said, "it was very odd her giving

174

you such a late appointment. You signed your letter 'William Smith,' and I can't help thinking that she recognized the 'William.' Not enough to be sure, but enough to make her give you that late appointment when practically everyone else would have gone. They shut at half past five nominally. Mr. Davies used to hang about a bit. That evening he'd forgotten something and came back, poor old boy."

"Why poor old boy?"

"He's dead, William."

"How?"

"He had a street accident on December the seventh."

He repeated the date—"December the seventh—"

"The day after he saw you."

"The day after he recognized me?"

"Yes."

There was a pause. Then William said,

"He did recognize me?"

"Yes. He rang me up and said, 'I've just seen Mr. William.'"

"Do you think he said that to anyone else?"

"I don't know. He went to the office next day, and he went away in the evening. On the way home he was knocked down at a street-crossing and taken to hospital. He never recovered consciousness. I didn't hear about it until ten days ago. Bunny told me. It was the day I had extra time off. I lunched with Cyril. Brett and Bunny were there. There had been a bit of a hold-up about my money and Bunny had come up to see about it. We went away together in a taxi, and he told me the money would be all right now, but to let him know if it wasn't. They had been telling him Mr. Davies had muddled things up. William, I can't forgive them for that."

"Katharine—what are you saying?"

"They said he was past his work, and that he had muddled

175

up the accounts. Bunny told me. And he told me that Mr. Davies was dead. I didn't know till then. I went back to the flat and rang up Miss Jones. She told me about the accident, and when I pressed her I got the date. It was the seventh of December."

There was a pause. Then he said,

"Davies came to the office that day?"

"Yes."

He began, "Do you suppose—" and then broke off.

Katharine answered what he hadn't said.

"I don't know. I wrote to say not to tell anyone about seeing you. He would have had my letter that evening, but he never got home. He went to the office on the seventh. Perhaps he didn't tell anyone." She stopped. Then after quite a long time she said, "Perhaps he did."

CHAPTER 28

On the Saturday afternoon whilst William and Katharine were driving down to Ledstow Abigail Salt was having tea with Mr. Tattlecombe. He was half expecting that she would not come, and quite prepared to be in a huff about it. Influenza or no influenza, he didn't see why she should dance attendance on Emily when her own flesh and blood with his leg only just out of a splint was expecting her. Human nature being what it is, he was almost disappointed when she turned up punctually to the moment and, taking off her coat and gloves, went into the little upstairs kitchen to make the tea— Mrs. Bastable having gone down to Ealing to see her husband's eldest sister, who was a retired elementary school-mistress.

Sipping his first cup, Abel reflected that it was extraordinary how much better the tea tasted, with the same water, the same tea-leaves, the same gas stove, and the same pot. Tea made by Abby was, and probably always would be, superior to tea made by Mrs. Bastable. The same thing with coffee, with soup, with everything. He felt mollified and forgave her the sin of omission which, after all, she hadn't committed. Emily had not been preferred, he himself had not been neglected. Abigail had made buttered toast of a very superlative kind. He remembered with a shudder that Mrs. Bastable had offered to make it before she went and leave it "keeping hot." He had been rather firm with her about that, and she had departed sniffing.

He ate Abigail's toast with a good deal of satisfaction whilst she explained how kind it was of Miss Simpson to come in and keep an eye on Emily. "She was round to enquire last night, and when I mentioned that you were expecting me today and I didn't know quite what to do about it, she offered at once. Ellen Simpson's a good friend, though I don't say she hasn't got trying ways sometimes, but I suppose we're all like that. It isn't everybody I could leave with Emily, even if she's pretty much herself again—up yesterday and most of today, though she hasn't been out. But I told her she'd better be lying down in her own room whilst I was out, and I gave her the wireless. If she wanted anything, I told her, Ellen would be just across the passage in the parlour and she'd bring her her tea, but better not try and talk too much—they might get disagreeing about something."

This was such a long speech for Abigail that Abel Tattle-combe began to feel very faintly disturbed. He was no more interested in Ellen Simpson than he was in Emily Salt. He

177

didn't mind which of them had been left to look after the other, and Abby knew it. He wouldn't have cared if they had been on desert islands at the North Pole. Ellen Simpson had eyebrows that met in the middle, and she always contradicted everybody flat. When after his wife died she had started agreeing with him, and Abby had begun asking her to meet him at tea, he had been very much alarmed and he had spoken out. Abby couldn't possibly think that he wanted to talk about Ellen Simpson.

He took another piece of buttered toast and said,

"You've got something on your mind."

Mrs. Salt's fair, fresh-complexioned face remained impassive. The blue eyes which were so much like Abel's maintained their quiet gaze. She lifted her cup, drank from it, and set it down before she answered him.

"Well, I won't say I'm not glad to find you alone."

Abel wagged his head. He could do it quite comfortably now that the stiffness was gone.

"You knew very well I was going to be alone. Mrs. Bastable has gone to see her sister-in-law at Ealing. She will come home in very low spirits because Miss Bastable always treats her as if she ought to be in the infants' class. What have you got on your mind?" Then, without waiting for a reply, "I suppose it's Emily."

"Well, yes, it is."

Abel grunted.

"What's she been doing?"

"She has been having influenza. On Tuesday night she was very feverish. She wandered in her mind and talked a lot of nonsense. I was glad there wasn't anyone there to hear her."

"What did she say?"

Abigail hesitated.

"She was out of her head. You can't take notice of what anyone says when they are in a fever."

Abel's bushy eyebrows twitched. Women—look at them! Look at Abby! Had she come here on purpose to tell him what Emily had said, or hadn't she? Could she get it out without a lot of sticking and fussing? Not a bit of it! He said crossly,

"Are you going to tell me what she said?"

There was an answering spark in the eyes that were so much like his own.

"Yes, I am, but I won't be bustled. I came here on purpose, but it isn't an easy thing to say, and you've never liked poor Emily. I've had a duty to her and I've done my best. It hasn't always been easy, and now I've come to the place where I've got to think about my duty to others, and that isn't easy either—not after all these years of thinking about Emily first. I've come to where I've got to speak to someone, and you're my brother and you're mixed up with it."

Abel Tattlecombe finished his piece of toast and reached for another. He wasn't going to let Emily Salt put him off his tea. If the toast wasn't eaten hot it would be spoiled, and it was much too good to spoil.

"What did Emily say?"

Abby wasn't eating at all. She folded her hands in her lap and looked at him.

"I'm going to tell you. But you've got to make up your mind to look at it the way you would if it wasn't Emily. You've got to judge righteous judgment, Abel, and not just think the way you want to. You've never liked Emily, but you're a just man, and you've got not to let it weigh with you. You've got to judge the way you would if I was telling you this about somebody else."

Abel wagged his head.

"That's not possible, Abby. You've got to judge people according to what you know about them. There's things I know about Emily. If I've got to use my judgment about her, it's no use telling me I've got to put those things out of my head, because I don't believe the Lord means us to do that, and anyhow it can't be done. But I'll do my best to be fair."

Abigail gave a quiet sigh. Abel always had been set in his ways. She said,

"Well, I'll tell you. And you mustn't make too much of it, for she was clean out of her head. She woke up crying out, and when I went to her she didn't know me—only stared and said, 'I did it—I did it.' So I said, 'I'll get you a drink, my dear.' But when I came back with it she was talking nineteen to the dozen. All a lot of rubbish it sounded like."

The picture came up in her mind as she spoke—Emily wild enough to frighten you, with her eyes fixed and burning, and a hot, shaking hand. She hadn't been frightened at the time—she had known too many sick people for that—but when she looked back it frightened her a little more each time.

"What did she say, Abby?"

She could give the words, but she could never give the horrid way they had come—sometimes in a cold whisper that chilled your blood, sometimes, and quite suddenly, in a scream which made you feel thankful there wasn't anyone else in the house. Under that habitual look of calm Abigail Salt was deeply perturbed. She said in her quiet voice,

"She was angry about your will."

"She had no call to know anything about it."

Abigail nodded.

"She heard you telling me. I couldn't get her to see that it was all right for me, and nothing to do with her. She's got the kind of mind that takes hold of things and can't let go.

180

She got worked up to feel that William Smith was doing me an injury—and her."

Abel continued to eat buttered toast. He said with angry contempt,

"She's crazy! You're not telling me what she said."

Abigail sighed again.

"I'm trying to make you understand."

He pushed over his cup, and filled it. Even with the trouble she was in, she took care that it should be just to his liking. If it came to that, she wasn't in any hurry to tell him what Emily had said. She wouldn't be telling him at all if it wasn't that her conscience wouldn't let her hold it back.

He sipped from his newly filled cup, fixed his eyes upon her severely, and said,

"Now, Abby."

CHAPTER 29

Miss Silver had a busy two days. On Saturday morning, after a short telephone conversation, she put on her hat and coat and went round to New Scotland Yard, where she was received by Sergeant Abbott and presently conducted by him into the presence of Chief Detective Inspector Lamb.

Frank Abbott, as always, derived a sardonic amusement from the ensuing ritual. Having met as old friends, with a hearty handshake on one side and a ladylike one on the other, Miss Silver hoped that the Chief Inspector was well, and enquired after his family.

"And Mrs. Lamb? I trust she is in very good health . . . And your daughters? Lily's little boy must be at a most delightful age."

His daughters were the Chief Inspector's weakness. He permitted himself to expatiate on the infant talents of little Ernie.

"They would call him after me, and they say he looks like me too, poor little beggar."

Miss Silver beamed.

"He could not, I am sure, have a worthier ambition. And your second daughter, Violet? Her engagement—"

Lamb shook his head.

"Broken off—and just as well, if you ask me. Naval officer and a nice enough chap, but when he'd been away two years and come back they didn't want to go on with it. She's got a good confidential job at the Admiralty, and too many friends to want to make up her mind in a hurry."

"And Myrtle?"

His youngest daughter was the core of Lamb's heart.

"Wants to train as a nurse," he said. "Her mother worries over it. Thinks she'll catch something, but I tell her nurses don't."

Miss Silver opined that it was a noble profession. They came to business with a "Well now, what can we do for you?" and one of her delicate coughs.

Seated in an upright chair, her own back as straight, her neatly shod feet in black woollen stockings and Oxford shoes planted side by side upon the office carpet, her hands in their black knitted gloves folded in the lap of a well worn cloth coat, a little tippet of elderly yellowish fur about her neck, and a hat of several years standing enlivened by a bunch of purple pansies on her head, Miss Silver gave her whole attention to the case of William Smith.

"I find myself in a difficult situation," she said.

"Well, what can we do to help you?"

This was Lamb at his most accessible. There had been times in the past when it was he who had been the recipient of help which, however tactfully proffered, had slightly ruffled his temper and their relations. It was not disagreeable to have Miss Silver asking for assistance.

She said, "You are so kind," and then got briskly to her case.

"I have some reason to believe that an elderly clerk of the name of Davies was murdered on the seventh of December last. The death followed on a street accident after which he was taken to hospital and is said not to have recovered consciousness. I believe that he was pushed. Here is a memorandum of his place of employment, his private address, and the hospital to which he was taken. I should like to know whether he said anything at all before he died, and I should like to see a transcript of the evidence at the inquest."

Lamb turned his eyes upon her. Brown in colour and slightly protuberant, they had been compared by his irreverent subordinate to the sweets known as bullseyes. He asked,

"Why do you think he was murdered?"

"He had just recognized someone who had been missing for seven years, and whose return may prove to be a serious embarrassment to the firm for which he was working."

The Chief Inspector's face assumed a tolerant expression.

"Well now, I should call that a bit far-fetched. There are quite enough accidents to elderly people without calling in murder to account for them."

Miss Silver coughed.

"That is very true. But in this case the life of the person recognized by Mr. Davies has been attempted, certainly on three, and possibly on a fourth occasion. One of these at-

183

tempts was witnessed by Sergeant Abbott."

Lamb shifted in his chair, brought a refrigerating gaze to bear upon that elegant young man, and said in tones of disfavour,

"So you're mixed up in this, are you? I might have known it."

"Well, sir—"

Miss Silver interposed.

"Permit me, Chief Inspector—"

She presented the case of William Smith in as short and concise a manner as was possible—the loss of memory and identity; the recognition by Mr. Davies, by Katharine, by Frank Abbott; Mr. Tattlecombe's "accident"; the first and second attacks on William; the tampering with the wheel of his car.

When she had finished Frank took up the tale. He described the attack, telling the Chief Inspector, as he had told Miss Silver, that he was convinced a second blow had been intended, and that in the circumstances it would almost certainly have proved fatal.

Lamb grunted.

"Not much to go on," he said.

Miss Silver gave a slight protesting cough.

"It is difficult to believe in such a series of coincidences. An accident to Mr. Davies just after he had recognized William Smith. An accident on that same evening to Mr. Tattlecombe in circumstances which rendered it possible that he had been mistaken for William Smith. Two separate attacks on William Smith after visiting Mr. Tattlecombe in Selby Street. And now the tampering with the wheel of his car. The trouble is that suspicion appears to be equally divided between someone connected with the firm of Eversleys' and someone in the household at Selby Street. It is difficult to see

184

how anyone in the firm could have been aware that William Smith would pay those visits to Mr. Tattlecombe. He did not even go by appointment, and this would seem to make it likely that Miss Emily Salt may have been the assailant. She appears to be a person of unstable mentality, and to have resented Mr. Tattlecombe's testamentary dispositions in favour of William Smith. She is, I am informed, a tall and powerful woman. Mr. Tattlecombe's mackintosh was hanging in the hall. It would, I think, be difficult to tell a woman wearing such a garment from a man on the kind of night Sergeant Abbott has described. The first attack on William Smith was almost at Mrs. Salt's door. On the second occasion Emily Salt could easily have followed him. It is not easy to see how anyone from the firm could have done so. On the other hand it seems impossible to suspect Emily Salt of the death of Mr. Davies, or of the accident to Mr. Tattlecombe, since she and her sister-in-law Mrs. Salt were present at a chapel social on the evening of December the seventh. I have made a few local enquiries, and I find Mrs. and Miss Salt were assisting in the preparations between five and seven, and that they were back in the hall before eight o'clock, where they remained until half past ten. It would not, therefore, have been possible for Emily Salt to be concerned in these two 'accidents,' and during the period when the wheel was tampered with she was laid up in bed with influenza under the care of Mrs. Salt. I find myself unable to believe that two independent and unconnected series of attempts are being made upon William Smith, yet on the evidence at present before us it is very difficult to attribute all these attempts to the same agency."

The Chief Inspector smiled. He said drily,

"If they ever were attempts, Miss Silver."

There was a pause, lightly tinged with something not

amounting to displeasure but tending that way. When she thought it had lasted long enough, Miss Silver coughed and said,

"I am, naturally, not asking you to accept conclusions on which you have only hearsay evidence, and as to which I am not myself fully satisfied. I merely invite you to pursue some discreet investigations. You can call for the evidence in that inquest. You can, perhaps, discover whether either of the Eversley partners, Mr. Cyril and Mr. Brett, are in financial difficulties. I would not press you if I were not quite seriously troubled as to the personal safety of William Smith."

Lamb continued to survey her with that tolerant smile.

"William Smith being William Eversley?"

"Precisely. He is also the senior partner, with a controlling interest in the business. When I add that Mrs. Eversley told me that her dividends were not forthcoming until there was active intervention on the part of a third trustee—Mr. Cyril and Mr. Brett Eversley being the other two—you will, I think, be prepared to admit that there are some grounds for my apprehension."

Lamb frowned. He was remembering previous occasions on which Miss Silver had entertained apprehensions which had been rather dreadfully realized. He tapped the table and said,

"Eversley won't thank you for stirring up trouble about his firm."

Miss Silver drew herself up.

"That is the very last thing which I have in mind." She relaxed suddenly into one of her charming smiles. "Indeed, Chief Inspector, I have far too much confidence in your delicacy and discretion to suggest, as you yourself appear to be suggesting, that your department cannot make some discreet enquiries without precipitating a scandal."

Lamb threw up his hands and broke into a hearty laugh.

"Well, well—when you put it like that! Just give Frank here all the particulars you want, and I'll see what we can do. You'll have to excuse me—I've got a conference. And you know, if I hadn't, I'd be afraid to stay. Some day you'll be getting me into trouble."

Miss Silver coughed.

"There is just one thing more."

He had drawn back his chair and laid a big hand on the arm preparatory to rising. Checking momentarily, he restrained a frown and said in a good-humoured voice,

"Now, now, you mustn't keep me, or I shall be getting into the trouble I was talking about."

Miss Silver assumed a gracious and friendly air.

"Your time is indeed valuable and I will not trespass upon it. I would merely ask that you will have a person who is closely connected with this case placed under constant observation."

Lamb withdrew his hand, placed it upon a solid knee, and leaned forward a little.

"What person?"

"Miss Mavis Jones."

"Why?"

Miss Silver submitted her reasons in an efficient manner, observing in conclusion,

"I would not urge this course upon you if I were not persuaded of its vital importance."

Lamb was really frowning now.

"Can't say I see much case for it myself."

Miss Silver met his look with a very grave one.

"My dear Chief Inspector, I have before now urged that a similar course of action should be taken. I beg that you will recall those occasions and decide for yourself whether my requests were then justified."

Lamb again remembered with some unwillingness that when Miss Silver's suggestions had in the past been disregarded the consequences had not always been such as to minister to his peace of mind. It came to him in the blunt, plain English which we talk in our own minds that there were men who would be alive today if he had done what Miss Silver had asked him.

Her voice interrupted his thought persuasively.

"I do really believe that Mr. William Eversley's life is in very grave danger."

He got to his feet in a hurry.

"Now, now, you know, you're making me late. I suppose you'll have to have your way—you generally do. Tell Frank what you want, and we'll look after it for you."

Miss Silver smiled upon him benignly.

"You are always so kind."

When the door closed behind him after a cordial handshake Frank Abbott observed with malice,

"You've got him rattled, you know. He thinks you keep a broomstick, and the unlicenced broomstick is naturally anathema to any government department, which would rather let its murderers go free than have them brought to book in an unorthodox manner."

Miss Silver regarded him with indulgent reproof.

"My dear Frank, you talk great nonsense."

CHAPTER 30

It was at a little after six o'clock on Saturday evening that the
telephone bell rang in Miss Silver's sitting-room. She lifted
the receiver and heard an unknown male voice say with a
trace of country accent,

"Can I speak to Miss Silver?"

She gave her slight preliminary cough.

"Miss Silver speaking."

"Miss Maud Silver—the private enquiry agent?"

"Yes."

The voice said. "My name is Tattlecombe—Abel Tattlecombe. Does that convey anything to you?"

"Certainly, Mr. Tattlecombe."

At his end of the line Abel ran a hand through his thick
grey hair. Not having Miss Silver's address, he had had to
pick her out from among all the other Silvers in the telephone-
book, and there was always the chance that he might have
picked the wrong one. He felt a good deal of relief, and was
able to achieve an easier manner.

"Then I'm right in thinking that it was you that Mrs. Smith
was telling me about—Mrs. William Smith."

Miss Silver coughed again.

"Did she tell you about me?"

"Yes, she did. She works here. I expect she told you that.
She came up and talked to me, wanting the afternoon off so
she could go and see you."

"Yes, Mr. Tattlecombe?"

189

"Well, I was agreeable. I would like to say I think a lot of William Smith. Mrs. Smith, she's troubled about him, and so am I. She told me she'd been to see you, and she wanted to go again. She said your name, but she didn't mention any address, so I had to go to the telephone directory to find you. The fact is I've got things on my mind, and I think you ought to know what they are."

"Yes, Mr. Tattlecombe?"

Abel ran his hand through his hair again. He couldn't think what Abby was going to say to him. But it wasn't any good. There are things you can keep to yourself, and things you can't. Why, look at Abby—she couldn't keep it—had to come round and load it off on to him. Well then, he wasn't keeping it either. His conscience wouldn't let him. You can't play about with people's lives, and he wasn't going to be a party to it. He said firmly,

"There's things you ought to know, and the way I'm placed I can't come and tell you about them—my leg's only just out of a splint. Would it be possible for you to come here?"

Miss Silver coughed and said, "Perfectly possible, Mr. Tattlecombe."

Abel rang off with a slightly defiant feeling that he had burned his boats.

He had gone downstairs into the empty shop to telephone. He could manage the stairs if he took them slowly one step at a time and nobody hustled him. He had rather an enjoyable prowl about the shop and the workshop whilst he waited. The doctor said to use the leg, and this was as good a way as any. The new animals pleased him a good deal. He took a look into Miss Cole's books, and was gratified.

When Miss Silver knocked as he had bidden her he went to let her in, walking stiffly, but not allowing himself to limp. What he saw when she emerged into the light had a very reassuring effect. Mr. Tattlecombe knew a lady when he saw one. He considered that Miss Silver was a lady. She was dressed in very much the same way as his sister Abigail. Her clothes were not made of such handsome material, and they had been worn for a considerably longer time, but they were the same sort of clothes. Suitable was the word which he would have used. None of your mutton dressed as lamb. An elderly lady should be suitably attired. Just what he would have done if the private enquiry agent whom he had as it were plucked blindly from the pages of the telephone directory, had walked in upon him in high heels, a skirt to her knee, powdered, lipsticked, and waving a cigarette, it is really quite impossible to say. He was, fortunately, not to be subjected to any such ordeal.

Upstairs, and able to view one another in the unshaded light of his sitting-room, it was with mutual approbation that they did so, Miss Silver's mental comment being, "A very nice, respectable man." When they were seated and she had seen that his leg-rest was comfortably placed, there was one of those slight pauses. It was broken by Mr. Tattlecombe.

"Well, ma'am," he said, "It was very good of you to come."

Miss Silver offered a deprecating smile and a "Not at all."

Abel continued.

"The fact is, I think a lot of William Smith. He's been as good as a grandson to me here. I lost mine that was in the prison camp with him in Germany, and what one man can do to take another one's place—well, William's done that and more. His wife's been to see you. She'll have told you about me being struck down, and William too—and pushed after that to throw him under a bus when he was waiting on an island."

"Yes, she told me."

There was a second pause. It lasted longer than the first

one. In the end Abel Tattlecombe fixed his round blue eyes on her face and said in a tone of portent,

"My sister had tea with me today."

Miss Silver inclined her head without speaking.

"Mrs. Salt—Mrs. Abigail Salt, that's her name—176 Selby Street."

Miss Silver repeated her former acknowledgement.

Abel pursued the theme.

"That's where I was when I came out of hospital—that's where I made my will leaving the business to William Smith. And that's where he was struck down after coming to see me." He paused, and added, "Both times."

Miss Silver coughed.

"So Mrs. Smith informed me."

Abel brightened. He rubbed the top of his right ear vigorously and said,

"Did she tell you about Emily Salt?"

"Yes."

Abel let his hand fall with a clap upon his knee.

"How ever my sister Abby has put up with her all these years passes me. But it can't go on. Something's got to be done about it, and so I told her this afternoon. 'She'll be far better off in a home,' I said, 'and no risk to others.' And Abby—well, for once she hadn't got anything to say for a bit, and then come out with a piece she'd said before, about Emily being in a fever and not rightly knowing what she was saying."

With a neat disentangling movement Miss Silver extracted the pith of this discourse.

"Your sister came here to tell you of something Miss Salt had said during her recent illness?"

Abel wagged his head.

192

"Influenza," he said gloomily—"and clean out of her wits."

Miss Silver, sitting extraordinarily upright on a small Victorian chair inherited from a previous generation of Tattlecombes, clasped her hands in her lap and enquired,

"What did she say?"

Abel rubbed his ear.

"Abby said she'd got a temperature of a hundred and three and she was laid there groaning. All of a sudden she shoots out her hand and gets Abby by the wrist. 'He ought to be dead,' she says, whispering fit to curdle your blood, and then she screams it out at the top of her voice over and over a dozen times, till Abby was afraid the neighbours would think there was a murder in the house. Abby did her best to quiet her, and presently she stopped and said just as if it was something quite ordinary, 'I did my best—both times. You'd think he'd be dead by now, wouldn't you?' Abby said to hush and lie down, and she went to get her a drink. When she came back, there was that Emily lying there staring, and saying, 'He's no right to have the money. It's very wicked of Abel.' Abby hushed her up and told her the same as she'd done before, that she didn't want my money—her husband left her plenty, and William was welcome. She says Emily just went on staring. She took the drink and stared at her over the cup and said, 'I thought you wanted me to.' Abby said sharp, 'Wanted you to do what?' and that Emily shifts her eyes and says, 'Oh, no—it wasn't you, was it?' and she finished her drink and went off to sleep. Abby says there was talking and muttering in the night, but nothing you could put words to, and in the morning her temperature was down. Well, you may say it wasn't much to go on and the woman was out of her head, but I could see there was more than that. I've known Abby too many years not to know when

193

she's got something on her mind, and in the end I got it out of her. Seems she went downstairs with William the night he was struck down. They were in the front parlour for a bit, talking about me. When she came back from letting him out she took notice that my mackintosh was gone from the hall stand. I'd got it on when I had my accident, so it went to the hospital and come on with me to Selby Street. It was torn, but not too bad, and Abby mended it up and hung it in the hall against my wanting it. Well, it passed in her mind that Emily might have slipped it on to go to the post, which she shouldn't have done, and Abby says she'd made up her mind to tell her as much. She went on up, and no Emily Salt. Presently she hears the front door and she goes down. There's my mackintosh back on the hall stand wringing damp, and Emily half way down the kitchen stairs. Abby says, 'Where have you been?' and she says, 'To the post.' Abby was going to mention the mackintosh, but that Emily didn't wait, she was off into the scullery and the tap running. Said she wanted a drink. Cold tap-water after going to the post on a January night! Well, Abby said no more, but there was something she thought about afterwards when it come out about William being struck down." He paused.

Miss Silver said, "Yes, Mr. Tattlecombe?"

He wagged his head in an emphatic manner.

"When she went down to see to the kitchen fire she missed the poker. It's a little short one she keeps handy at the side of the range. Well, it wasn't there, and she didn't stop to look for it, but come next morning she found it in the scullery."

There was a pause, followed by one pregnant word.

"Rusty," said Mr. Tattlecombe.

CHAPTER 31

"And where do we go from here?" said William.

It was Sunday morning, and they had finished breakfast. The day lay before them. It came to Katharine with a tremendous sense of relief that it wasn't for her to say what the next step was to be. She had done it all these weeks, but she didn't have to do it any more. It was very restful. She said,

"That is for you to say."

He pushed back his chair.

"Well, I don't know that there's much choice, really. I think we'd better go over and see Cyril. Has he still got Evendon?"

"Yes, but I don't know that he'll be there."

"He always used to go down there for the weekends—liked gloating over his collections. But of course you said Maud was dead—"

She nodded.

"Five years ago."

"And Sylvia's married. Doesn't he go down there now?"

"Oh, yes, I think so." She hesitated, and then said in a reluctant voice, "I think there's something going on with Mavis Jones."

He gave a whistle.

"I thought it was Brett!"

"So did I, but I think that's back history. I daresay I'm wrong about Cyril, but—well, you know how it is, if she's in the room he's got a sort of way of looking at her before

195

he answers, and I've thought she was being a bit proprie-
tary."

He whistled again.

"Poor old Cyril! He's rather a defenceless sort of chap—
not much good at saying no. And Mavis—Katharine, she
must have known me."

"Do you suppose she—told anyone?"

"I don't know."

"Cyril—or Brett?"

"I don't know, William."

He got up, walked to the window, looked out at the grey
sky, the grey street, and turned, frowning deeply.

"I don't think so—not Cyril—not either of them. Why
should she? If she was trying to kid herself it was just a likeness she wouldn't. You know, it's quite extraordinary how
convinced people can get themselves over something if they
don't want it to be true. She may have done that, or—" He
stopped short.

"Or what?"

He said, "Davies—Mr. Tattlecombe—me. If she made up
her mind to do anything about it she wouldn't tell Cyril or
Brett." Then quite suddenly he laughed. "That's rubbish—
it must be. Where's the motive? Besides, people don't do
things like that. It must be nonsense. I tell you what, you
ring up Evendon and find out if Cyril is there. If he is, say
you'd like to run over. Don't say anything about me. If he's
not there, find out where he is. He might be with Sylvia."

"I shouldn't think he would be. They aren't settled."

He came over and pulled her up.

"Well, come along and telephone! We can't do anything
until we know where he is."

It was the butler who answered, elderly, polite, and suave.
Mr. Eversley was at home but he had stepped out.

Katharine heard the news with relief. She said,

"It's Mrs. William Eversley, Soames. Will you tell Mr. Eversley when he comes in that I am very particularly anxious to see him, and that I am driving over. I'm speaking from the Cedar House, and I should be over in about an hour and a half. Will you tell him that?"

"Certainly, madam."

"I suppose Mr. Brett isn't there?"

"No, madam."

Katharine said, "Thank you," and rang off.

She turned round. William had his hands in his pockets. The thought went through her mind—"No one who knew him when he was a boy could possibly think he was anyone else."

He said, "Soames still there? Think he'll stand up to the shock of seeing me?"

She came to him then, slipping her hand inside his arm.

"You don't think we ought to break it to them first?"

She got a grave, steady look.

"No, I don't. I think we'll administer the shock."

It was about half an hour later that Sylvia rang up. Her voice was as pretty as herself, but it sounded distracted, as who should say, "Enter Tilburina, mad in white satin." If, however, she was mad at this moment, it was in the American sense.

"Is that Katharine? Soames says you rang up from the Cedar House."

"Right both times, darling."

"I'm not at Evendon. I wouldn't go. Jocko and I are at Huntinglea with his people. Soames rang up and said you were coming to lunch, and what about us. Of course Daddy put him up to it, and I just want to know if he was speaking the truth. Are you really going to be there for lunch? Or is it just a trap to get us there?"

Katharine felt a little bewildered.

"Well, I don't know about lunch. The fact is, something's happened, and I'm going over to see Cyril about it. After that—well, it just depends."

Sylvia sounded more distracted than ever.

"Then you've heard! Isn't it *grim*? Daddy wanted us to come over for the week-end and meet her, but I put my foot down flat."

"Sylvia, I don't think we're talking about the same thing—it doesn't make sense. Who did Cyril want you to go and meet?"

An angry sob came back along the line.

"That foul Jones woman—he's married her!"

Katharine said, *"No!"* on a quick in-drawn breath.

Twenty-five miles away Sylvia stamped her foot.

"Well, he has! He rang up last night to say so. He was so nervous he could hardly get it out, and I don't wonder. I kept saying *"No!"* just like you did, and he went on saying it over and over again. And then he wanted Jocko and me to come for the weekend, and I said, 'I won't'—just like that, and slammed down the receiver. So now he's got Soames to ring up and lure us by saying you're coming to lunch, and I thought I'd just find out if you really were. Because it might be Daddy gone all foxy, or it might be Soames trying to boil up a reconciliation—he's frightfully family-retainer, you know. So what about it? Jocko says what's the good of quarrelling with your father, even if he has married his secretary? And his father and mother say the same. You know how they are—all for peace and quiet life. And of course they're marvellous in-laws. But I'm not confronting that Jones woman alone. Jocko doesn't count. I want a fellow female at my back, so you've just got to be there, or I won't stay. Au revoir, *angel*—but if you're not there, it'll be *devil*, and I'll never speak to you again!"

By the time the conversation was over William had practically made himself a part of it by coming up close and propping his chin on Katharine's shoulder so as to get his ear next to the receiver. When she hung up his eyes were laughing. He said,

"Whatever else has changed, Sylvia hasn't. Jocko used to be a nice lad. What's he turned out like?"

"Pretty good, I think. They're blissfully happy. Did you hear what she said?"

"Most of it—something about Cyril and Miss Jones."

"William, he's married her!"

He whistled.

"Gosh! Well, I suppose he bought it."

Katharine felt a light shiver go over her, she didn't quite know why. Cyril and Mavis Jones—married—now! Why? Or wasn't there any reason? What reason could there be?

William said quickly, "Don't look like that—I won't have it!" He pulled her up close and kissed her. "I won't have it, I tell you—not for fifty thousand Cyrils and a million Mavis Joneses!"

She had to laugh then.

"Darling, what a perfectly appalling prospect!"

CHAPTER 32

Evendon had been a wedding present to Cyril Eversley from his father-in-law, the late Alfred Sherringham Upjohn, who, having accumulated a preposterous fortune, had decided that his daughter and sole heiress would be better off without most of it. He gave her husband what he described as a gentleman's landed estate, put a comfortable sum in trust for Sylvia, and spent the afternoon of his days erecting alms-houses for the old, and nurseries for the very young. As he had always been perfectly sure that whatever he did was right, it never occurred to him to doubt the wisdom of this proceeding, his only regret being that the war interfered with his building schemes. He was killed by a direct hit from a flying bomb early in '45, but his trustees were now able to continue the work he had planned. Mavis Jones' opinion was that he should have been declared insane and placed under restraint, but she had learned not to express this view to Cyril.

As William and Katharine drove in at the entrance gate and followed a winding drive, the trees were leafless overhead, their winter brown and grey broken here and there by clumps of evergreen or the shining mass of holly, berries still clinging to it here and there. The house, placed upon rising ground and set off by terraces, was modern—not too big to be run with a diminished staff, and planned for comfort.

Waiting for Soames to answer the door, Katharine would rather have been anywhere else. She was afraid, and part of her fear was for Cyril Eversley. That Mavis had recognized

William, she was sure. That she had told Cyril—was that sure, or wasn't it? Could Cyril know that William was alive and do nothing about it? Someone who knew William was alive had tried to do something about it—to Mr. Davies—to Mr. Tattlecombe—to William—and to William's car. It couldn't be Cyril. She had known him all her life. He wasn't cruel, or ruthless, or hard. He was a drifter—vague and dreamy. It couldn't be Cyril. The line of least resistance, yes. A desperate cutting of the Gordian knot, no.

The door swung in. Soames stood there waiting, all his manner gone. He said, "Mr. William!" in a gasping voice. His mouth opened and shut like a fish. He choked and said it again—"Mr. William!"

William clapped him on the shoulder.

"Hold up, Soames—I'm real. Look here, you'd better sit down for a minute. Where's Mr. Cyril?"

Soames stood by the chair to which he had been led, holding on to it, getting back his breath. He said,

"The study—" And then, "I'm all right, Mr. William. It was just—the shock—as you might say—"

William pushed him down on to the chair.

"You stay put. We'll go and find him."

But Soames was pulling himself up again. He put out his hand to Katharine, and she took it.

"If I may say, madam, how pleased—how very pleased I am—"

Cyril Eversley was in the study alone. As far as it was possible to retreat from the complications of this week-end, he had retreated. Whether you study in it or not, any room with that name is from time immemorial the private property of the man of the house, to which women are only admitted on sufferance. When, in addition to its private character, the man has surrounded himself with the Sunday papers, the

201

"Keep out" sign could hardly be more patently displayed. Cyril was not, however, at all sanguine. Mavis had been free of his private office for too long to consider that the hint could apply to her, and as to Sylvia—when had he ever wished to keep her out? She would come, and she would make a scene. Mavis had made one already. One—if it had stopped at that! The word could really only be used if today's scene was considered to be a prolongation of yesterday's.

He held up the *Sunday Times*, but he didn't read it. It gave him a very slight feeling of protection against somebody bursting in. Yesterday's scene had been about giving out their marriage. After saying that there was no hurry, Mavis had suddenly insisted on accompanying him to Evendon as his wife. He had had to announce his marriage to Soames. He had had to ring Sylvia up and break it to her. He hadn't wanted to do either of these things. The interview with Soames had left a decided chill upon the air. His telephone conversation with Sylvia had been quite disintegrating. This morning's scene with Mavis—if you were going to separate it from yesterday's scene—had had Sylvia's reception of the news as its theme-song. Why in heaven's name must women be so dramatic? The last thing he wanted was any fuss. Scenes made him feel positively unwell, and there were going to be more of them. Sylvia and Jocko were coming to lunch. Katharine was coming over—

A very faint gleam of light illumined the mental scene. Katharine mightn't like the idea of his marriage, but she wouldn't make a scene, and it was, not probable, just barely possible, that she might have a calming effect upon Sylvia.

He heard the door open, looked apprehensively over the top of the paper, and saw Katharine—transformed. He could not have analysed the impression she made on him. There was a glow, a bloom, a brightness. The paper dropped, and as he rose to his feet and she stretched out her hands to him and said, "Oh, Cyril, something wonderful's happened!" William came into the room behind her and shut the door. It all happened in just that moment, the rush and glow of emotion and William, and for the moment the whole unbelievable scene was believable and real. It was as if Katharine had created the kind of illusion which is created on the stage, where an imagined drama moves its audience to laughter or to tears.

Cyril Eversley found himself with a hand on William's shoulder and a voice that stammered his name. And then, before there was time for anything more, Mavis walked into the room. Whether she had encountered Soames and was prepared, or whether she had just walked in upon the situation, she maintained an extraordinary appearance of calm. She came to Cyril without hurry, allowed her glance to pass indifferently over Katharine, and to rest with a shade of hauteur upon William. Cyril's hand dropped, he stepped back. She said,

"Mr. William Smith, I think."

William smiled his usual pleasant smile.

"I don't think you do, Miss Jones."

"I am Mrs. Eversley." She turned to Cyril. "What is this man doing here?"

Cyril put a hand to his head. The moment was over. You didn't stay in the clouds, you came spinning down to earth with a crash.

He said, "It's William," and felt her hand close hard upon his arm.

"My dear Cyril, pull yourself together! This is Mr. William Smith, an assistant in a shop called Tattlecombe's Toy Bazaar. He came to see me about the manufacture of some toys for which he has taken out a patent. That must have been about six or seven weeks ago. Naturally I was struck, as you are, by a certain superficial likeness to your cousin William, but—"

Cyril pulled away.

"You saw him? Why didn't you tell me?"

"I didn't think the toys would interest you, and I thought you might find the likeness—upsetting."

William gave a short laugh.

"I'm sorry to contradict a lady, but it isn't a likeness. I'm William Eversley."

"Then why didn't you say so?"

"Because I didn't know. I'd had a bang on the head and I couldn't remember anything before '42. I'm sorry if I'm inconvenient, Cyril old chap, but it's me."

Mavis stared at him. Those fine eyes of hers could sustain a very long, cold stare.

"This story would have been a good deal more convincing if you had produced it before Mrs. William Eversley had been given the opportunity of coaching you for six or seven weeks."

Katharine's colour flamed. William said, "You're talking about my wife," and Mavis laughed.

"Nobody is disputing that, Mr. Smith. I'm sorry I didn't give her her right name just now. After knowing her so long as Mrs. William Eversley it's quite natural, I'm sure. But she's been Mrs. William Smith for just over a week now, hasn't she?" She swung round on Cyril with a sort of fierce triumph. "They were married yesterday week at St. James', Rasselas Square, just round the corner from where she's been living in Rasselas Mews. She married him as William Smith, and that's what he is. She saw the likeness the same as I saw it, and she saw how she could make use of it. She's had seven weeks to coach him, and a week's honeymoon to dot the i's

204

and cross the t's, with a brand-new husband all ready to walk into the firm and take William Eversley's place."

With every word she jarred Cyril's taste more painfully, but if one sense was outraged, another reinforced it. An aghast sense of self-preservation beheld the possible abyss and recoiled. Between the two, his by no means robust initiative was paralysed.

At this moment there came the sound of running feet. The door was flung open and Sylvia rushed into the room. It was rather like seeing a young colt rush a fence. She was all long limbs, uncontrolled but pliant with youth and grace. Her hair, her colouring, her eyes, were all as bright as a spring day. Her dark young husband followed her with a slightly abashed air. Sylvia took one look, uttered an ecstatic scream, and flung herself on William's neck.

"Sylly!"

"Billy!"

They hugged each other over the old nursery joke. With the tears running down her face and one arm still round William, Sylvia reached for Katharine and hugged her too.

"Angel darling lambs—when did it happen—why didn't you tell us? Jocko, it's William! He's come back—he's alive!" She let go suddenly and ran to Cyril. "Daddy, what's the matter? Why aren't you waving flags? It's William! It's my own blessed darling William! What's the matter with you?"

It would really have been better if Mavis had restrained herself, but she was quite unable to do so. She smiled in a superior manner and said,

"I am afraid you are making rather an embarrassing mistake, Sylvia. This is Katharine's new husband, Mr. Smith."

Sylvia had both hands clutching at her father's arm. She clutched as hard as she could and said,

"And who told you you could call her Katharine? If you

ask me, it's a piece of damned cheek! And if you start coming the stepmother over me you'll be sorry for it, so you'd better watch it! And if anyone says this isn't William—"

William came up quietly and put a hand on her shoulder. "Dry up, Sylvia!" He turned to Cyril. "Don't you think this is a bit of a crowd? I suggest that everyone goes away and leaves us to it. I lost my memory, but I've got it back again. It came back quite suddenly in the night. I don't think you've really got any doubts, but if you have, I don't think I shall have any difficulty in clearing them out of the way. This is all a bit emotional, don't you think? Katharine, suppose you take Sylvia away. And perhaps"—he paused—"your wife would leave us too."

Sylvia moved, flung her arms round his neck again, murmured, ran to Katharine, and went out with her, pulling Jocko by the sleeve.

Mavis said, "No!" And then, "Cyril, don't be a fool! You haven't got anything to say to this man, and you don't want to listen to him either. You want to see your solicitor."

Cyril looked at her, and looked away. Then he looked at William. There was something of wretchedness in the look, something of defeat.

William said, "Don't be an ass, Cyril! You don't want to drag a solicitor into this, do you? If your wife won't leave us, what about coming for a drive in my car? We'll really do better by ourselves, you know."

Cyril passed a hand over his brow. There was sweat on it. He said,

"You'd better go, Mavis."

It was he who got the cold stare this time. It carried an icy, dominant anger.

"And leave him to talk you round—to talk you into the sort of admissions you'll be ready to kick yourself for when you see a solicitor and he tells you just what a fool you've been! I'm not going! And you're not going a step without me!"

William said quietly, "Very well then—Katharine and I will go. But you had better think what you are doing. Cyril doesn't even pretend that he hasn't recognized me. It's very inconvenient of me, I know, but I've come back and I've got to be reckoned with. Well, it's up to you what sort of reckoning it's going to be. There will be things to be settled up. We can make a family matter of it and fix things in a friendly way as between cousins, or you can call in your solicitor, and I can call in mine, and we can make a business matter of it as between partners. Brett will have to take sides with one of us, there'll be some sort of a dog-fight, and it will all be very bad for business. If you want to have it that way you can. What you'd better understand here and now is that you can't have it both ways. You'll have to make up your mind, Cyril. You can't start the dog-fight and then call it off and switch over to a friendly arrangement. You know, you'd really very much better have a talk with me now."

Mavis turned her anger on him.

"He's not having any talks with you, Mr. Smith, and you needn't think he is!"

William said in his most matter-of-fact voice,

"Oh, don't be silly. He knows perfectly well who I am, and so do you. Come on, Cyril, speak for yourself—do you recognize me, or don't you?"

This time there was appeal as well as defeat in Cyril's look. He put out a wavering hand to William and said,

"Send her away."

CHAPTER 33

"And if she could have killed me then and there she'd have done it," said William cheerfully.

They were driving back to the Cedar House through the early afternoon—mild, grey weather, and everything very peaceful.

"Where do you suppose she's gone?" said Katharine.

"Back to town to beat up Brett, I should think. She just pushed herself into a fur coat, new and quite expensive, and a small car, ditto. I suppose she's got rooms or something?"

"A flat. Rather a nice one, I believe. I should think Cyril's been paying the rent." She laughed and said, "That's gossip."

"Whose?"

"Brett's."

William looked straight in front of him, frowning.

"How does she stand with Brett these days?"

"I don't know."

"You don't think she told him she'd seen me? I didn't think so myself, but—well, I don't know."

Katharine said quickly, "Oh, no, she couldn't have."

"Why?"

"Because he went on asking me to marry him." She laughed a little. "You needn't worry, darling—he isn't in love with me, and never has been. I think he just thought I'd do nicely to settle down with."

"You say he went on asking you. Do you mean after Mavis saw me?"

"Oh, yes. He wrote to me just after that, and he rang me up—well, actually it was the night before we were married. I don't know how he found out where I was. So, you see, Mavis couldn't have told him about seeing you."

William fell into a dead silence for the best part of a mile. Then he said,

"I think the business is in a pretty fair mess. Cyril has obviously got the wind up, and Mavis was uncommon anxious to make him hold his tongue. I didn't press him—I thought we'd better get the family reunion part of it over first. But he had a bit of a breakdown and said one or two rather odd things."

"What sort of things?"

"Well, I should think there's been some funny business about your money, because he blattered out something about Brett wanting to marry you and that would have made it all right, and then something about Mavis saying so. It was all muddled up, you know, because the poor chap rather went to pieces, but I got the impression that Mavis had been pretty keen on the idea of Brett putting things square by marrying you."

Katharine's colour brightened dangerously.

"Kind of him, and of her, but I kept on saying no."

William didn't take any notice of that.

"The thing is, I got the idea that Mavis had gone on being keen right up to the present moment. Cyril rather put it forward to show that she couldn't have recognized me when I went to see her in December, because if she had she wouldn't have been pressing Brett to marry you."

She made a quick angry sound.

"William, I shall scream if you go on talking as if I was something on a bargain-basement counter waiting to be picked up!"

He gave a fleeting grin, put out a hand and patted her, and was sober again.

"She certainly did recognize me, but she must have known that I didn't recognize her. Well, she had my address. She'd make enquiries, and she'd hear all about William Smith having lost his memory. I wonder if she came along on the night of December the seventh and pushed Mr. Tattlecombe under that car—not as Mr. Tattlecombe of course, but thinking it was me. You see, she didn't know what he looked like, or anything about him. She may just have been meaning to give the layout a once-over. Or she may have had some kind of a plan for getting me to come out. And then the door opens and someone does come out—right size, hair looking the right colour with the light shining from behind—" He paused and added cheerfully, "I wonder how long it was before she found out that she hadn't bumped me off."

Katharine didn't say anything at all. William went on again.

"It's all theory of course, but it might quite easily have been that way. I'm practically sure there's been some funny business with the accounts. Well, my coming back would mean a show-down. It must have been an awful shock when I walked in on William Smith's appointment. I'll say this for the Jones, she didn't bat an eyelid. But the position would be fairly grim. First line of defence my loss of memory. No depending on it. Anyone might recognize me, and once you start bumping into people you're apt to go on. If Brett could get you to marry him, that would be a second line. They'd reckon on my not wanting to make things difficult for you, and if I happened to meet with an accident, there wouldn't ever be any question about the marriage."

"William, I said I'd scream, and I will. I wouldn't have married Brett *ever!*"

"But they weren't to know that," said William reasonably. "He's always been considered a very fascinating chap."

At about this time Miss Silver was entering the cold, hygienic precincts of St. Luke's Hospital in company with Sergeant Abbott, who had invited her over the telephone in the following terms.

"The Chief says I can take you along if you don't mind being a friend of the deceased."

After rather passing from hand to hand, they found themselves in the brisk and businesslike presence of the Sister to whose ward Mr. Davies had been carried on the night of his accident. To her was presently added a couple of student nurses, one of whom had been on day and the other on night duty during the few hours that elapsed before he died. All three concurred in saying that Mr. Davies had uttered nothing more intelligible than a groan.

Frank Abbott got to his feet. The prettier of the two nurses looked at him admiringly. He said,

"Well, thank you very much, Sister."

Miss Silver coughed.

"What about the patients on either side of him in the ward?"

The Sister's gracious smile of dismissal chilled off.

"I am afraid they would not be of any help to you. You see, the screens were round his bed, and as you have heard, he was unconscious."

"Perhaps if you will be so good as to let me have their names and addresses, just for my own satisfaction—"

"Oh, certainly, but I am afraid—the man on the right died on the following day. Yates, on the other side, is still with us. As a matter of fact he goes out tomorrow. He had rather a severe relapse."

Miss Silver looked at Sergeant Abbott in a pointed manner, and he obliged.

"Perhaps if we could just see this man Yates—"

They found Mr. Yates, a friendly talkative Cockney, quite disposed for company. They were presently left with him, and after a few preliminaries he was asked whether he remembered an accident case in the next bed on December 7th.

"Acourse I do. It's me leg that's been bad, not me 'ead. Only in for a few hours, poor bloke. Old gentleman like 'im hadn't got no business dodging around in front of cars after dark—see? The h'eye isn't quick enough—see? You get flummoxed and down you go. Pity."

"Did he say anything at all?"

"The screens was round his bed," said Mr. Yates. "Always know a bloke's going to pop off when they puts the screens round him. Started doing it to me once, but I soon put 'em to rights. It was that little red-headed nurse—pretty gal. And I says to her, 'You put those screens round me, and I'll knock 'em over—see?' She says, 'Oh, Yates!' and I says, 'Don't you Oh Yates me! There wasn't no one to put screens round when I was born. Eight in a room we was, and if I'm agoing to die I can do it just as well in a crowd as being born—see? Only I ain't agoing to die, and you can go and tell Sister so with my love.' So she says, 'Oh, Yates!' again and goes for Sister. But I never 'ad no screens."

Miss Silver leaned forward.

"A very commendable spirit," she said. "Mr. Yates, are you quite sure that poor Mr. Davies didn't say anything?"

Yates put his head on one side. He had a little puckered monkey face. His eyes were dancing bright.

"Well, there wasn't nothing you could call a message, if that's what you're looking for."

Miss Silver inclined her head graciously.

212

"Just anything you heard him say, Mr. Yates—even if it was only a word or two."

"Well, it wasn't nothing really. I shouldn't 'ave heard it only my leg was bad and I couldn't seem to get off. There was a bloke down at the far end of the ward playing up, and Nurse trying to settle 'im, when I heard the old bloke behind the screens call out. Not loud—see? 'Joan,' he said—leastways that's what it sounded like."

"Joan, or Jones?" said Miss Silver.

"I dunno—might 'ave been either—you pays your money and you takes your choice. If 'e'd got anyone belonging to 'im name of Joan, then you can take it it was Joan. And if 'e'd got anyone belonging to 'im name of Jones, then you can take it it was Jones. It might just as well 'ave been one as the other. So if it's going to be any comfort to anyone, you'd better make up your mind which way you want it to be and stick to it—see?"

Miss Silver coughed.

"What else did he say?"

Mr. Yates nodded brightly.

"Said she didn't believe 'im—jus' like that, 'She didn't be-lieve me.' " He puckered up the whole of one side of his face in a monkey grin. "Coo, lumme, I could 'ave told 'im that! Waste of time thinking up lies to tell 'em. 'Orrid unbelieving minds women's got. So I says, 'Never mind, chum,' I says, 'you just take it easy.' And 'e says, 'She pushed me.' 'She didn't ought to have done that, chum,' I says, and 'e gives a kind of groan and starts muttering. And bimeby 'e stops and I can't 'ear nothing, so when Nurse comes along I tells 'er. 'I think 'e's gone,' I says, and so 'e was."

Frank Abbott said, "Did you tell anyone he'd spoken to you?"

Mr. Yates shook his head.

"Nobody arst me. And next day I'ad my h'operation, and after that I was crool bad."

Emerging upon the street, Frank Abbott said,

"It's about as much good as a sick head ache so far as evidence goes, but I suppose one might describe it as local colour."

Miss Silver coughed.

"I should not advise your describing it in that manner to Chief Detective Inspector Lamb."

CHAPTER 34

William and Katharine came back to Rasselas Mews on the Sunday night. Katharine could hardly believe that they had been away for something less than thirty-six hours. So much, so very much, had happened in that short, strange space of time. She was Katharine Eversley again, for one thing. There was a strangeness in that. To come back to the name of her girlhood, to the name of the bride of the last year before the war, and the name which she had borne through the bitter years of widowhood, and to come back to it with the bitterness all gone and happiness flooding in—this in itself made day before yesterday seem like something which had been left behind a long time ago.

There was a parcel on the doorstep at the top of the flight of twelve steps which led to the front door. William stubbed his toe against it in the dark. They took it into the sitting-room and found a cardboard box wrapped in brown paper. When the paper was removed a two-pound jar appeared. It was labelled Apple Honey, and it had a scrap of paper tied round the neck on which was written in an upright, old-fashioned hand, "With kind regards—Abigail Salt."

Katharine said, "How frightfully good of her. It's the same as she gave us for tea when we went there, and we said how nice it was. We'll have some tomorrow."

William said, "All right. I say, it's twelve o'clock. Get off to bed! I'll just put the car away. A bit of luck, there being room for it here. I should hate to have to trail back from Ellery Street."

Katharine put the apple honey away.

They had decided that they must go to business as usual on Monday morning. With Brett an uncertain quantity, seven years' arrears of business waiting, and a visit to his solicitor imperative since whether actually alive or not, he was legally dead, William could still feel and say that Mr. Tattlecombe must come first.

"There's a very nice chap, a friend of Ernie's—I've been wanting to get hold of him for some time. He's a good salesman, and I think he'd suit Mr. Tattlecombe down to the ground. The business he's in has just changed hands, and I don't think he cares about the new people. If I could bring the old man round to thinking what an acquisition he'd be, it would soften the blow a bit—I'm afraid it is going to be a blow. Well, that'll just about take up the morning. Then, I think, we'll get the rest of the day off. I'll have to get the legal side going. Is Mr. Hall still in the firm?"

"Oh, yes."

"Then that ought to make it all quite easy. You can ring up from the shop and make an appointment, and we'll go along together. Then there's Brett—I suppose someone will have broken it to him by then."

215

"Mavis might—"

"Cyril's bound to have done something about it, I expect. They'll both be at the office."

"William—there's Miss Silver—"

"Well, you can ring her up now before we start. She lives at the address you've got, doesn't she—it's not just an office?"

They were having breakfast. There was a pleasant smell of coffee and bacon. Katharine began to get up, but was pulled back again.

"Not a step till you've finished what's on your plate! Cold bacon is about the nastiest food on earth. Five minutes isn't going to make any difference to Miss Silver."

The bacon finished and the coffee drunk, 15 Montague Mansions was rung up. Miss Silver expressed herself as highly gratified at the return of Mr. William Eversley's memory.

"It should certainly simplify matters. And you say Mr. Cyril Eversley and his daughter have recognized him? That is all to the good."

Katharine said, "Miss Silver—"

"Yes, my dear?"

"Miss Silver, Cyril's secretary—that Miss Jones who saw William when he called on the firm in December—he's married her."

Miss Silver said, "Dear me!"

"I suppose I ought to have seen it coming, but I didn't think he'd be such a fool."

Miss Silver coughed.

"It is never safe to rely on that with a gentleman—especially in the case of a secretary. They are so much thrown together, and he had probably come to depend on her."

"Oh, she'd got him completely under her thumb—you

216

could see that. But she couldn't quite manage to make him say he didn't recognize William, so she lost her temper and flung off to town in her new car—a wedding present, I suppose."

There was a little more talk. Miss Silver said,

"I would like to see you both. Would some time today be possible?"

Katharine hesitated, half looked over her shoulder at William who shook his head, and turned back again.

"I don't know—I'm afraid not. We've got to see Mr. Tattlecombe and our solicitor—and William will have to see his cousins. Perhaps I—"

Miss Silver said firmly, "I think it is important that I should see Mr. William Eversley."

"I don't know—perhaps this evening—" She looked round again, caught William's nod, and went on. "About half past eight, unless anything unforeseen turns up—is that all right? . . . Goodbye, and thank you very much."

William had a teasing look.

"What did you mean by something unforeseen turning up?"

All at once Katharine wished she hadn't said it. It came echoing back on her like sound out of a dark cave. She didn't like it. She was quite pale as she said,

"I don't know."

William said cheerfully, "We must take care not to get run over," and she didn't like that either. Then he kissed her and said they were going to be late if they didn't hurry.

CHAPTER 35

Mr. Tattlecombe took it hard. After saying that it was a Blow but that he supposed it was the Lord's will, he ran both hands through his hair, fixed round blue eyes upon William and Katharine, and observed that it didn't matter, because he was past the three score years and ten already and it wouldn't be for long. From there to a lonely deathbed, with no one to close his eyes or so much as put up a stone, was an easy short cut.

At just what point in the proceedings it occurred to Katharine that he was enjoying himself, she didn't quite know, but she found herself holding his hand and saying, "Dear Mr. Tattlecombe, please don't talk like that or I shall cry."

Abel was distinctly gratified. He sat there as pink and healthy as a baby with his grey hair all fuzzed up and said there was no call to drop a tear, because we must all come to it and there would be nobody left to grieve.

William said firmly, "That's not quite fair, Mr. Tattlecombe. There's Mrs. Salt, and there's me, and Mrs. Bastable, and Miss Cole, and Katharine—you know very well we'd all grieve. And now I'd like you to listen to what I've been thinking. There's that friend of Ernie's, Jim Willis—" He proceeded to put forward his plan whilst Abel looked blankly over the top of his head.

When he had finished what he had in mind to say, there was one of those silences. It had prolonged itself to a really dreadful extent before Mr. Tattlecombe broke it with a heavy sigh.

"Very kind of you, William, and I've no doubt he's a steady, good-living young man—Ernie always did have the right sort of friends—but there'll be no need for an assistant in the grave."

"I wasn't talking about the grave, I was talking about the shop, and you're going to need an assistant there. I don't want you to think I'm going to give up my interest or just walk out and leave you, because I wouldn't think of it. But you must see for yourself that there'll be a good deal of business to attend to with Eversleys', and that I'll have to attend to it personally. Now my idea would be to get Jim to come in as soon as he can so that I can put him in the way of things."

By the time they left him the gloom had to some slight extent lifted. There were fewer references to the tomb and to Abel's rather gloomy estimate as to the appropriate age for retirement to it. There were even some gleams of interest in Jim Willis, and an early recollection or two of his coming about the house with Ernie. In fact the worst was over.

Just before they went away Katharine said how kind it was of Mrs. Salt to send them a pot of her apple honey.

Abel nodded.

"She said she was going to. My cousin Sarah Hill sends it to her. I've got a pot or two myself. Sarah won't let on how it's made, but she lets us have some every year. Abby said something about bringing a pot round here for you tomorrow. That Emily's all right again, and she's coming to have tea with me. She said she'd bring it along then and leave it for you. You'll like it."

Katharine said, "It's lovely. We had some when we went

to tea with her. But we've had our pot already—we found it waiting for us when we got back to the flat last night. I was going to ring Mrs. Salt up and thank her, but William said she would rather have a letter, so I'm going to write to her as soon as we get home. It was very kind."

Abel wagged his head.

"She must have taken it round herself," he said. "But Sunday evening she'd have been in chapel—never misses, wet or dry—" He paused, and then added, "William's right about the telephone. It took a long time before she'd have it put in, and she wouldn't have done it then if I hadn't put it to her that one or other of us might be took suddenly, and no chance of a last word if it wasn't for being able to call up and say so."

It was half past twelve before William parked his car in the yard at Eversleys' and walked round the building to the front door. The factory stood on the outer edge of the London fringe. It did not seem to have suffered any bomb damage, but even from the outside it had rather a going-down-hill appearance. His previous visit had been paid after dark. He took time now to look about him. The neighbourhood had changed a good deal. The big electrical works opposite was new. Marsdens', which had towered up a couple of hundred yards away, was gone—the site cleared, new foundations rising. Looked as if there had been a direct hit there.

When he had had a look round he went inside. This time he wasn't going to be put off with seeing Miss Jones. He went up the stairs and into the outer office. A girl looked up from her typing, and he asked,

"Is Mr. Cyril Eversley in?"

She said, "No."

"Mr. Brett?"

"Yes."

William said, "Then I'll just go through and see him. You needn't announce me."

He left her fluttering behind him and went out of the other door and along the passage. Brett's room used to be at the end. He wondered if he had changed it.

Apparently not. There was his name on the door, like everything else a good deal the worse for wear. He turned the handle and went in. This time there wasn't going to be any surprise. Cyril would have been on the telephone—possibly Mavis too, but certainly Cyril. The only question was how Brett was going to take it. There was just a moment after he got inside the door, and then it was,

"William—my dear chap!" and his hand was being wrung.

Well, that was that, and a considerable relief. He looked at Brett, and found him a little heavier, a little older, but essentially the same. In fact after the first moment it was difficult to see any change at all. The warmth, the charm, were paramount.

"My dear chap, I never was so pleased in my life! Cyril got me on the telephone an hour ago—said he'd been trying to get hold of me ever since you turned up yesterday. Well—" he laughed with a sound of real enjoyment—"I was week-ending, and one doesn't hurry back on a Monday morning—at least I don't. There isn't all that much business to attend to. I wish there were. I'm afraid things aren't quite what they were when you went away."

William said, "So I gathered from Cyril."

Brett's eyebrows rose. The dark eyes under them took on a rueful, laughing expression.

"We got through the war, but that's about all you can say." The laughter flickered out. "Look here, William, it's no good making any bones about it, we're in the devil of a mess."

There was a pause before William said,

"What sort of a mess, Brett?"

Brett Eversley looked him straight in the face and said, "Katharine's money's gone."

Katharine, waiting in the flat, picked up the telephone receiver and heard William's voice sounding rather faint and far away.

"That you, Kath?"

She said, "Yes."

"Look here, darling, I can't possibly get back to lunch. We're up to the eyes in business . . . Yes, Brett's here. I'm speaking from his office. We're going into things together. Cyril's still at Evendon. About that appointment with Mr. Hall—I can't keep it. Brett rang through and caught him before he went out to lunch, so he knows I'm back, and I'll be seeing him tomorrow."

"When will you be home?"

"I'll try and make it by five—but don't wait tea."

She said, "Of course I will. We'll have apple honey."

She hung up and went back to the table, which was set for lunch. There was a savoury stew in a casserole keeping hot in the kitchen, but the cold shape was at the far end, and a little cut glass dish of Abigail Salt's apple honey. Katharine picked it up and put it away in the glass-fronted cupboard. She wasn't going to start on it without William. She took out the remains of a pot of raspberry jam instead. Then she went to the kitchen to fetch the casserole.

It was well after five before William came home. He looked at the tea-table drawn up in front of the fire, at the whole warm glow of the room, and at Katharine. Then he kissed her. She said,

"How did you get on, darling?"

"It's the real devil of a mess, Kath."

She said, "Well, don't bother about it now. Have your tea."

He kept his arm about. her.

"Presently." Then after a moment, "You know, I think Brett is really glad I'm back."

"Was he—nice?"

William gave a sort of half laugh.

"Perfectly charming. Brett's got a brain if he'd use it. Cyril hasn't—at least not the kind that's any good to himself or anyone else. And I don't mean that unkindly either. What I do mean is that Brett has got brains enough to see that it would have to be one thing or the other. I'd either got to be William Smith who was trying it on, or he'd got to get busy with the fatted calf and all the trimmings—that was obvious. And he wouldn't want more than one look at me to see that the William Smith idea wouldn't wash, so he did the thing handsomely. And of course it was very good business, because they've got themselves well on to the wrong side of the law, and Brett doesn't want to go to prison."

Katharine said, "Oh—"

"Your money's gone, Kath."

She said "Oh—" again.

"It was the old game. They took a bit to pull the firm round, and then took more to bolster it up. They'd got to the point where they'd have been ruined if you married. Brett skated away from that, but of course it's why he was trying to marry you."

Katharine's lip quivered.

"There couldn't be any other reason, could there, darling?"

"Well, you said yourself he wasn't in love with you," said William reasonably. "Thank goodness! There are quite enough complications without that. What I really set out to say was that I think Brett would have put up a pretty good show of being glad to see me whether he was or not, because he's got brains enough to know which side his bread is buttered. But I've got a hunch that he really was glad to see me. I don't think he could put on an act that would take me in."

Katharine nodded. William always could see through people. He seemed so simple and easy, and in a way he was, but he saw through most brick walls. She said,

"What are you going to do about them—about Brett and Cyril?"

"Oh, Cyril can retire. Evendon, if it'll run to it. He's no use to the firm. Brett—" he grinned suddenly—"Brett can turn on the famous charm and go out and get us orders for the Wurzel toys. I'm going large on them, and I think they'll pull us out of the mess. Gosh, I'm hungry! We had a sandwich lunch. Make the tea while I go and get washed."

He came back to find Katharine standing at the table with the teapot in her hand. But she wasn't looking at it, she was looking at something on the other side of the table. He got the impression that she had been looking at it for some time—something about her expression, something fixed. As he came up to her, she put the teapot down and said without any expression at all,

"There's a dead fly."

"*Flies*—at this time of year?"

"There are always some in the Mews—no proper larders, and people are careless. But it's dead."

He said, "What—" and all of a sudden her hand came out and caught at his. The room was warm, but the hand was very cold. She said,

"There's another. Wait!"

They both looked at the table. Beyond Carol's bright green lacquer tray with the teapot, sugar-basin and cups there was a loaf of brown bread, a plate of scones, a seed cake, a dish of butter pats, and the flat cut-glass dish heaped with Abigail

Salt's apple honey. It was a lovely translucent amber colour. There was a dead fly on it. As they stood there looking, a second fly came buzzing and circling down. It settled on the apple honey, plunged its tiny proboscis down into the jelly, quivered, and rolled over dead.

Katharine's ice-cold hand stiffened on William's warm one in a frantic grip. Neither of them spoke. When the telephone bell rang Katharine's grip loosened. She went to the writing-table, lifted the receiver mechanically. What she heard was Miss Silver's voice.

"Mrs. Eversley?"

"Yes."

"You have received a pot of apple preserve from Mrs. Salt?"

"Yes."

"Do not on any account partake of it. You have not done so?"

"No."

The tension was sufficiently relieved for Miss Silver to cough.

"I am truly thankful to hear it. May I speak to Mr. William Eversley?"

William took the receiver. He put an arm round Katharine and heard Miss Silver say,

"There has been a very grave development. I am speaking from Selby Street. We are awaiting the arrival of the police. I think that you and Mrs. Eversley should come here at once. The matter concerns you deeply. Will you bring with you the pot of apple preserve which Mrs. Eversley tells me you have not tasted. It should not be touched with the hand, but replaced in its wrappings in such a manner as not to disturb any possible fingerprints."

After a moment William said, "All right," and hung up. He and Katharine stood looking at one another.

225

CHAPTER 36

Miss Silver had rung the front door bell of 176 Selby Street about half an hour earlier. She came by appointment, and was most unwillingly received. That she was received at all was due to the fact that in the course of her brief telephone conversation with Mrs. Salt she had taken it upon herself to quote Mr. Tattlecombe with some authority.

"He would, I think, advise you to see me."

Abigail's voice came back stiffly.

"I do not always follow my brother's advice."

Miss Silver coughed.

"In this instance you would, I think, be well advised to do so."

"Can you tell me why?"

"He thought you would find it preferable to a more official visit."

Abigail Salt said in an expressionless voice,

"You can come at five o'clock."

Conducted to the upstairs parlour, Miss Silver seated herself and the interview began. In her quiet, restrained manner, Mrs. Salt was formidable. She took her own seat immediately below a grim photographic enlargement representing her mother-in-law in an alarming widow's cap and a jetted chain strongly suggestive of a fetter. All the furniture in this room had belonged to old Mrs. Salt. It was out of date, without having attained to being antique, but it was solid and handsome, and had cost quite a lot in its day. Amid these surroundings Abigail Salt felt herself to be entrenched in the family tradition. The Salts had been well-to-do, respectable chapel people for a hundred years, and that is far enough for anyone to go back. The clock on the mantelpiece had come from the Great Exhibition of 1851.

Miss Silver could appreciate both the atmosphere and Mrs. Salt's demeanour. She slightly inclined her head and observed,

"It is very kind of you to see me."

Receiving no reply, she pursued her theme.

"Kind, and if I may say so, very wise."

Abigail sat quite still with folded hands. She wore the dress reserved for Sundays and tea-parties. She wore her Honiton lace collar and her diamond brooch. These things gave her moral support. What she did not know was that they told Miss Silver she felt in need of it. She looked at her visitor's well worn coat, at the rubbed fur about her neck, at the black felt hat which she would have considered too shabby to go out in, at the black woollen gloves which were such a contrast to the fur-lined pair reposing in her bedroom drawer next door. When, in spite of all this attention to all this detail, her eyes unwillingly returned to Miss Silver's face, she looked away again almost at once.

Miss Silver gave her slight cough.

"I will be quite frank with you, Mrs. Salt. Mr. Tattlecombe asked me to go and see him on Saturday evening, and when I did so he communicated to me the substance of his conversation with you that afternoon."

Abigail pressed her lips together so tightly that they became a mere pale line. She said nothing.

Miss Silver continued.

"You must, of course, be aware of the very serious nature of that conversation. What you told Mr. Tattlecombe

227

amounted to an admission that it was your sister-in-law who assaulted Mr. William Smith. You spoke of finding Mr. Tattlecombe's raincoat wet, and the kitchen poker out of its place and rusty."

Abigail opened those closed lips and said,

"I spoke to my brother in confidence."

"Mr. Tattlecombe is very much attached to Mr. Smith. He believes his life to be in danger."

"That is absurd."

"I do not think so. On the occasion of your brother's accident he declared, and has since maintained, that he was 'struck down.' That blow was, I believe, intended for William Smith. The second attempt was the one to which I have just referred. All the evidence points to Miss Salt as the assailant. On the third occasion, which might very well have proved fatal, William Smith was on his way back from a visit to this house. He was pushed in the back with a stick whilst waiting to cross the road from an island, and would have been thrown under a motor-omnibus if he had not been saved by the promptitude and strength of the gentleman next to him in the crowd. In the latest attempt one of the wheels of his car was loosened."

"My sister-in-law knows nothing at all about cars. And she was laid up all last week with an attack of influenza."

"So Mr. Tattlecombe informed me. I do not attribute the attack on your brother or the attempt on the car to Miss Emily Salt. I believe that the other two attempts can be attributed to her. You will see of course, as I have done from the first, that two people are involved. Miss Emily Salt is one of them. I have come to you to find out who is the other, and what is the connection between them."

Abigail Salt sat there in her handsome dress, the grey curls of her hair neatly ordered, her eyes as round and blue as her brother's, her cheeks rosy, her lips unnaturally compressed. She opened them to say,

"I can't help you."

Miss Silver looked at her very steadily.

"I think you can. I do not wish to be misleading. When I say I have come to you to find out who is the second person concerned in this affair I mean that I have come to you to discover the link between this person and Miss Emily Salt. The person's identity is known. Where you can help me is—"

"Miss Silver, I can't help you."

"I believe you can."

"I know of no such person."

Miss Silver put up a hand in its black woollen glove.

"Mrs. Salt, I only ask that you will answer a few questions. If I do not ask them, the police will do so."

The colour deepened in Abigail's cheeks.

"You can ask your questions. I can't say whether I can answer them."

Miss Silver smiled gravely.

"I feel sure that you will endeavour to do so. Pray do not think that I do not appreciate the difficulty of your position. You have had a heavy charge in the care of Miss Emily Salt. You cannot have fulfilled it without being aware of certain things. Will you tell me whether she has ever shown any tendency to violence before?"

There was a silence. When it had lasted some time Miss Silver said gently,

"I see."

Abigail looked away.

"It was a long time ago. She was jealous. I don't want you to think it was worse than it was. I had a maid in the house then—a very nice, superior girl. She came to me and said that Emily had tried to push her down the stairs. I have thought it best not to have a resident maid since then. Emily gets jealous."

"And she was jealous of William Smith?"

"My brother had made a will in his favour. She was vexed on my account."

Miss Silver inclined her head.

"I can see that she has been an anxious charge. These unstable temperaments are easily moved to jealousy and passion. They fall readily under the domination of a stronger will. I am seeking for evidence of such a domination. This is where I feel that you can help me."

Abigail said, "No."

She got another of those grave smiles.

"I hope you can, and that if you can you will. Come, Mrs. Salt—when you look back, is there no one in the family, no friend or connection, with such an influence as I have described? If you can think of anyone of the sort, pray do not hesitate to tell me. You will not harm any innocent person, and you may be protecting your sister-in-law as well as William Smith. If, as I suspect, her peculiarities have been worked upon and she has been used as a tool, she may be in very grave danger. A tool which is no longer needed is quickly discarded by the criminal who has used it, and the discard is apt to be final."

The gravity of Miss Silver's voice and expression shook Abigail Salt. Her immobility was gone. She said in a different voice,

"That sounds dreadful."

The answer came back with an added gravity.

"It might be even more dreadful than it sounds. Mrs. Salt, what associates, what friends, what connections has your sister-in-law had?"

"Very few. She doesn't make friends. As long as my

230

mother-in-law lived she treated Emily as if she was a child. She was very stern with her—she directed everything she did. She would never admit that there was anything wrong. I think sometimes that if she had been differently treated she might have been different. She wasn't allowed to do the same as other girls did. She hardly ever saw anyone outside the family—unless you count going to chapel."

Miss Silver shook her head.

"As you say, Mrs. Salt, most unwise treatment. But if there were no outside connections, was there perhaps anything inside the family circle?"

"There's no one—" She broke off and then went on again. "There was a niece of hers—it's some years ago now—Emily took one of her violent fancies for her. She gets them sometimes—they make her very tiresome. I was very glad when it faded."

"You say a niece?"

Abigail hesitated.

"Well, in a way. The fact is I don't know much about her. There was one of my husband's sisters made a runaway marriage and the quarrel was never made up. I never met her, and the family never spoke about it. Then just before the war Emily met a cousin who said that a daughter of Mary's had turned up. I forget how she'd come across her. She said she recognized her from her likeness to my mother-in-law." Abigail half turned and indicated the grim enlargement on the wall. "That's how she was when I knew her, but she was considered very goodlooking when she was young. You'd never think it, would you? Those enlargements don't flatter anyone, but I've got a photograph in that album over there that shows you what she was like. I think her father was partly Italian. He had a restaurant in Bristol and he'd an Italian name, but her mother was English. Mary, the daughter who ran away, was like her, and by all accounts her daughter was too."

"Yes, Mrs. Salt?"

"Well, there isn't much more. Emily went to see this May, and she took one of her crazes about her. It was very tiresome indeed. Always running round with pots out of my jam-cupboard, or half a chicken, or the best part of a tongue, and no sooner any money in her pocket than it was out of it again—gloves for May—stockings for May—handbags. I put up with it because there wasn't anything I could do and I hoped it would come to an end of itself, because presents or no presents, I didn't think anyone would go on putting up with Emily for long—not unless they had to."

The silence maintained through all the years of her life with Emily had been forcibly broken. Through the breach there came flooding in the realization of just what that association had cost Abigail Salt in friendship, in service, in constant daily effort.

Miss Silver answered words which had not been spoken. "It must have been a great strain."

Abigail said, "Yes." A fleeting expression of surprise crossed her face. It may have been caused by her own recognition of what the strain had been, or she may have been wondering how Miss Silver came to know about it. After a moment she went on speaking.

"May got tired of it—anyone would. There must have been a scene. Emily came home in the worst state I've ever seen her in. I couldn't do anything with her. In the end I had to get the doctor, a thing I hadn't had to do since my husband died."

"What did he say, Mrs. Salt?"

Words which she had never repeated came from Abigail now.

"He said she might do herself or someone else a mischief."
Her colour changed, the surprised look came back. She said,
"I've never told anyone before."

"Did he say anything else?"

"He said she ought to be in a home. But she quieted down
again and got back to her usual."

"That was before the war?"

"Just before—that July or August."

"And was that all? Was there no recurrence of the friendship?"

Abigail hesitated.

"Well, that's just what I can't say. I've thought sometimes—"

"Yes, Mrs. Salt?"

"Well, there's been something going on for the last two
months, and I've wondered if it was that May again or—
somebody else. Emily's taken to slipping out in the evenings
like she used to do—and not so natural in the winter. If I
asked her where she'd been, she'd put herself in a state. I
did put it to her point-blank, was she seeing May again, and
she said she wasn't. But it was just the same thing all over
again—money just running away and food gone from the
larder. There was a whole shape once when I'd got someone
coming to supper, and no longer ago than this week-end a
pot of my apple honey, which I had set aside all ready to
leave at my brother's for William Smith and his wife."

Miss Silver coughed.

"Mrs. Salt, what is the name of this niece of Miss Emily
Salt's?"

"May—"

"But what surname?"

"Well, I believe it is Woods—Mrs. Woods—or Wood—I
can't really say which."

"And her maiden name?"

"I really don't know. Her mother ran away, as I told you, and the family never mentioned her. And Emily always spoke of this daughter as May, and to begin with when she spoke of her a good deal—I don't know—I got the idea—but perhaps I had better not say."

Miss Silver said firmly, "I think it would be better if you did."

A slight frown appeared upon Abigail's smooth forehead.

"Well, it was just an idea I got that there was something—" She hesitated, and then came out with, "not too respectable. There was a good flat, and everything nice, but nothing about who the husband was or what he did—only that he came there sometimes, and that if he was coming May would ring up and put Emily off. I thought it sounded as if there was something wrong, and after the first once or twice Emily didn't say anything more, and I thought perhaps she'd been told to hold her tongue."

There was a pause, after which Miss Silver gave a slight thoughtful cough.

"Mrs. Salt, have you ever heard of Eversleys'?"

Abigail's eyes remained perfectly blank. She said,

"No—" and then, "Mrs. Smith was a Miss Eversley."

Miss Silver looked at her in a very searching manner.

"William Smith is Mr. William Eversley. He has recovered his memory, and has been recognized by members of his family. He has a controlling interest in the firm, and there are some who may find his return inconvenient. Do you know anything at all about this?"

Abigail said in a bewildered voice,

"Oh, no—how could I?"

Miss Silver continued to look at her.

"I should like to put that same question to Miss Emily Salt."

"To Emily?"

"Yes, please, Mrs. Salt."

Abigail got up and went out of the room. She left the door open behind her. Miss Silver heard her cross the passage and knock. After a moment the knock was repeated, and after that there was the sound of an opening door.

Abigail came back looking disturbed.

"She must be out. Her coat is gone, and her hat. I don't know why I didn't hear her go."

Miss Silver said, "She may not have wished you to do so." And then, "Perhaps I may wait until she returns. I think you spoke of a photograph of your mother-in-law. I should be interested to see it."

The photograph-album lay, as it had done in old Mrs. Salt's time, upon the highly polished pedestal table which occupied the centre of the room. In order that the polish might sustain no damage a crocheted woollen mat, originally moss-green relieved with salmon but now all gone away to a dim shade resembling lichen, had been interposed. The covers of the album were very highly embossed, and linked by a massive gilt clasp.

Drawing her chair to the table, Miss Silver watched with interest whilst a succession of Salt portraits were displayed, all very glossy and in a high state of preservation owing to the fact that they had hardly ever been allowed to see the light of day. They were of two sizes, cabinet and *carte-de-visite*, each photograph embedded in the thick cream-laid boards which formed the pages of the album—young men with beards; middle-aged men with muttonchop whiskers and the high wing collar popularized by William Ewart Gladstone; a little girl with striped stockings and a round comb in her hair, looking as if she had escaped from one of Tenniel's illustrations to *Alice in Wonderland*; ladies with heavy braided skirts stretched over a crinoline; girls of the early eighties in jutting bustles and little tilted hats; babies smothered in pelisses; and dreadful little boys with curls and sailor suits.

At intervals Miss Silver murmured, "So interesting—" With a case mounting to its climax, she could still become absorbed in these pages from a family history which was in miniature the history of a rather splendid age. Here was a cross-section of the great middle class to which England owes so much, constantly replenished on the one hand from those who by dint of perseverance, push, and brains had fought their way up from below, and on the other from those off-shoots of the aristocracy and landed gentry who as continually passed into it in the pursuit of a livelihood in trade, farming, or one of the lesser professions.

Abigail turned a page and disclosed an empty space. Her smooth forehead contracted. She said in a puzzled voice,

"It should be here. Who can possibly have taken it out?" And then in a quick, vexed way, "It must have been Emily. She must have wished to show it to May. She used to say there was a strong likeness. But it is really very wrong of her—she shouldn't have done it!"

It was at this moment that Emily Salt entered the house. The opening and closing of the front door was plainly heard in the parlour. And then there was a pause. Abigail closed the album and laid it back upon the woolly mat. She rose to her feet and leaned over the table to fasten the heavy gold clasp. All this occupied the shortest possible space of time, but it was long enough.

Emily Salt shut the door behind her. She put her latchkey back in her bag and took something else out. She went towards the foot of the stairs.

Up in the parlour they heard her fall. With a startled look

236

on her face Abigail went to the door, opened it, and called over the banisters,

"Emily!"

But the word was hardly out of her mouth before she was running down. Miss Silver followed her. Emily Salt lay dead across the bottom step with part of a stick of chocolate clutched in her gloved right hand.

CHAPTER 37

Abigail got slowly to her feet. She had knelt beside the body, turned the glove back from the wrist and felt for a pulse that was not there. Now she stood up and put a hand on the newel-post to steady herself.

"She's dead—"

Miss Silver had been kneeling too. She also rose. Her face was very grave.

Abigail said in an expressionless voice, "Her heart was all right—the doctor said so—"

Miss Silver came to her.

"You will want all your courage, Mrs. Salt. I fear that it was poison."

"Oh, no!"

"I think cyanide. There is the suddenness, the appearance, and the distinctive odour. We must not touch her or disturb anything. Scotland Yard must be informed at once."

Abigail Salt's eyes had filled with tears. They had a be-wildered look. The tears began to run slowly down over her cheeks, which had lost nearly all their rosy colour.

She held on tightly to the newel and said,

"But why?"

"Can you not think of any reason, Mrs. Salt? Where is your telephone? The police must be notified."

Abigail said, "It's here—in this downstairs room."

They went into the sitting-room to which she had taken William Smith on the night he was attacked. In a very brisk and businesslike manner Miss Silver asked if she might speak with Sergeant Abbott or Chief Inspector Lamb. When she heard Frank Abbott's voice she said briefly,

"A shocking fatality has occurred. I am speaking from 176 Selby Street. Miss Emily Salt has just entered the house and dropped down dead. I suspect cyanide."

She heard him whistle at the other end of the line.

"Suicide?"

"I did not say so. The person who was to be watched—is there any information from that quarter?"

"Yes—let me see—Donald reported that she had returned to town at midday yesterday."

"I already knew that."

"He followed her to her flat. You always know everything, but I just wonder whether you know that she has been living there as Mrs. Woods."

Miss Silver coughed.

"I have been suspecting it for the last half hour. It supplies the link for which I have been looking."

As she hung up the receiver her mind was working rapidly. The indispensable link had been established. Mavis Jones had been for fifteen years a confidential secretary. It appeared that she was now Mrs. Cyril Eversley, but that for a good many years out of the fifteen she had occupied a very comfortable flat as Mrs. Woods. And Mrs. Woods was Mary Salt's daughter and Emily Salt's niece May. She stood there thinking of Emily Salt's abnormal mentality, her crazy devotion to this new-found niece, its fading—and its recurrence "about two months ago."

About two months ago—when William Smith had paid a visit to Eversleys' and been recognized by the old clerk. About two months ago—when Mr. Tattlecombe had been struck down and Mr. Yates had heard the casualty in the bed next to him mutter something that might have been "Joan" or "Jones," and then, "She pushed me." That was the beginning of it—death of Mr. Davies—accident to Mr. Tattlecombe. Attacks on William Smith—the tampering with his car—that was how it went on. And now the death of Emily Salt—was that the end?

Emily Salt was dead—thought focussed on that. Why? She thought Emily had been an instrument, and that the instrument had been discarded. When do you discard an instrument? The answer appeared in a very bright light. When it has done its work—when it might be dangerous to keep it. But the work for which this instrument had been required was the destruction of William Smith.

An instrument is only discarded when its work is done and it would be dangerous to keep it.

What work?

The destruction of William Smith.

How?

Into that very bright light in her mind there came a single word. It was the word with which she had accounted to Abigail for the death of Emily Salt.

Cyanide.

Perhaps concealed in the stick of chocolate still clasped in her hand. Cyanide can be concealed in other things besides chocolate. Quick and clear came the picture of Abigail Salt telling her about the pot of apple honey. "A pot of my apple honey which I had set aside all ready to leave at my brother's for William Smith and his wife."

She turned upon Abigail.

"Mrs. Salt—you missed a pot of apple honey."

There was a look of surprise, a slight start. The words seemed so irrelevant, the occasion so trifling.

"Yes."

"You told me that you had put it aside. Did you mean that it was packed up?"

"Yes, I had done it up all ready to take."

"Was there any message enclosed?"

"Just a line, 'With kind regards—Abigail Salt.' Miss Silver—"

Miss Silver was opening her bag. She took out a notebook, consulted it, found the telephone number she required, and dialled with steady fingers. When she heard the receiver lifted at the other end of the line she spoke. Her voice was steady too.

"Mrs. Eversley?"

No one but herself was to know with what a feeling of thankfulness she heard Katharine's voice say, "Yes."

CHAPTER 38

Sudden death has its own dreadful routine. Those who serve it came into Abigail Salt's house and went about their business there without reference to her—Detective Sergeant Abbott, a police surgeon, a police photographer, a fingerprint man. Miss Silver sat with Abigail in the upstairs parlour whilst they were at their work. Presently Katharine joined them there. William was making a statement downstairs. They had put an outer covering right over the pot of apple honey and its contents and brought it with them. They had brought the little cut-glass dish heaped up with amber jelly, the two dead flies still lying on it.

Katharine was very white and still. She went over to Abigail Salt and took her hand.

"I'm so sorry, Mrs. Salt—so dreadfully sorry. She couldn't have known what she was doing."

Abigail looked at her.

"I put it out all ready to take round when I went to see Abel tomorrow. She must have taken it last night when I was at chapel. But I never thought—"

"You mean the apple honey? It was very good of you." An uncontrollable shudder went over her. She let go of Abigail's hand, looked round for a chair, and sat down.

Abigail Salt said in a steady, expressionless voice,

"I don't suppose any of us will ever fancy it again."

Katharine's ungloved hands took hold of one another. She said very low,

"William was late. I was vexed because he was so late, but it saved his life. We were going to have the apple honey for tea—I had put it out in a little glass dish. Then William came, and we talked. I saw there was a dead fly on the honey. Then we saw another one come down and settle." The shudder came back. "It just fell over dead. Then Miss Silver rang."

Miss Silver coughed briskly.

"A most providential escape, dear Mrs. Eversley. Let us be thankful for it."

At this moment the door opened and Sergeant Abbott looked in. He caught Miss Silver's eye and beckoned her. She went out.

"Look here," he said, "the doctor seems pretty sure about its being cyanide. I gather that you know about this pot of apple honey the Eversleys have brought along. It seems to have killed two flies, and was probably intended to kill them. Emily Salt's fingerprints are all over the wrappings and the pot. I don't suppose there's much doubt that she conveyed the parcel to Rasselas Mews. William Eversley says they found it on the doorstep on Sunday night when they got back from Ledstow. But there was a message from Mrs. Salt inside—" He paused and looked at Miss Silver.

She said in her firmest voice,

"Yes, she was intending to leave it at the Toy Bazaar for them. She was having tea there with her brother tomorrow. It was already packed up."

Frank looked at her with his faint quizzical smile. "What a mine of information you are! But here is something that I can tell you, and I think you'll be interested. I told you Donald was shadowing Miss Jones. You did a very good bit of work there, getting the Chief to agree to it."

Miss Silver coughed.

"I considered it of the very first importance."

"I think you were right. She went off down to Evendon with Cyril Eversley on Saturday afternoon. The village fairly buzzed with the news that they were married. Donald put up at the Duck and heard all about it. General verdict that Cyril had made a fool of himself. Sunday morning Donald hung about—saw the William Eversleys arrive—didn't of course know who they were. Saw another young couple roll up. Cyril's daughter and her husband, William tells me, though Donald wasn't to know that either. And then in a brace of shakes out comes Mrs. Cyril Eversley in her brand new car, and Donald grabs his motor-bike and follows her all the way to her flat. That's when he finds out that she's been living there as Mrs. Woods. Well, he rings up and reports. Evans goes along to relieve him at about four o'clock. The lady hasn't shown up, but it looks as if she's going out again, because her car is still outside. She comes out about six and drives off. Evans follows her. She pulls up in Morden Road, just round the corner from Selby Street. A woman comes along with a parcel and gets in. Evans hears her say, 'I've got it.' They drive off together, and Evans follows them to a cul-de-sac behind Rasselas Mews—only of course he's not thinking about the Mews, because he's just been put on to watch Mrs. Cyril Eversley."

"Yes, Frank?"

"Evans was puzzled. They just sit in the car. It's a dark place, practically unlighted. He can't make out what they're doing. He strolls past once, and thinks they are opening a parcel. It doesn't seem to be his business. Presently the passenger gets out and goes off round the corner with her parcel, and Mrs. Eversley goes home. She parks her car, and doesn't show up again. Grey takes over at midnight. Nothing doing. Evans on again this morning. Mrs. Eversley doesn't show up. Donald on again at four. I've asked them to contact him and telephone his report to me here."

As he spoke, William Eversley came up the stairs and the telephone bell rang. William went into the parlour. Frank and Miss Silver went down to the ground floor room where the telephone was.

The body of Emily Salt was gone from the hall. A constable in uniform came out of the sitting-room and said, "For you, Sergeant."

Frank crossed the floor and took up the receiver. Miss Silver, standing just inside the door, could hear the measured rise and fall of a deep male voice. It was, in her opinion, the

243

voice of Chief Inspector Lamb, a circumstance which engaged her most interested attention.

Frank Abbott said, "Yes, sir." And then, "Not much doubt about its being cyanide." After a pause he said, "No, they're all right. They had a narrow shave—a pot of poisoned honey. Holt's taken it off for analysis. . . . Yes, they're here. It was a very narrow shave." Finally, after a considerable interval, "Well, that just about puts the lid on it! . . . All right, sir, we're finishing here." He hung up and turned.

Miss Silver had closed the door. She said,

"Well, Frank?"

"That was the Chief."

"So I supposed."

"Could you hear what he was saying?"

Her glance reproved him.

"I made no endeavour to do so."

"But you wouldn't mind if I were to tell you?"

"I should be very much interested."

"Well then, here you are. I think we've got her cold. Donald says she came out just after five, went round and collected her car—she keeps it in a garage just behind the flats—and went off to the same place as before, Morden Road. The same woman came to meet her. Evans couldn't see her face, but the description fits Emily Salt—tall and thin, shapeless coat, squashed-down hat. She got into the car. He heard her say, 'I can't stay. Abby doesn't know I'm out.' Mrs. Cyril Eversley said something, but he didn't hear what it was. The door was shut, and they sat in the car and talked for about five minutes. Then Emily Salt got out. She stood with the door in her hand and said, 'It's ever so good of you, May. I love chocolate.' Mrs. Cyril leaned across from the driving-seat, and this time Donald heard what she said. It's pretty damning. She said, 'Mind you don't eat it in the street. You won't,

244

will you?' Emily Salt said, 'No, no, I'll put it in my bag. I won't eat it till I get in.' Then she said, 'I'll be seeing you soon, won't I?' and Mrs. Cyril said, 'Oh, yes.' And that was all. Emily Salt went back round the corner into Selby Street and into the house, where she ate her chocolate and died. And Mrs. Cyril Eversley went home with the comfortable feeling that she had disposed of all her worries. If William Eversley was poisoned by the apple honey which Mrs. Salt had sent him, and Emily Salt committed suicide with the same poison, it was all very distressing, but everyone knew that Emily had always been crazy, and that she had a spite against William because Mr. Tattlecombe had made a will in his favour instead of leaving what he had to Abigail, and so indirectly to Emily herself. Mrs. Cyril must be feeling quite sure that no one can possibly connect her with Emily or with the crime. And if you hadn't practically blackmailed the Chief into having her followed, she would be perfectly right."

Miss Silver looked quite horrified.

"My dear Frank—blackmail—what a shocking expression!"

That faint smile reached his eyes.

"Revered preceptress—" he murmured, and then was grave again. "The Chief is sending Donald along to arrest her now," he said grimly.

CHAPTER 39

Frank Abbott had been perfectly right about Mavis Eversley. She was feeling extremely well pleased with herself. Difficulty after difficulty had presented itself—you might even say reverse after reverse—but she had not allowed herself to be discouraged. She had persevered, and now awaited the confirmation of a triumphant success. Thinking it all over, she could not see where the plan could go wrong. There was, of course, just the bare possibility that the apple honey would kill Katharine and leave William alive. It was a possibility and she faced it, but it was so very unlikely. Katharine would be making the tea, pouring it out, looking after William. He would almost certainly begin eating before she did. He had always had an excellent appetite. There had been family jokes about his fondness for jam. She felt comfortably sure that he would be in a hurry to help himself to Abigail Salt's apple honey. The minute Emily had mentioned it in one of her grumbles she had known that it was just the thing to do the trick. She would be rid of William and of Emily by the same clever stroke. William had got to go. Cyril and Brett might be fools enough to think they could do a patched-up deal with him. Brett and his "We're all falling on each other's necks and killing fatted calves" when she called him up this morning at the office! More idiots they, and poor-spirited idiots at that! They would just be under William's thumb for ever and ever, and never dare say "Boo!" to him. But even if she could bring herself to it, none of that was going to get

Mavis Jones out of the mess. William wasn't Cyril or Brett—nobody was going to throw any dust in his eyes. He was one of the thorough kind, and he was as good at figures as she was herself. When he came to go into the books it wouldn't take him long to find out what she'd been doing for the last seven years, and when he found out, she didn't think he was going to have much mercy, or that either Brett or Cyril would lift a finger to save her. They were none too secure themselves, and to put it bluntly, she'd been robbing them for years.

No—William was bound to go. And the way she'd brought it off, she got rid of Emily too. And just about time—ringing her up every time Abigail went out, pouring out her crazy spite about men, about William—thank goodness she only knew him as William Smith—about Abel Tattlecombe and his will. What a crashing bore! She could be dangerous too, if she went a little bit more crazy and tattled to Abigail. She hadn't done it so far. Emily was secretive—liked to feel no one knew about "May." Heavens, how she hated the name—the crazy, smarmy way of going on—the whining, grumbling voice on the telephone! How she hated Emily Salt!

By this time, with any luck at all, she was rid of her, and rid of William too, and without one atom of risk. She had never let Emily come to the flat. She used to come to her old place seven years ago—that was when she was having her affair with Brett—but never here, never once. They had met, when it was necessary, in some out of the way tea-room, but there had been as little of it as possible. It would be quite a clear case. A crazy woman would have poisoned William Eversley and then committed suicide. The only person to be blamed would be Abigail Salt who ought to have had her put away in a home years ago. That would be the end of it, and very nice too. William gone, Emily gone, and that damned

Salt family pride in the dust. They had turned her mother out—they hadn't cared whether the child lived or died. And who came out on top now?

Her thoughts slid to Katharine. She had kept her to the last. Katharine—Sylvia's pretty, angry voice rang in her ears—"And who told you you could call her Katharine?" If she had needed to have her purpose edged, that slap in the face would have done it. From the business point of view she wanted Katharine dead, because there would never be any question of those trust funds then—they came back to Cyril and Brett. But as far as her own private feelings went, it would be a considerable satisfaction to them to let Katharine live and suffer.

She turned to thinking of the future. She would make it up with Cyril of course, and they must pull the firm out of the mess. It could be done. Those toys of William's—they had better take them up. Properly handled and pushed, there would be big money in them. Every child in the country would be wanting them. Even under the urgent pressure of danger it had outraged her business sense to turn them down as she had had to do in December. Now they could go straight ahead with them. She looked on and saw her own firm hands on the reins at Eversleys'. She had a sense of power, domination, success. The way lay straight and open before her. She had never had anyone to help her except herself—her own wits, her own courage, her own skill in shaping the event to serve her purpose. And this was where it had brought her.

The front door bell jarred suddenly in the silence of the flat. For a moment she wasn't sure whether it was the telephone. She thought of Brett, of Cyril—ringing up to say William was dead. Then the bell rang again, and she knew it was the front door.

248

Cyril? No—Brett said he was still at Evendon this morning—he wasn't coming up. But it might be Brett—

She opened the door, and saw two strange men standing there. One of them stepped forward. His hand dropped on her shoulder. He said her name, and he got as far as "I have a warrant for your arrest," and then she twisted free, everything in her shrieking, "No—no—*no!*" She reached the bedroom, banged the door, and locked it. There was time. There was just, just time.

When they broke the lock, she was there on the floor— dead like Emily Salt.

CHAPTER 40

In the next few days two inquests were held in two separate districts of London. Neither of them took long or attracted very much attention. The verdict in each case was suicide whilst the balance of the mind was disturbed. There was apparently nothing to connect May Woods, 39, married, with Emily Salt, 58, single, except the fact that they had both poisoned themselves by taking cyanide.

Where justice has no end to be served, it is not the policy of the police to provide the public with a dish of scandal at the expense of innocent survivors. Since neither Evans nor Donald was called as a witness, there was simply nothing to connect the two deaths. In the case of Emily Salt, the doctor who had attended her during a recent attack of influenza stated that she was, he considered, decidedly unhinged, and that he had advised her sister-in-law that it might be better if she could be placed under some restraint. Mrs. Salt and Miss Silver deposed to hearing her enter the house, and to finding her dead at the foot of the stairs. The police surgeon gave evidence as to the cause of death, and that was all. There was no mention of a pot of apple honey.

At the inquest on Mrs. Woods it was stated that on receiving a visit from a police officer she locked herself in her room, and when the door was broken down she was found to have taken a fatal dose of poison. The Coroner enquired whether Mrs. Woods had reason to suppose that she would be arrested. On receiving an affirmative reply he asked whether the police had any further evidence to offer, and was told that they had not. The deceased was identified as Mrs. May Woods by the caretaker of the block of flats in which she had resided for the past five years.

At Eversleys' it became known that Miss Jones was dead. Cyril Eversley wore a black tie and stayed away from the office. He had been too profoundly shocked to realize that before very long he would be experiencing an almost equal degree of relief.

On the day after the two inquests Miss Silver dispensed coffee and conversation to Frank Abbott and to William and Katharine. It was icy cold outside, with a north wind full of little pricking points of snow, but Miss Silver's room with its blue curtains drawn, a fire blazing, and cakes and coffee displayed beside it, was bright and comfortable. A warm, cheerful light illuminated the patterned wallpaper, the photogravures in their yellow maple frames, Miss Silver's gallery of photographs, and Miss Silver herself in a utility silk purchased in the last year of the war and worn one year for Sundays, a second for every day, and now come down to evening wear with the addition of a black velvet coatee— a most comfortable and treasured garment, so time-honoured as to be verging upon the legendary.

Frank Abbott, very much off duty, looked across at William and said,

"Good production, don't you think? No fuss, no scandal, no headlines in the papers—in fact what the eye doesn't see the heart needn't grieve over."

William said, "Yes, it was a good show—very well managed. We're very grateful. You can't afford that sort of publicity when you're trying to get a business on its legs again."

Frank lifted his coffee-cup.

"Well, here's luck—" his eyes went to Katharine—"to you both."

She smiled at him.

"You'll come and see us sometimes, won't you?"

"I'd like to—if I shan't have unpleasant associations. You've had a rotten time."

She shook her head.

"The bad part's gone. We'll keep the friends we've made—Mr. Tattlecombe, and Mrs. Salt, and Miss Silver, and you."

Miss Silver smiled, then gave her slight cough.

"I saw Mrs. Salt this afternoon. She told me one or two things which interested me extremely. I had been trying to think where this series of crimes and attempted crimes could really be said to have begun. In nearly every case one finds that the seed of a crime has been present in thought for a long time before it germinates and passes into action. There are, perhaps, years during which selfish, ruthless, ambitious, and despotic tendencies could, and should, be checked and eliminated. In the case of Emily Salt, in the case of Mavis Jones, we have to go a long way back. When I went to see Mrs. Salt I was very much struck by an enlarged portrait of her mother-in-law, Mrs. Harriet Salt, the mother of Emily and the grandmother of Mavis Jones. The features must always have been marked. In youth, Mrs. Salt tells me, they were remarkably handsome, but they had become harsh. The face as actually pictured was that of a ruthless despot. I learned this afternoon that the camera had not traduced her. It was under her iron domination that Emily Salt became the warped creature that she was. She might never have been very bright, but she need not have been repressed, thwarted, and bullied. With kindlier treatment her affections could have been developed and useful occupations found for her. She was not allowed to make friends, so all her capacity for affection was dammed up and became abnormal, manifesting itself in a crazy devotion which could only prove unwelcome to its object. A very sad case."

Frank Abbott lifted a quizzical eyebrow.

"Is the late Miss Mavis Jones, alias May Woods, a sad case too?"

Miss Silver looked at him gravely.

"I think so, Frank. She was a wicked and unscrupulous woman. She might have been something very different. Her mother, as you know, was Mary Salt, Harriet Salt's eldest daughter. She was, by all accounts, a handsome, high-spirited girl with a strong resemblance to her mother. When Abigail Salt first mentioned her she spoke of a runaway marriage, but I learned this afternoon that so far as the family knew no marriage had taken place. Mary Salt was going to have a child, and her mother turned her out. No one knows what happened to her or to her child for several years after that. Her name was never mentioned. The family closed its ranks. For what follows, Emily Salt is the authority. When she was seeing a good deal of her niece just before the war she told Abigail that Mary Salt, after working her fingers to the bone to keep her child, had married a man called Jones, an elderly valetudinarian. I think he had been a school-

252

master. Mavis got a secondary school education, matriculated, and took a course in typing and shorthand. Her mother died when she was sixteen. Mr. Jones was then quite sunk in invalidism, and the sister who came to look after him turned Mavis out. This is, of course, her own account. She must have been about twenty-three when she entered your firm's employment, Mr. Eversley. She had excellent abilities, a prepossessing appearance, and assured manners. She became Mr. Cyril Eversley's secretary—in what year?"

William said, "Thirty-seven or thirty-eight. She was very efficient."

"Oh, yes—a clever, efficient woman who came to rely on her own cleverness and efficiency to such an extent that she allowed these qualities to dominate her. I do not know, Mr. Eversley, whether you have yet been able to make a thorough examination of the books of your firm, but I would advise you to do so. I can only account for her subsequent actions on the supposition that your return to the firm would have involved her in criminal proceedings."

William said, "Yes, I think so."

Miss Silver coughed and proceeded.

"Her marriage to Mr. Cyril Eversley was, of course, designed to afford her some protection. But it was not enough. She must have been conscious of defalcations too serious to be condoned. We now come to the tragic affair of Mr. Davies. I think we must conclude, Mr. Eversley, that when Mavis Jones opened your typed letter asking for an interview she received a shock. You signed it in your own handwriting, William Smith. She must have seen the first part of the signature too often not to have been struck by it. With only one word to go on, she could not be sure, but she was enough impressed to give you an appointment at an hour when neither of the partners would be there and the staff would be preparing to leave."

William said, "One of the girls in the office remembers her pushing Davies off early. As a matter of fact she defeated her own ends. She hustled him, he forgot something, and he came back for it. That's what he told you, wasn't it, Kath?"

She said, "Yes."

"That's when he ran into me. Of course I didn't know him from Adam. The poor old chap went away feeling quite dazed and rang Katharine up. She isn't sure whether she told him not to say anything or not. She wrote it to him next day, but he never got the letter."

Miss Silver had picked up her knitting. The two blue coatees were finished and packed up ready for the post. A cardigan for the baby's mother, her niece Ethel Burkett, was now upon the needles. About half an inch of deep bright cherry-red could be discerned—most warm, most cheerful, most comfortable. Knitting rapidly and without effort, she gave it a passing glance of admiration and reverted to the analysis of crime.

"If Mr. Davies had been more reticent, there is very little doubt that he would have been alive today. I think there can be no doubt that he sought Miss Jones out and told her of his encounter. She probably tried to make him believe that he had been deceived by some chance likeness—she may even have commented on it herself. But when she discovered that he was in possession of her visitor's address she must have decided that it was all too dangerous. Consider the evidence of Mr. Yates who occupied the bed next to that in which poor Mr. Davies died. The official account stated that he had passed away without speaking, which of course only meant that the nurses had not heard him speak. Mr. Yates, however, heard him say three things—the first a name which

254

he took to be Joan or Jones, and after that two disconnected sentences, 'She didn't believe me,' and, 'She pushed me.' I think there can be no doubt that Mavis Jones followed him from the office and found the opportunity she was looking for. He was pushed under a car and fatally injured. On that same evening Mr. Tattlecombe met with a very similar accident. Here we have no direct evidence. One can only weigh the probabilities and draw an inference. I think that Mavis Jones went down to Ellery Street that night to have a look at the lie of the land. I do not think it probable that she had any definite plan. It is possible, but I do not think that the probabilities lie that way. It was getting on for half past ten at night, and she had no means of knowing whether William Smith lived on the premises, but, as it must have seemed to her perverted mind, fortune favoured her. The door opened and a man came out and crossed the pavement. She would have seen him as a dark shape against the light of the open door. In height and build he resembled William Smith. It must be remembered that though she would know Mr. Tattlecombe quite well by name as the brother of Abigail Salt, she had never seen him. What she saw now was a strong, upright figure, and the light striking upon a thick head of light-coloured hair. Mr. Tattlecombe's hair is grey, and Mr. Eversley's is fair. I think they would look very much the same at night with the light coming from behind. Mr. Tattlecombe has always maintained that he was 'struck down.' I believe Mavis Jones pushed him, as she had pushed Mr. Davies."

Katharine said, "It sounds too horribly cold-blooded."

Miss Silver continued to knit with great rapidity.

"It is a commonplace to say that one crime leads to another—'The lust of gain, in the spirit of Cain,' as Lord Tennyson so aptly says. And, if I may quote from a modern writer, 'If you take the first step, you will take the last.'"

255

Before the picture of Kipling as a modern the three young people sat dumb. Unconscious, Miss Silver pursued her theme.

"We do not know when Mavis Jones discovered her mistake. She must have thought it too dangerous to repeat the attempt immediately, and she does not seem to have known that Mrs. William Eversley had obtained a situation at the Toy Bazaar."

Katharine smiled faintly.

"I told the family that I'd taken a job and was going away, and I didn't give anyone my address. But—" she hesitated— "they did get to know where I was. At least Brett did—I don't know how."

Miss Silver's needles clicked.

"I think Mr. Brett Eversley rang you up late on Friday evening—the day before you married Mr. William Smith." She brought out the name with a smile.

Katharine said, "Yes."

"You had, I believe, taken tea with Mrs. Salt and Mr. Tattlecombe at Selby Street that afternoon. Your address was by that time known to them, and therefore to Emily Salt."

"I suppose so."

William said, "Mr. Tattlecombe had known the address for a day or two. Miss Cole had it when we engaged Katharine. She went to Mr. Tattlecombe to complain that I was going to see Katharine in the evenings. It wasn't her business of course, but Mrs. Bastable must have said something, and Miss Cole got worked up—she's like that. Anyhow Mrs. Salt came to the wedding, so there wasn't any secret about the address by then."

The strip of cherry-coloured wool on Miss Silver's needles had lengthened perceptibly. She said,

"Precisely. I think there can be very little doubt that Emily

Salt rang up Mavis Jones, and that Mavis Jones immediately imparted the information to Mr. Brett Eversley. I do not know whether she had a grudge against him, or whether she considered that protestations of devotion on his part might ease the situation as regards the firm.''

William said, "It might be a bit of both. He used to run round with her. But Brett wasn't in this business, you know. He wouldn't have let himself be used like that if he'd known I was alive—I would like that to be quite clear to everyone. My cousins have both welcomed me back, though it has put them in an awkward position financially. Whatever Mavis Jones was doing, it was all off her own bat.''

Miss Silver inclined her head.

"From what Mrs. Salt tells me it is evident that Miss Jones was not idle. The intimacy with Emily Salt had been resumed as far back as December. In this manner Mavis would know when Mr. Tattlecombe came to Selby Street for a period of convalescence, and she would be informed of any developments regarding William Smith. It was not hard for her to work up Emily Salt's grievance over Mr. Tattlecombe's will into a state which induced the poor unbalanced woman to make her two attempts upon Mr. Eversley's life.''

William said, "Those were Emily—I thought so all along. You know, I picked up a note on the pavement after the first one. It was from Mrs. Salt to Mr. Tattlecombe, and I couldn't think how it got there.''

Miss Silver coughed gently.

"She wore Mr. Tattlecombe's raincoat and used the kitchen poker. Mrs. Salt found the coat quite wet, and the poker rusty. You had a most providential escape, both then and when she endeavoured to push you off the island. The next attempt—the one in which the wheel of your car was loosened—was, I imagine, the work of Miss Jones. She had driven a car for some years. I use the word imagine advisedly, because the only evidence about this attempt is of a negative character. It could not have been the work of Emily Salt, since she was in bed at the time with a sharp attack of influenza. One of the difficulties of the case has been that two separate motives were apparent, and two entirely different suspects. Emily Salt had no possible interest in the attack on Mr. Davies, and a definite alibi for the time of Mr. Tattlecombe's accident—she was present with Mrs. Salt at a chapel social. She also had an alibi on the occasion of the attempt on the car. And it did not appear possible to connect Mavis Jones with the two attacks on Mr. Eversley, since both his visits to Mr. Tattlecombe were unpremeditated and she could not have known of them beforehand. At the same time I felt quite unable to believe that there was no connection between these two sets of attempts on Mr. Eversley's life. There had to be a link, and I went to Mrs. Salt to find out what it was." She turned to Frank Abbott with a smile. "Excellent work done by Detective Donald and Detective Evans helped to make the whole position clear. In the light of their evidence I think there can be no doubt at all that Mavis Jones rang Emily Salt up on the Sunday evening. She would know that it was quite safe to do so, as Mrs. Salt never missed evening chapel. During that conversation she told Emily to meet her just round the corner in Morden Road, thus avoiding the possibility of her car being seen in Selby Street. Either at this time or perhaps on some previous occasion Emily must have mentioned the pot of apple honey. It would be a grievance that this very special preserve should be given away, and to the very people of whom she already felt a crazy jealousy. What is certain is that she was told to bring the pot of apple honey with her, and that she did so. Detective Evans actually saw the parcel being unwrapped while the two women were sitting in the car in the cul-de-sac behind Rasselas Mews. I feel sure that Mavis Jones avoided touching it, but that she superintended the proceedings and supplied the cyanide. As you will have heard, analysis shows that practically the whole of the poison must have been in the top of the jar and had been decanted into the little cut-glass dish which Mrs. William Eversley set out upon her tea-table. How the cyanide was obtained, we do not know."

William frowned and said, "My cousins tell me there was a wasp's nest outside the office window last summer—some cyanide was bought to deal with it."

Miss Silver gave a reproving cough.

"There should be more restraint upon the sale of these dangerous poisons. Procedure is at present sadly lax. A great deal of crime would be avoided if the means were not to hand. Miss Jones probably had no evil intentions when she put the surplus cyanide away. She may have forgotten that she had done so. She may have come across it by accident, or she may have remembered it—we have no means of knowing. But if she had not had this poison ready to her hand she might not have resolved upon this last, most ruthless crime which would rid her of Mr. William Eversley and of Emily Salt by a single stroke and leave her, as she supposed, in a position of complete security." She paused for a moment and sighed. "The triumphing of the wicked is short. It is all very sad, very regrettable, but I think we now know how it happened. As I said before, some excellent work has been done. I trust that Chief Detective Inspector Lamb is aware of how much I have valued his very kind co-operation."

Frank Abbott bent over the fire, poker in hand, his face not quite under control. He had a picture of Lamb with empurpled cheeks and bulging eyes being graciously thanked for his co-operation. Maudie was marvellous—she really was.

From her moralizing to her quotations from the moderns (!), from her strict hair-net to the toes of her beaded shoes, she was unique and he adored her. Her reproving cough came to his ears.

"My dear Frank, you are really spoiling the fire. It did very well as it was."

William and Katharine walked home together. Curious how quickly a place could become home when you were happy there. This wasn't Carol's flat any more—it was theirs, it was home. Because wherever they were together would be home. Coming into it with Katharine, William got the feeling which he had always had when he came into the house in his dream—the feeling of safety, the feeling of something shared, the feeling of home. He couldn't put it into words. He could only put his arms round Katharine and hold her close.

THE END